LITERARY NOIR:
A SERIES OF SUSPENSE

Other Novels by Cornell Woolrich

Cover Charge (1926)
Children of the Ritz (1927)
Times Square (1929)
A Young Man's Heart (1930)
The Time of Her Life (1931)
Manhattan Love Song (1932)
The Bride Wore Black (1940)
The Black Curtain (1941)
Marihuana (1941, originally as by William Irish)
The Black Alibi (1942)
The Black Angel (1943, based on his 1935 story "Murder in Wax")
The Black Path of Fear (1944)
Deadline at Dawn (1944, originally as by William Irish)
Night Has a Thousand Eyes (1945, originally as by George Hopley)
Waltz into Darkness (1947, originally as by William Irish)
Rendezvous in Black (1948)
I Married a Dead Man (1948, originally as by William Irish)
Savage Bride (1950)
Fright (1950, originally as George Hopley)
You'll Never See Me Again (1951)
Strangler's Serenade (1951, originally as by William Irish)
Hotel Room (1958)
Death is My Dancing Partner (1959)
The Doom Stone (1960, previously serialized in *Argosy* 1939)

Woolrich also published over 200 short stories and various novellas.

Praise for Cornell Woolrich

"Along with Raymond Chandler, Cornell Woolrich practically invented the genre of noir."
—Newsday

"Critical sobriety is out of the question so long as this master of terror-in-the-commonplace exerts his spell."
—Anthony Boucher, *The New York Times Book Review*

"Revered by mystery fans, students of film noir, and lovers of hardboiled crime fiction and detective novels, Cornell Woolrich remains almost unknown to the general reading public. His obscurity persists even though his Hollywood pedigree rivals or exceeds that of Cain, Chandler, and Hammett. What Woolrich lacked in literary prestige he made up for in suspense. Nobody was better at it."
—Richard Dooling, from his Introduction to the Modern Library print edition of *Rendezvous in Black*

"He was the greatest writer of suspense fiction that ever lived."
—Francis M. Nevins, Cornell Woolrich Biographer

LITERARY NOIR:
A SERIES OF SUSPENSE

• VOLUME 1 •
SOLVE THE CRIME / WHODUNIT?

BY CORNELL WOOLRICH

Published in collaboration with Renaissance Literary & Talent
Post Office Box 17379
Beverly Hills, California 90209
www.renaissancemgmt.net

Murder, Obliquely

All at Once, No Alice

Silent as the Grave

After Dinner Story

Death at the Burlesque

Red Liberty
Originally published in *Dime Detective*,
Vol. 18, No. 4, July 1, 1935
Copyright © 1962, 1935 Popular Publications, Inc.

Preview of Death
Originally published in *Dime Detective*,
Vol. 15, No. 1, November 15, 1934
Copyright © 1961,1934 by Popular Publications, Inc.
Copyright © 2014 JPMorgan Chase Bank, N.A. as Trustee for
The Claire Woolrich Memorial Scholarship Fund,
American Rights Management Company, LLC

ISBN: 978-1-950369-02-7

Cover art: Abigail Larson
www.abigaillarson.com

CONTENTS

INTRODUCTION

The spirit of *Literary Noir: A Series of Suspense* is very much in line with that of past collections by Cornell Woolrich. The vast majority of his short stories and novellas—of which there are hundreds—weren't originally published in book form, but in monthly detective noir and mystery magazines such as *Ellery Queen's Mystery Magazine, Dime Detective, Rex Stout's Mystery Monthly, Street & Smith's Detective Story, Black Mask, College Humor, Detective Fiction Weekly, Argosy* and many more. Years after the original magazine collections, Woolrich, alongside many different publishers, thematically curated multiple book series containing his shorter stories, which were a huge success. All of the tales within *Literary Noir: A Series of Suspense* were at one point included in such various collections. Some of the more well-known series are: *Darkness at Dawn, The Dancing Detective, The After Dinner Story Collection, Angels of Darkness, Blind Date with Death* and *Borrowed Crime.*

When it came time for a new publication, Woolrich would often take the opportunity to re-write the journey or the ending for these characters and pass them off as a never-before-seen story, mixed in with older collections of materials. Many of the stories you'll read throughout these volumes are in their original (and only) form, while others were once published under a different title and are now the second or third version.

Volume One: *Solve the Crime/Whodunit*? Within this Volume, you'll step into some of the most imaginative, high-tension and dangerous worlds of Cornell Woolrich. At the center of each story is a protagonist desperate to solve a crime, or you, the reader, trying to figure out *whodunit* up until the last page. Follow Woolrich's everyday characters turned into detectives, seasoned detectives on the hunt for psychotic killers, endangered

Hollywood and burlesque starlets, vengeful family members stopping at nothing for justice, and spouses desperately seeking the sometimes horrific truth about their partners. Volume One includes some of Woolrich's most powerful, emotional and chilling noir literature with an underlying theme of his personal journey throughout the economic depression of the 1930's, and as a failed screenwriter in Hollywood at the end of the silent era.

With great recognition and being coined the father of "Pulp-fiction," Woolrich came into many Radio, TV and Film adaptation offers for his works. Within the stories of Volume One, two were adapted for radio and eventually, television. NBC Radio's *Molle Mystery Theatre* aired *After-Dinner Story* in 1939 and *Silent as the Grave* in 1945, and both made their TV debut on CBS in 1949 which, at the time, were 30-minute live television episodes. *After Dinner Story* was a part of a series called *Suspense* with Otto Krueger, and *Silent as the Grave* as a part of *Silver Theatre* with Marsha Hunt and George Reeves. With the success of the first adaptations, both titles were later adapted for other television and radio shows throughout the following decades. The emotional force behind both stories coupled with a stunning climax makes them ideal choices for radio and television adaptations.

Please enjoy the latest collection of Cornell Woolrich's short stories.

MURDER, OBLIQUELY

Murder, Obliquely is a rewrite of *Death Escapes the Eye* which was originally published in *The Shadow Mystery Magazine* in 1947. This version was published over 10 years later in the short story collection *Violence,* Part II: "Love and Murder" and retains the basic plot but differs in the minor, yet important, details about the characters. *Murder, Obliquely* is one of the last stories in which Woolrich wrote from the point-of-view of a woman, the protagonist, and falls into a more unique whodunit trope than others.

HE OTHER NIGHT at a party I met my last love again. By last, I don't mean latest, I mean my first and yet my final one. We said the things you say, holding tall glasses in our hands to keep us company.

"Where've you been?"

"Around. And you?"

"Here and there."

Then there wasn't anything more to say. Love is bad for conversation; dead love, I mean. We drifted on. In opposite directions, not together.

It isn't often that I see him any more. But when I do, I wonder whatever really *did* become of her.

I first met him through Jean. Jean collects people, as a velvet evening wrap collects lint. People she has no emotional need for. She is very happily married. In an insulting, slurring way. I've never heard her speak a civil word to, or of, him. Example: "Oh, I don't know why." (shrug) "I had a spare twin bed and it seemed a shame to let it go to waste." She is the most gregarious one-man woman I know. Or else she keeps going through brambles, I can't say. Possibly it has to do with her face. She is not beautiful by wide-screen standards. But there is a winsome, elfin quality to her expression of face. I am not beautiful, either. The similarity ends there, right there.

Even when I was young, I was always the fifth wheel on the wagon. The other girl they had to ring in an extra man for, on dates. She never brought one of her own along. Never had one to bring. And these telephone-directory swains never repeated themselves. It was always someone else, the next time around. Once had been enough, for the one before.

Jean and her husband, the Cipher, stopped by for me in a cab at six thirty, and the three of us went on together from there. The Cipher wore glasses, was beginning to show baldness, and grew on you slowly. You found yourself beginning to like him after a time lag of about six months. The nickname, Jean's creation, was not inappropriate at that. The Cipher was singularly uncommunicative, on any and all subjects, after five o'clock in the afternoon. He was resting from business, she and I supposed. "He has a voice," she had once assured me. "I called for him one day, and I heard it through the office door. I wasn't at all certain until then."

He said, on the present occasion, " 'Lo, Annie," in a taciturn growl as I joined them in the cab; and that, we knew, was all we were likely to get for the next hour to come, so it had to do. But " 'Lo, Annie," when it's sincere and sturdy and reliable, isn't bad, either. In fact, it may be better than a lot of facile patter. Jean had settled for it, and Jean was smarter when it came to men than I could ever hope to be.

Number 657 was one of the tall monoliths that run along Park Avenue like a picket fence from 45th to 96th; but a picket fence that doesn't do its job. It doesn't seem to keep anyone out; everyone gets in.

"Mr. Dwight Billings," Jean said to the braided receptionist.

"Sixth floor," he said.

We entered an elevator that was a trifle small. Space, presumably, was so expensive in this building that only a minimum could be spared for its utilities. We stepped out into a foyer, and there was only a single door facing us. A colored man opened it. His accent was pure university. "Good evening, Mrs. Medill, Miss Ainsley, Sir. If you'll allow me." He took the Cipher's hat. "If you ladies would care—" He indicated a feminine guest room to one side.

Jean and I went in and left our wraps there, and looked at our faces in a wide, triple-winged vanity mirror. She unlidded a cut-crystal power receptacle, being Jean, and sniffed at it. "Quite good," she said. "Coty's, unless I'm slipping. Rachel for brunettes, and"—she unlidded a second one on the opposite side—"flesh for blondes. Evidently there are no redheads on his list."

I didn't answer. I've been redheaded since I was twenty.

We rejoined the Cipher in the central gallery. It ran on for a length of about three rooms, cutting a wide swath through the apartment, and then you stopped, and turned to your left, and came down two steps onto the floor of the drawing room. It was artfully constructed for dramatic entrances, that room.

Overhead hung two rock-crystal chandeliers. One was lighted and sparkled like a rhinestone hornet's nest inhabited by fireflies. The other was unlighted, and showed cool blue with frosty crystalline shadow. A man was sitting behind the upturned ebony lid of a grand piano. Desultory notes of "None but the Lonely Heart," played with one hand alone, stopped short at the bustle of our coming down the two steps. Then he stood up and came forward, one hand out for Jean.

I like to study people. Even people that I think I'm going to see only once.

He was tall and he was thirty-five; brown eyes and lightish hair, blond when he was still a boy. He was like—how shall I say it? Everyone's glimpsed someone, just once in her life, that she thought would've been just the right one for her. I say would've, because it always works out the same way. Either it's too late and he's already married, or if he isn't, some other girl gets across the room to him first. But it's a kindly arrangement, because if you had got across the room to him first yourself, then you would have found that he wasn't just the right one for you after all. This way, the other girl is the one finds it out, and you yourself don't get any of the pain.

What's the good of trying to describe him? He was—well, how *was* that man that you didn't quite get over to in time?

I like to study people. People that I know I'm going to see lots more than just once. That I want to, that I've got to.

"This is Annie," Jean was saying in that careless way of hers.

7

Nothing could be done about that. I'd given up trying. All the "Anyas" and "Annettes" when I was seventeen and eighteen hadn't helped any. I was back to plain Annie again, this time to stay. Good old Annie, there's a good girl.

We all sat down. He looked well sitting; not too far forward, not too far back. Not too straight, not too sunken. Couldn't he do anything wrong? He should do something wrong. This wasn't good for me.

We talked for a while, as people do, entering on the preliminaries of social intercourse. We said a lot of things; we said nothing. His man brought in a frost-clouded shaker and poured Bacardis and offered them to us. The talk that was talk for the sake of making talk went on, at quickened pace now, lubricated by the cocktails.

"How did you happen to get hold of all this?" Jean blurted out in that pseudonaïve way of hers. We were at the table now.

"An aunt," he smiled. "The right kind."

"Old and rich," she quickly supplied.

"Fond of me," he contributed.

"Dead," she topped him.

"It's a co-operative, she owned it, and when she died two years ago, I found it on my hands."

"Why don't I find things like that on my hands?" Jean wondered innocently.

"I didn't know what to do about it, so I moved in here, along with Luthe. He's my man. The estate takes care of the upkeep, so that what it amounts to practically is I'm living here rent-free."

I kept wondering what he did. I didn't know how to go about asking, though. Jean did. It was a great convenience having her along, I couldn't help reflecting.

"Well, what do you do?" she pressed him.

"Nothing," he said bluntly. "Simply—nothing."

She burst out with enthusiasm. "Now, there's a man after my own heart! Let me shake hands with you." And she proceeded vigorously to do so.

"I did have a job until this—this windfall descended upon

me," he said. "I even kept it up for a while afterwards—at first. And then I got up too late for work one day after a party, and it felt good not to go to work, so I said to myself 'Why haven't I done this before?' and I never did go back from then on."

The Cipher made his hourly utterance at this point. "I admire you," he stated emphatically. "That's the way all of us have felt at one time or another. Only, you had spunk enough to go ahead and carry it out."

"Do you always carry out the things you feel like doing, stray impulses that come along?" Jean asked him mischievously. "If you do, I'd hate to be the lady in front of you in a theater seat wearing one of those tall, obliterating hats."

"Pretty nearly always," he said with grim determination. "Pretty nearly always."

And you could tell he wasn't joking.

We left early. He closed the door, and we could hear his step going away down the corridor inside. He had a fine, firm, crisp tread; clean-cut, without any slurring. He even walked right.

She stood there looking at me with her brows raised.

"Why are your brows up?" I asked, finally.

"Are they up?"

"Well, they don't grow that way."

She let them down at length. Presently she remarked, as if to herself, "He's unhappy." She turned back to me for corroboration. "Don't you think so? Couldn't you notice?"

"Women," observed the Cipher, eying the cab ceiling light.

She ignored him. "Some girl, probably." She pondered the matter. Then she nodded confirmation of her own line of reasoning. "He's the broody type, would let it get him."

"I couldn't see anything the matter with him," the Cipher put in. "What did you expect the poor fellow to do, stand on his hands?"

"Men," she said crushingly.

"I think I saw her," I told her.

"What was she like?" she wanted to know eagerly.

"Not good for him," I said somberly. "Or anyone else. She was inside a frame in one of the rooms there. He had the door closed, I guess so we wouldn't look in, but the key was still in it on the outside. It said: 'To my Dwight,' down in a lower corner, but her own name wasn't signed. As though," I went on resentfully, "there could be no possible danger of confusion, there was only one of her in his life."

"Ho, you were busy!" she reveled.

"She must use the room sometimes. Stay over," I said bitterly. "It was all in peach and marabou."

"He's a big boy now," Jean drawled extenuatingly. "And he is a bachelor. And they do say there's an awful lot of it going on."

"That will do," said the Cipher with mock primness.

And so we began to know him, the little that you could. The little that he would let you. Or perhaps I should say, the little that we were capable of.

I had him at my place, and then Jean had him at hers. It went better there. Anything always did at Jean's place. Even a funeral would have been lively. We were all even now. I don't know why you have to be, but you have to be. Then he called, in about a week, and invited us to dine with him again, starting the thing over.

Jean, it was obvious, already didn't view the prospect with any great enthusiasm. "I'm not going to stay too late," she remarked. "You come away blue. I don't mind anyone being lovesick, but not if I have to sit and watch it."

I didn't answer. I was trying to decide what I was going to wear.

The dinner was just as good as the first time. He was just as hard to get to know as ever.

After we'd left the table, Luthe kept coming to the door with telephone calls. Effect without cause; you never heard it ring. Dwight just shook his head in refusal each time. I counted about five or six times it happened. It got on Dwight's nerves finally.

"Not anyone, understand?" he said sharply. "Not anyone at

all."

Jean looked into her drink as though she were wondering whether it were big enough to drown herself in.

The next thing, Luthe had come back to the door again, in spite of the recent blanket injunction he'd been given.

Dwight turned his head abruptly. "I thought I told you—"

Luthe beamed at him. Wordlessly a message passed between them. I don't know how they did it, but it was sent and it was understood.

"No!" Dwight gasped incredulously. And then I saw his face light up as I'd never seen it light up yet. There was only one way to describe it. It was the face of a man deliriously in love. The face of a man who had thought all along he'd lost something, and now found it was being returned to him. That it was his once more.

It hurt me a little to see that light on his face. Second-degree burns, most likely, from foolishly trying to get too near.

The telepathic currents continued to flow back and forth between the two of them. Luthe was all white teeth. "Sure enough," he grinned.

Dwight choked on some sort of too-turgid happiness brimming up all over him. "Luthe, you're not fooling me? Don't do that."

"Don't I know the right voice?"

"When did she get back?"

"You better find that out for yourself."

He went into a sudden flurry of—I don't know what you'd call it—altruistic ecstasy. "More drinks for everybody! Annie, Jean, another. Champagne this time, Luthe. I'll join you in it, be right back!" And as he zigzagged to get out of the room in the shortest time possible, he passed close by where I was sitting, and in a sudden blind effusion—it must have been blind, it must have been—he bent and elatedly kissed the top of my head.

He didn't walk down the gallery out there. You could hear him running. It was a long thing, and he ran the whole length of it; then his footsteps stopped, and he'd arrived; he was there, he was talking to her.

I sat very still, as though I were afraid of spilling a drop of the champagne Luthe had just poured for me.

Nothing was said.

There was a muffled thud, outside there, about where the footsteps had ended. As when a chair goes over, perhaps. A little less sharply defined than that. Or when you sway unexpectedly and bump your head upon a table or against a doorframe.

Luthe looked up sharply. Then he hastened over and looked out, down the gallery. He hurried from sight, in that direction.

We waited there, holding our champagne.

He took a long time to come back to us.

Jean got up and wandered over to the radio console, and studied it. But then she didn't turn it on. There was more and better drama here, on the outside of it. I'd been hoping she wouldn't. She came back again presently and reseated herself about where she'd been before.

It must have been about ten minutes. Then he came walking in again. A little tiredly, a little inertly. There was a neat little patch of adhesive up on his temple, back from the eye.

"I got a little bump on the head," he smiled. "Luthe insisted on giving me first aid. Sorry I was so long."

His face was too white for that. It was drawn, it was sick. You don't get that look on your face even when you half knock yourself out. It was behind the eyes, mostly; inside them.

"She's said good-by—whoever she is," I said to myself.

I took a sip of champagne. Funny how quickly it worked through you, making you glow, making you feel happy, even such a small sip.

Luthe had come in with a drink for him. It was straight brandy. It was a giant. It wasn't a drink for conviviality; it was a restorative.

He looked at it dubiously while Luthe stood there holding it for him. Then he looked up into Luthe's face, as though appealing to some superior wisdom, more than he himself had at the moment. "That won't help much, will it?" I heard him say almost inaudibly.

"No, that won't help much," Luthe agreed ruefully.

Luthe turned away with it, set it aside someplace, went out without it.

We tried to pick up the pieces of the conversation. Even Jean chipped in now, her humanitarian instincts aroused.

I kept watching his flayed face. I wondered if we were being cruel or kind.

"Don't you think we'd better be getting along," I suggested.

"No, don't go yet," he said, almost alarmedly. "Wait a little while longer, can't you? It's good to have you here. I feel sort of—"

He didn't finish it, but I knew the word: lonely.

We stayed on, by common consent. Even the Cipher forbore looking at his watch, that gesture with which he had a habit of harrying Jean, any evening, anywhere—but home.

It would have been a case of leaving just as the curtain was about to go up, though we didn't know it.

Suddenly drama had come fuming in around us, like a flash flood.

Luthe reappeared, went to him, bent down and said something. This time wholly inaudibly.

Dwight looked up at him, first in complete disbelief. Then in consternation. Then he pointed to the floor. I caught the word. "Here?"

Luthe nodded.

I caught the next two words too. "With him?" I saw him wince, as if in imminence of unendurable pain.

"All right," he said finally, and gave his hand an abrupt little twist of permission. "All right."

I got it then. There's somebody else; that was her first message, the one that floored him. But not only that: she's come right here with the somebody else.

He was a bad actor. No, I shouldn't say that. We were in the wings, watching him; we were backstage. All actors are bad when you watch them from behind-scenes. He was a good actor from out front. And that was from where he was meant to be seen.

He got up and he went over quickly to where Luthe had parked that brandy bombshell. And suddenly the glass was empty. I never saw a drink go down so fast. It must have flowed in a steady stream, without a stop for breath between. He did it with his back to us, but I saw him do it just the same. Then he wagged his head and coughed a little, and it was all down.

It wasn't a restorative now, it was more an anesthetic.

Then he slung himself to the arm of the settee I was on, and lighted a cigarette, not without a little digital difficulty, and he was ready for the curtain to go up. On the last act of something or other.

His timing was good, too.

Luthe showed up at the gallery opening, announced formally: "Mr. and Mrs. Stone."

She came out onto the entrance apron, two steps above the rest of us. She, and a husband tailing her. But what it amounted to was: she came out onto the entrance apron. He might just as well not have been there.

She was familiar with the stage management of this particular entryway, knew just how to get the most out of it. Knew just how long to stand motionless, and then resume progress down into the room. Knew how to kill him. Or, since she'd already done that pretty successfully, perhaps I'd better say, knew how to give him the shot of adrenalin that would bring him back to life, so that she could kill him all over again. To be in love with her as he was, I couldn't help thinking, must be a continuous succession of death throes. Without any final release. I imagined I could feel his wrist, hidden behind me, bounce a little, from a quickened pulse.

She stood there like a mannequin at a fashion display modeling a mink coat. Even the price tag was there in full view, if you had keen enough eyes; and mine were. Inscribed *"To the highest bidder, anytime, anywhere."*

She had a lot of advantages over the picture I'd seen of her. She was in color; skin like the underpetals of newly opened June rosebuds, blue eyes, golden-blonde hair. And the picture, for its part, had one advantage over her, in my estimate: it couldn't breathe.

She had on that mink she was modeling, literally. Three-quarters length, flaring, swagger. She was holding it open at just the right place, with one hand. Under it she had on an evening gown of white brocaded satin. The V-incision at the bodice went too low. But evidently not for her; after all, she had to make the most of everything she had, and not leave anything to assumption. She had a double string of pearls close around her neck, and a diamond clip at the tip of each ear.

They have the worst taste in women, all of them. Who is to explain their taste in women?

She came forward, down the steps and into the room. Perfume came with her, and the fact that she had hip sockets. The bodice incision deepened, too, if anything.

I kept protesting inwardly, But there must be something more than just what I can see. There *must* be something more. To make him fall and hit his head at the telephone; to make him down a glass of brandy straight to keep from moaning with pain. To make his pulse rivet the way it is against the back of this settee. As though he had a woodpecker hidden in it.

I kept waiting for it to come out, and it didn't. It wasn't there. It was all there at first glance, and beyond that there was nothing more. And most of it, at that, was the mink, the pearls, the diamonds and the incision.

She was the sort of girl who got whistled at, passing street corners. Her two hands went out toward him, not just one. A diamond bracelet around one wrist shifted back a little toward the elbow, as they did so.

"Billy!" she crowed. And her two hands caught hold of his two, and spread his arms out wide, then drew them close together, then spread them wide again. In a sort of horizontal handshake.

So she called him Billy. That would be about right for her, too. Probably "Billy-boy" when there were fewer than three total strangers present at one time.

"Well, Bernette!" he said in a deep, slow voice that came

through hollow, as from inside a mask.

One pair of hands separated, then the other. His were the ones dropped away first, so the impulse must have come from him.

"What happened?" she said. "We were cut off." I saw her glance at the court plaster. "Billy!" she squealed delightedly. "You didn't *faint*, did you? Was it that much of a shock?" She glanced around toward her oncoming fellow arrival, as if to say: "See? See what an effect I still have on him?" I read the look perfectly; it was a flicker of triumphant self-esteem.

The nonentity who had come in with her was only now reaching us; he'd crossed the room more slowly.

He was a good deal younger than either one of them; particularly Dwight. Twenty-three perhaps, or five. He had a mane of black hair, a little too oleaginous for my taste, carefully brushed upward and back. It smelled a little of cheap alcoholic tonic when he got too near you. He had thick black brows, and the sort of a beard that leaves a bluish cast on the face even when it is closely shaven. He was good-looking in a juvenile sort of way. His face needed a soda-jerk's white cocked hat to complete it. It was crying for something like that; it was made to go under it. And something told me it had, only very recently.

Her hand slipped possessively back, and landed on his shoulder, and drew him forward the added final pace or two that he hadn't had the social courage to navigate unaided.

"I want you to meet my very new husband. Just breaking in." Then she said, "You two should know each other." And she motioned imperiously. "Go on, shake hands. Don't be bashful. Dwight. Harry. *My* Dwight. *My* Harry."

Dwight's crisp intelligent eyes bored into him like awls; you could almost see the look spiraling around and around and around as it penetrated into the sawdust. You could almost see the sawdust come spilling out.

It's not the substitution itself, I thought; it's the insult of *such* a substitution.

The wait was just long enough to have a special meaning; you could make of it what you willed. Finally Dwight shook his hand.

"You're a very lucky—young fellow, young fellow."

I wondered what word he would have liked to use in place of "young fellow."

"I feel like I know you already," the husband said sheepishly. "I've heard a lot about you."

"That's very kind of Bernette," Dwight said dryly.

I wondered where she'd got him. He had the dark, slicked-back good looks that would hit her type between the eyes.

Then again, why differentiate? They went well together. They belonged together.

The line of distinction didn't run between him and her; it ran between her and Dwight. And part of her, at that, belonged on one side of the line, and part belonged on the other. The mink coat and the pearls and the diamond clips belonged on Dwight's side of the line; and she herself belonged on the other side of it. She wasn't even an integrated personality. The husband, with all his cheapness and callowness, at least was.

Dwight introduced the rest of us; introduced us, after I already knew her better than he ever had or ever would, with a pitiless clarity that he would never have.

Jean might have aroused her antagonistic interest, I could see that, but the married title deflected it as quickly as the introduction was made. Then when it came to myself, one quick comprehensive look from head to foot, and she decided, you could tell, there was nothing to worry about *there*.

"Drinks for Mr. and Mrs.—" Dwight said to Luthe. He couldn't get the name yet. Or didn't want to.

"Stone," the husband supplied embarrassedly, instead of letting the embarrassment fall on Dwight, where it rightfully belonged.

She at least was perfectly self-possessed, knew her way around in this house. "My usual, Luthe. That hasn't changed. And how are you, anyway?"

Luthe bowed and said coldly that he was all right, but she hadn't waited to hear. The back of her head was to him once more.

Their drinks were brought, and there was a slow maneuvering for position. Not physical position, mental. She lounged back upon the settee as though she owned it, and the whole place with it; as she must have sat there so very many times before. Tasted her drink. Nodded patronizingly to Luthe: "As good as ever."

Dwight, for his part, singled out the husband, stalked him, so to speak, until he had him backed against a wall. You could see the process step by step. And then finally, "By the way, what line are you in, Stone?"

The husband floundered badly. "Well, right now—I'm not—"

She stepped into the breach quickly, leaving Jean, with whom she had been talking, hanging on midword. "Harry's just looking around right now. I want him to take his time." Then she added quickly, just a shade too quickly, "Oh, by the way, remind me; there's something I want to speak to you about before I leave, Billy." And then went back to Jean again.

That told me why she'd dragged him up here with her like this. Not to flaunt him; she had no thought of profitless cruelty. The goose that had laid its golden yolks for one might lay them for two as well. Why discard it entirely?

"Where'd you go for your honeymoon, Bernette?" Dwight asked her.

She took a second, as though this required care. She was right, it did. "We took a run up to Lake Arrow."

He turned to the husband. "Beautiful, isn't it? How'd you like it?" Then back to her again, without waiting for the answer he hadn't wanted anyway. "How is the old lodge? Is Emil still there?"

She took a second. "Emil's still there," she said reticently.

"Did you remember me to him?"

She took two seconds this time. "No," she said reluctantly, mostly into the empty upper part of her glass, as though he were in there. "He didn't ask about you."

He shook his head and clicked with mock ruefulness. "Forgetful, isn't he? Has he done anything about changing that godawful wallpaper in the corner bedroom yet?" He explained to me, with magnificent impartiality: "He was always going to. It was yellow, and looked as though somebody had thrown up at two-second intervals all over it." He turned and flicked the punch line at her. "Remember, Bernette?"

It was now she who addressed the husband.

"We were both up there at the same time, once. I went up there on my vacation. And Billy went up there on his vacation. At the same time. And the room that Billy had, had this godawful wallpaper."

"At the same time," I thought I heard Dwight murmur, but it wasn't a general remark.

"I know, you told me," the husband said uneasily.

I saw the way his eyes shifted. It's not that he doesn't know, I translated; it's that he doesn't want to be forced into admitting publicly that he knows.

I watched them at the end, when they were about to go. Watched Dwight and her. When the good-by had been said and the expressions of pleasure at meeting had been spoken all around—and not meant anywhere. They reversed the order of their entry into the room. The husband left first, and passed from sight down the gallery, like a well-rehearsed actor who clears the stage for a key speech he knows is to be made at this point. While she lingered behind a moment in studied dilatoriness, picking up her twinkling little pouch from where she had left it, pausing an instant to see if her face was right in a mirror on the way.

Then all at once, as if at random afterthought: "Could I see you for a minute, Billy?"

They went over to the side of the room together, and their voices faded from sound. It became a pantomime. You had to read between the attitudes.

I didn't watch. I began talking animatedly to Jean. I didn't miss a gesture, an expression of their faces, a flicker of their eyes. I got everything but the words. I didn't need the words.

She glanced, as she spoke, toward the vacant gallery opening, just once and briefly.

Talking about the husband.

She took a button of Dwight's jacket with her fingers, twined it a little.

Ingratiation. Asking him something, some favor.

She stopped speaking. The burden of the dialogue had been shifted to him. He began.

He shook his head almost imperceptibly. You could scarcely see him do it. But not uncertainly, definitely. Refusal. His hand had strayed toward his billfold pocket. Then it left it again still empty.

No money for the husband.

The dialogue was now dead. Both had stopped speaking. There was nothing more to be said.

She stood there at a complete loss. It was something that had never happened to her, with him, before. She didn't know how to go ahead. She didn't know how to get herself out of it.

He moved finally, and that broke the transfixion.

They came back toward us. Their voices heightened to audibility once more.

"Well—good night, Billy," she said lamely. She was still out of breath—mentally—from the rebuff.

"You don't mind if I don't see you to the door, do you?" He wanted to avoid that unchaperoned stretch between us and it, wanted to escape having to pass along there alone with her, and being subject to a still more importunate renewal of the plea.

"I can find the way," she said wanly.

She left. I had him all to myself for a moment, at least the exterior of him.

Not for long, just between the acts. It wasn't over yet. Suddenly, over his shoulder, I saw she'd reappeared at the lower end of the room, was standing there.

"Billy, talk to Luthe, will you? What's the matter with him? Has he had a drink or something? I can't get him to give me my coat." And her whole form shook slightly with appreciative risibility.

He called and Luthe appeared almost instantly there beside

her in the gallery opening, holding the mink lining-forward in both arms. Like someone who has been waiting in the wings the whole time and takes just a single step forward to appear and play his part.

"Luthe, what are you doing?" he said amiably. "Is that Mrs. Stone's coat you're holding?" And before she could interject "Of course it is!" which it was obvious she was about to do, he added: "Read the label in the pocket lining and see what it says."

Luthe dutifully peered down into the folds of satin and read, "Miss Bernette Brady."

There was a pause, while we all got it, including herself. It was Miss Brady's coat, but not—any longer—Mrs. Stone's. Dwight stepped over to a desk, lowered the slab, and hastily inked something on a card. And then he went to her with it and handed it to her. "Bernette," he said, "take this with you."

It was an ordinary visiting or name card. She held it bracketed by two corners and scanned it diagonally, puzzled.

"What's this for?"

"I'll call him and make an appointment for you," he said quietly. "Go in and talk to him. The whole thing'll be over in no time."

"What do I need a lawyer for?" she blurted out.

I understood then, without the aid of the card. An annulment.

Anger began to smolder in her eyes. She gave him warning, but a warning that was already too late to avert the brewing storm. "That isn't funny."

"I'm not trying to be funny."

Her fingers made two or three quick motions and pieces of cardboard sputtered from them.

"Think it over," he urged, a second too late.

"I just did," she blazed. "Just then." She quirked her head sideward, then back toward him again. "Is Luthe going to give me my coat?"

"Come back for it," he drawled soothingly. "It'll be here—waiting for you—any time you say …."

Her voice was hoarse now, splintered. "Then let's be

consistent, shall we? How about it?"

Her hands wrestled furiously at the back of her neck. The pearls sidled down the bodice incision. She trapped them there with a raging slap, balled them up, flung them. They fell short of his face, they were probably too light, but they struck the bosom of his shirt with a click and rustle.

"Bernette, I have people here. They're not interested in our private discussions."

"You should have thought of that sooner." Her hands were at her earlobe now. "You want them to know you gave me things, don't you? You don't have to tell them! I'll tell them!" The ear clips fell on the carpet at his feet, one considerably in advance of the other.

"You can't carry that out down to its ultimate ...."

"I can't, hunh? You think these people being here is going to stop me, hunh? The hell with them! The hell with you yourself! I'll show you! I'll show you what I think of you!"

She was beside herself with rage. There was a rending of satin, and suddenly the dress peeled off spirally, like a tattered paper wrapper coming off her. Then she kicked with one long silk-cased leg, and it fluttered farther away.

She had a beautiful figure. That registered on my petrified mind, I recall. We sat there frozen.

"Keep your eyes down, ducky," I heard Jean warn the Cipher in a sardonic undertone. "I'll tell you when you can look up."

For a moment she posed there, quivering, a monotoned apparition all in flesh tints, the undraped skin and the pale-pink silk of vestigial garments blending almost indistinguishably.

Then she gave a choked cry of inexpressible aversion, and darted from sight.

Dwight raised his own voice then, but not in rage, only for it to carry to a distance. "Luthe, that raincoat in the hall! Put it over her."

A door slammed viciously somewhere far down the gallery.

None of us said anything. What is there that can be said following such a thing?

Jean was the first one to speak, after the long somewhat numbed silence that followed. And, probably unintentionally, her matter-of-fact minor-keyed remark struck me as the most hilariously malapropos thing I had ever heard. I wanted to burst out laughing at it.

She stirred and said with mincing politeness: "I really think we should be going now."

A six-week interval, then. It must have been fully that; I didn't time it exactly. Oh, why lie? Why write this at all, if not truthfully? I counted every week, every day, every hour. I didn't tally them up, that was all. At least once every day I had to remind myself, unnecessarily, "I haven't seen him since that explosive night. That makes it a day more, that I haven't seen him." It worked out at something like six weeks.

Nothing happened. No word. No sight. No sign.

Was he with her once more? Was he with somebody else entirely different? Was he alone, with nobody at all? Where was he? What was he doing? Was he still in New York? Had he gone somewhere else?

I had it bad. Real bad.

Finally I sent him a little note. Just a little note. Oh, such a very little note. *"... I haven't heard anything from you in some time now—"*

A coward's note. A liar's note; a liar even to myself.

The phone rang the next afternoon. I made a mess of it. I dropped the phone. I burned myself on a cigarette. I had to trample the cigarette out first. Then I hung onto the phone with both hands, when I'd once retrieved it.

He said things. The words didn't matter; it was just the voice they were pitched in.

Then he said: "I don't dare ask you and the Medills to come up here after what happened that last time."

"Dare," I said faintly. "Go on, dare."

"All right, would you?" he said. "Let's all have dinner together and—"

When I told Jean that he had called, about fifteen minutes later, she said the strangest thing. I should have resented it, but she said it so softly, so understandingly, that it never occurred to me until later that I should have resented it.

"I know," Jean said. "I can tell."

She murmured presently, "I think we should. I think it'd be good for us."

How tactful of her, I thought gratefully, to use the plural.

So back we went, the three of us, for another glimpse at this real-life peepshow that went on and on with never an intermission, even though there was not always someone there to watch it.

He was alone. But my heart and my hopes clouded at the very first sight of him as we came in; they knew. He was too happy. His face was too bright and smooth; there was love hovering somewhere close by, even though it wasn't in sight at the moment. Its reflection was all over him. He was animated, he was engaging, he made himself pleasant to be with.

But as for the source of this felicity, the wellspring, you couldn't tell anything. If I hadn't known him as he'd been in the beginning, I might have thought that was his nature. He was alone, just with Luthe. We were only four at the table, one to each side of it, with candles and a hand-carved ship model in the center of it.

Then when we left the table, I remember, we paired off unconventionally. I don't think it was a deliberate maneuver on anyone's part, it just happened that way. Certainly, I didn't scheme it; it was not the sorting of partners I would have preferred. Nor did he. And the Cipher least of all. He never schemed anything. That left only Jean; I hadn't been watching her ....

I think I do recall her linking an arm to mine, which held me to her. And then she leaned back to the table a moment and reached for a final grape or mint, which resulted in reversing the order of our departure. At any rate, the two men obliviously preceded us, deep in some weighty conversation; she and I followed after. We gave them a good headstart, too. She walked with deliberate slowness, and I perforce had to follow suit.

She stopped short midway down the gallery, well before we had emerged into view of the drawing room, which the two men had already entered.

"I have premonitions of a run," she said. "I don't trust these sheers." But what she did was jog her elbow into my side, in a sort of wordless message or signal, as she turned aside and went in through the nearest doorway. That doorway.

I turned and followed her; that was what her nudge had summoned me to do.

Lights went on, and the big bed leaped into view in the background.

She went toward the full-length mirror in a closet door. She went through the motions of validating her excuse for stepping in here; raised her skirt, cocked her leg askew toward the mirror, dropped her skirt again. Then she reached out and purposefully took hold of the faceted glass knob of the closet door.

"Jean," I said with chaste misgivings. "Don't do that."

I saw she was going to anyway.

She swept it wide, the door, with malignant efficiency, and stood back with it so that I could see, and looked at me, not it, as she did so.

Satins and silks, glistening metallic tissues, flowered prints; and in the middle of all of them, like a queen amidst her ladies in waiting, that regal mink.

Then there was a blinding silvery flash as the electric light flooded across the mirror, and the door swept back into place.

"Back again," she said, brittlely. "This time, for keeps." And, I thought, what an apt word.

But for long moments afterward, long after the other things had faded and been effaced, it still seemed as if I could see the rich darkness of that mink, through glass and all, as if shadowed against some X-ray apparatus. Then finally it, too, dimmed and was gone, and there was just clear mirror left. With somebody's woeful, heartsick face on it. My own.

She put out the light as she shepherded me across the threshold; I remember the room was dark as we left it behind. I remember that so well. So very well.

She held her arm around me tight as we walked slowly down the remainder of the gallery.

I needed it.

"Tune in the Stadium concert, Luthe," he suggested at one point. "It must be time for it."

I wondered what he wanted that for.

Some very feverish dance band drumming filtered out.

"If that's the Stadium concert," Jean said, "they've certainly picked up bad habits."

"Luthe," he said good-naturedly, "what're you doing over there? I said the open-air concert, at the Lewisohn Stadium."

"I can't seem to get it. What station is it on?"

"ABC, I think."

"I'm on ABC now. Doesn't seem to be it."

"Does it?" agreed Jean, pounding her ear and giving her head a shake to clear it, as a particularly virulent trombone snarl assailed us.

"Call up the broadcasting station and find out," he suggested.

Luthe came back.

"No wonder. It's been called off on account of rain. Giving it tomorrow night instead."

"It's not raining down here," Jean said. She returned from the window. "It's bone-dry out. Do you even have special weather arrangements for Park Avenue?" she queried.

"Look who we are," he answered her. A little distraitly, I thought, as though he were thinking of something else. "What time is it now, Luthe?" he asked.

She arrived about an hour and a half later. Perhaps even two hours. I don't know; since I hadn't been expecting her, I wasn't clocking her exactly. If he was, he'd kept it to himself; you couldn't notice it. No more parenthetic requests for the time, after that first one.

There was one thing noticeable about her arrival. I mean, even over and above the usual flashlight-powder brilliance of her arrival anywhere, anytime. It was that she was not announced. She simply entered, as one does where one belongs. Suddenly, from nowhere, she had taken her stance there on the auction block (as I called it after that first time). Then, after flamboyant pause and pose there, she was coming down the steps to join us.

He'd made a few improvements in her. Surface ones only; that was the only part of her he could reach, I suppose. Or maybe he needed more time. Her dress was a little higher at the neck, now, and the phantom price tag had been taken off. You got her value after awhile, but not immediately, at first sight.

She'd even acquired an accent. I mean an accent of good, cultivated English; and since it was false, on her it was an accent.

When she walked, she even managed to use the soles of her feet and not her hips so much any more. I wondered if he'd used telephone directories on her head for that, or just clouted her there each time one of them swayed, until she'd stopped it.

Or maybe she was just a good mimic, was getting it all by suction, by being dunked into the company of the right people more and more often. For my money, she'd had all the other makings of a good sponge right from the start; why not in that way, too?

"You remember Annie and Jean, and Paul," he said.

"Oh yes, of cowass; how are you?" she leered affably. She was very much the lady of the manor, making us at home in her own domain. "Sorry I'm so late. I stayed on to the very end."

"Did you?" he said.

And I thought, Where? Then, No! It can't be! This is too good to be true ....

But she rushed on, as though speaking the very lines I would have given her myself. She wanted to make a good impression, avoid the cardinal social sin of falling mute, not having anything to say; all those unsure of themselves are mortally afraid of it. So the fact of saying something was more important than the content of what it was she said.

"Couldn't tear myself away. You should have come with me, Billy. It was heavenly. Simply heavenly." Business of rolling the eyes upward and taking a deep, soulful breath.

"What'd they play first?" he said tightly.

"Shostakovich," she said with an air of vainglory, as when one has newly mastered a difficult word and delights in showing one's prowess with it.

You couldn't tell she'd said anything. His face was a little whiter than before, but it was a slow process; it took long minutes to complete itself. Until finally he was pale, but the cause had long been left behind by that time, would not have been easy to trace any more.

She caught something, however. She was not dense.

"Didn't I pronounce it well?" she asked, darting him a look.

"Too well," he said.

She was uneasy now.

She didn't like us. She was hampered by our being there; couldn't defend herself properly against whatever the threat was. And although she didn't know what it was herself, as yet, she couldn't even make the attempt to find out, because of our continuing presence.

She sat for a moment with the drink he'd given her, made a knot with her neck pearls about one finger, let it unravel again. Then she stood up, put her drink down over where they originally came from.

"I have a headache," she said, and touched two fingers to the side of her head. To show us, I suppose, that that was where it was, in her head.

"Shostakovich always gives me a headache, too," Jean said sweetly to her husband.

She shot Jean a quick look of hostility, but there was nothing she could do about it. There was nothing to get her teeth into. If she'd picked it up, that would have been claiming it for her own.

"If you'll excuse me now," she said.

She was asking him, though, not the rest of us. She was a little bit afraid. She wanted to get out of this false situation. She didn't know what it was, but she wanted to extricate herself.

"You don't have to stand on ceremony with us, Bernette." He didn't even turn to look at her, but went ahead dabbling in drinks.

I thought of the old Spanish saying, *Aqui tiene usted su casa.* My house is yours. And it probably was as little valid in the present circumstance as in the original flowery exaggeration.

"But you just came," the Cipher said. He was only trying to be cordial, the poor benighted soul. He hadn't stepped aside into that room with us.

Jean and I simply looked at each other. I could almost lip-read what she was about to say before it came out. "She hasn't far to go." I nearly died for a minute as I saw her lips give a preliminary flicker. Then she curbed herself. That would have been going too far. I breathed again.

She made her good nights lamely, and yet with a sort of surly defiance. As if to say, I may have lost this skirmish, but I haven't even begun to fight yet. This was on ground of your choosing; wait till he's without his allies, and must come looking for me on ground of my own choosing. We'll see whose flag runs down then.

She even reached out and shook hands with him. Or at least, sought out his, took it up, then dropped it again; all the volition coming from hers.

Oh, really, I protested inwardly. You don't do that from room to room.

She climbed the steps, she turned galleryward, she passed from view. Tall and voluptuous in her black summer dress, her head held high, her chin out. A little cigarette smoke that had emanated from her on the way lingered behind her for a moment or two. Then that dissolved, too.

And that's all the trace you leave behind in this world, sometimes: a little cigarette smoke, quickly blown away.

Presently another figure passed the gallery opening, coming from farther back in the apartment, but going the same way she had. Handsome, well-dressed, almost unrecognizable for a moment in his tactfully-cut suit and snap-brim hat. There wasn't a garish detail of attire from head to foot. He would have passed without obtruding himself upon us, but Dwight turned his head.

"Going now?"

"Yes, sir. Good night." He tipped his hat to the rest of us, and left.

This time you could hear the outside apartment door close after him. Not like the time before.

"Luthe goes home out to Long Island one night a week to visit his mother, and this is his night for it." He shook his head. "He's studying law. I wish I lived as quietly and as decently as he does."

We left soon afterward ourselves.

As we moved down the gallery in leisurely deliberation, I looked ahead. That room that Jean and I had been in before was lighted now, not dark as we had left it. The door was partly ajar, and the light coming from it lay on the floor outside in a pale crosswise bar or stripe.

Then as we neared it, some unseen agency pushed it unobtrusively closed, from the inside. I could see the yellow outshine narrow and snuff out, well before we had reached it.

We were kept waiting for the elevator for some time. Finally, when it appeared, it was being run by a gnarled elderly individual in fireman's overalls, quite *declassé* for this building. There was no night doorman on duty below when we got there, either.

"What happened?" Jean asked curiously. "Where's all the brass?"

"Walked off," he said. "Wildcat strike. The management fired one of the fellows, and so they all quit. Less'n 'n hour ago. They ain't nobody at all to run the back elevator. I'm practic'ly running this whole building single-handed, right now. You'll have to get your own taxi, folks. Can't leave this car."

"She stayed," I breathed desolately, while the Cipher was off in quest of one.

"Just wait till he gets her alone, though," Jean chuckled. "She'll have a lot of explaining to do. I'd give anything to hear what's going on between the two of them right now."

He was waiting for me, the driver. I'd dropped them off first.

"I've lost something. Look, you'll have to take a run back with me a minute."

He meshed gears. "To where the other folks got out?"

"No, the first place. Where we all got in."

I'd lost something. A door key. Or pride. Or self-respect. Something like that.

"Want me to wait?" he said when we'd arrived.

"No, you'd better let me pay you. I don't want you clocking me the whole time I'm in there."

"You may have a wait for another, lady, at this hour."

He looked me too straight in the eye, I thought. The remark didn't warrant such a piercing gaze. And he had no need to crinkle the corners of his eyes like that; it gave his glance too familiarly knowing an aspect.

I dropped my own eyes primly. "Keep the rest."

The same elderly pinch hitter was still servicing the building's elevators single-handed. "They ain't nobody at all looking after the back one," he complained unasked.

I felt like saying, "You said that before," but I didn't.

He took me up without announcing me. I got out and I knocked at Dwight's door. The car went down and left me alone there.

No one came. I knocked again, more urgently, less tentatively. I tripped the Louis XVI gilt knocker, finally. That carried somewhat better, since it had a metal sounding board, not a wooden one.

Suddenly his voice said, "Who is it?" Too quickly for this last summons to have been the one that brought him; it must have been the first one after all, and he had been waiting there behind the door.

"Annie," I whispered, as though there were someone else around to overhear.

The door opened, but very grudgingly. Little more than a crevice at first. Then at sight of me, it widened to more normal width. But not full width of passage, for he stood there in the way; simply full width enough to allow unhampered conversation.

31

He was in a lounging robe. His shirt was tieless above it, and the collar band was unfastened. It had a peculiar effect on me: not the robe nor the lack of tie, simply the undone collar band; it made me feel like a wife.

"Don't look so stunned. Am I that frightening?" I couldn't resist saying. "Didn't you hear me give you my name through the door?"

"No," he said, "I missed it." Then he changed that to: "I thought I heard someone whisper, but I wasn't sure."

I didn't quite believe him, somehow. If he'd heard the whisper, then he'd heard the name whispered, I felt sure. I didn't resent the implication of a fib; quite the contrary. It was complimentary. It allowed me to believe—if I chose to, and I did—that my name effected the opening of the door, that another name would not have been able to. Castles in a foyer.

"Did I get you out of bed?" I said.

He smiled. It was a sort of vacant smile. The smile with which you wait for someone to go away. The smile that you give at a door when you are waiting to close it. Waiting to be allowed to close it, and held powerless by breeding. It had no real candlepower behind it, that smile. "No," he said, "I was just getting ready, by easy stages."

His face looked very pale, I thought; unnaturally so. I hadn't noticed it the first moment or two, but I gradually became aware of it now. I thought it must be the wretched foyer light, and I hoped I didn't look as pale to him as he did to me. I take pallor easily from unsatisfactory lights. The thing to do was to get inside away from it.

"It's my outside door key," I said. "I can't get into my house."

"It couldn't have been up here," he said. "I would have—I would have found it myself right after you left." He gestured helplessly with one hand, in a sort of rotary way. "It must have been in the taxi. Did you look in the taxi?"

The light was the most uncomplimentary thing I'd ever seen. It made him look almost ghastly.

"It wasn't in the taxi," I insisted. "I looked and looked. We even picked up the seat cushions." I waited for him to shift, but he didn't. "Won't you let me come in a moment and look?"

He was equally insistent. We were both strainedly civil but extremely insistent. "But it isn't up here, I tell you. It couldn't be, Annie, don't you see? If it was, I would have come across it by now myself."

I sighed exasperatedly. "But did you look for it? Did you know it was lost, until I told you so myself just now, here at the door? Then if you didn't look for it, how do you know it isn't there?"

"Well, I—I went over the place, I—" He decided not to say that, whatever it was to have been.

"But if you didn't know what it was that was lost, you couldn't have had your eye out for it specifically," I kept on, sugaring my stubbornness with reasonableness. "If you'd only let me step in for a moment and see for myself …."

I waited.

He waited, for my waiting to end.

I tried another tack. "Oh," I murmured deprecatingly, turning my head aside, as if to myself, as if in afterthought, "you're not alone. I'm sorry. I didn't mean to …."

It worked. I saw a livid flash, like the glancing reflection from a sun-blotted mirror, sweep across his face. Just for an instant. If it was fear, and it must have been of a kind, it was a new fear at this point: fear of being misunderstood, and no longer fear of my entering. He stepped back like magic, drawing the door with him.

"You're mistaken," he said tersely. "Come in."

And then as I did, and as he closed the door after me and pressed it sealed with his palm in one or two places, he added, and still quite tautly, "Whatever gave you that idea?" And turned to look the question at me, as well as ask it.

"After all," I drawled reassuringly. "I'm not anyone's grandmother."

This point, however, was evidently of importance to him, for some intangible reason that escaped me. Certainly I'd never detected any trait of primness in him before. "I never was so alone in my life," he said somewhat crossly. "Even Luthe went out home."

"I know," I reminded him. "He left while we were still here."

I had been thinking mainly of somebody else, not Luthe.

We moved slowly down the gallery, I preceding him.

She was gone, just as Jean had said she would be. The door that I had seen slyly closing before, shutting off its escaping beam of light, was standing starkly open now, and the room was dark. It looked gloomy in there, unutterably depressing, at that hour of the night.

"In here, maybe," I suggested, wickedly. I wasn't supposed to have been in there.

I heard him draw some sort of a crucial breath.

"No," he said quite flatly. "You didn't."

"I may have, just the same." I took a step as though to go in.

"No," he said, tautly, almost shrilly, as though I were getting on his nerves. He reached out before me and drew the door closed in my face.

I glanced at him in mild surprise, at the use of such a sharp tone of voice for such a trifling matter. The look I caught on his face was even more surprising. For a moment, all his good looks were gone. He was ugly in mood and ugly of face.

Then, with an effort, he banished the puckered grimace, let his expression smooth out again. Even tried on a thin smile for size, but it didn't fit very well and soon dropped off again.

Meanwhile, he'd withdrawn the key and the door was now locked fast.

"Why do you do that?" I asked mildly.

"I always keep it that way," he said. "It's not supposed to be left open. Luthe must have done that."

But Luthe had gone home before we had.

"Well, won't you let me go in and look at least?" I coaxed. I thought: I still love him, even when his face is all ugly and weazened like that. How strange; I thought it was largely his looks that had me smitten, and now I see that it isn't.

"But you weren't in there, so how could it get in there?"

34

"I was. I was in there once earlier tonight. I don't know whether you knew it or not, but I strayed in there one time this evening."

He looked at me, and he looked at the door. "Wasn't that a breach of manners on your part?" he suggested stiffly.

"There are no manners between a man and woman," I said. "There are only manners, good or bad, between a man and a man, or a woman and a woman."

He gave the cryptic answer, "Oh?"

Why do I drive him like this, I wondered? To see how far I can go? To make him fully aware of my being here alone with him? I didn't know myself.

We stood and looked at each other for a moment, he waiting for me to make the next move.

"Well, I'll have to get along without it," I said. "My key, I mean."

"Sorry."

"He wants me to go," I said, as though speaking ruefully to a third person. "He can't wait until I do."

What could he say then? What could anyone have said, except in overt offense? And that, you see, was why I'd said it. Though it was true, my saying so forced him to deny it, obliged him to act in contradiction to it. Though he didn't want to, and I knew that he didn't want to, and he knew that I knew that he didn't want to.

"No," he said deprecatingly. "No, not at all." And then warmed gradually to his own insistence; picked up speed with it as he went along. "Come inside. Away from that door." (As though my departure from a fixed point was now what he wanted to obtain, and if he could obtain it only by having me all the way in, rather than by having me leave, then he'd have me all the way in.) He motioned the way with his arm and he turned to accompany me. And kept up meanwhile the running fire of his invitation at a considerably accelerated tempo, until it ended up by being almost staccato. "Come inside and we'll have a drink together. Just you and me. Just the two of us alone. As a matter of fact, I need company, this minute."

On the rebound, I thought. On the rebound; I may get him that way. They say you do. Oh, what do I care how, if only I do.

I went down the steps, and he went down close beside me. His swinging arm grazed mine as we did so, and it did something to me. It was like sticking your elbow into an electrical outlet.

That drawing room of his had never looked vaster and more somber. There was something almost funereal about it, as though there were a corpse embalmed somewhere nearby, and we were about to sit up and keep vigil over it. There was only one lamp lighted, and it was the wrong one. It made great bat-wing shadows around the walls, from the upraised piano lid and other immovables, and now added our own two long, willowy emanations.

He saw me look at it, and said, "I'll fix that."

I let him turn on one more, just to take some of the curse off the gruesomeness, but then when I saw him go for the wall switch that would have turned on a blaze overhead I quickly interposed, "Not too many." You don't make very good love under a thousand-watt current.

I sat down on the sofa. He made our drinks for us, and then came over with them, and then sat down in the next state.

"No, here," I said. "My eyesight isn't that good."

He grinned and brought his drink over, and we sat half-turned toward each other, like the arms of a parenthesis. A parenthesis that holds nothing in it but blank space.

I saw to it that it soon collapsed of its own emptiness, and one of the arms was tilted rakishly toward the other.

I tongued my drink.

"It was a pretty bad jolt," I admitted thoughtfully.

"What was?"

"You don't have to pretend with me."

"Oh," he said lamely.

"You're still pretending," I chided him. "You're pretending that you haven't thought of it; that I'm the one just now brought it back to your mind for the first time. When all along it hasn't left your mind, not for a single moment since."

He tried to drown his face in his drink, the way he pushed it down into it. "Please," he said, and made a grimace. "Not now. Do we have to—? Don't let's talk about it now."

"Oh, that much it hurts," I said softly.

The parenthesis had become a double line, touching from top to bottom.

"Why don't you put iodine on it?" I suggested.

He made a ghastly shambles of a smile. "Is there any for such things?"

"Here's the bottle, right beside you," I offered. "And there's no death's head on the label."

That symbol seemed to frighten him for a moment, or at least be highly unwelcome. He screwed up his eyes tight, and I saw him give his head a shake, as though to rid it of that particular thought.

"It stings for a minute, and then you heal," I purred. "You heal clean. No festering. And then you're well again; even the mark goes away. And you have a new love." I dropped my voice to a breath. "Won't you try—iodine?"

So close his face was to mine, so close; all he had to do ....

Then he turned it a little; oh, a very, tactful little. The wrong way; so that the distance had widened a little. And he could breathe without mingling his breath with mine. Which seemed to be what he wanted.

"Don't you understand me, Dwight? I'm making love to you. And if I'm awkward about it, it's because women aren't very good at it. Can't you help me out a little?"

I saw the look on his face. Sick horror. I wish I hadn't, but I did. I never thought just a look on a face could hurt so.

"Would it be that bad? Would it be that unbearable, to be married to me?"

"Married?"

His backbone gave a slight twitch, as though a pin overlooked in his shirt had just pricked him. I caught him at it, slight as it was. That was no compliment, either, any more than the look on his face before had been.

"You've just been proposed to, Dwight. That was a proposal, just then. The first I've ever made."

He tried, first, to carry it off with a sickly grin. The implication: You're just joking, and I'm supposed to know you are, but you make me a little uncomfortable just the same.

I wouldn't let him; I wouldn't accept the premise.

"You don't laugh when a lady proposes to you," I said gently. "You don't laugh at her. You meet her on her own ground; you give her that much, at least."

He put his hand on my knee for a moment, but it was a touch of apology, of consolation; it wasn't what I wanted.

"I'm not—cut out—" He floundered. "It would be about the dirtiest trick I could play. I couldn't do that to you ...." And then finally, and more decidedly, like a snap-lock to the subject: "You'd be sorry."

"I want to be. Let me be. I'd rather be sorry—with you—than glad—with anyone else."

He looked down his nose now. He didn't say anything more. A sort of stubborn muteness had set in. That was his best defense; that was his only one. He probably knew it. Their instincts are just as valid as ours.

I had to do the talking. Someone had to. It would have been even worse to sit there in silence.

I took a sip of my drink. I sighed in feigned objectivity. "It's unfair, isn't it? A woman can refuse a man, and she doesn't have to feel any compunction. He's supposed to take it straight, and he does. But if a man refuses a woman, he has to try to spare her feelings at the same time."

He hadn't as a matter of fact made any such attempt until now; he did now, possibly because I had recalled his duty to him.

"You're a swell gal, Annie. It's you I'm thinking of. You don't know what you're asking. You don't want ME."

"You're getting your pronouns mixed," I said sadly.

All he could repeat was: "No, I mean it, you're a swell gal, Annie."

"You're a swell gal, Annie," I echoed desolately, "but you

don't ring the bell."

He made the mistake of putting his arm around my shoulder, in what was meant as a fraternal embrace, I suppose. He should have left his hands off me; it was hard enough without that.

I let my head go limp against him. I couldn't have kept it up straight if I'd tried. And I didn't try.

"Then on shorter terms," I whispered, closing my eyes. "As short as you wish."

He tried to jerk his arm away, as he realized this new danger, but I caught it from in front with mine, and held it there, around my shoulders, like a precious sable someone's trying to take away from you.

"Even just—for tonight. Just for—an hour. Do I have to speak any plainer than that? *Your* terms. Any terms at all."

He shuddered, and hit himself violently in the center of the forehead. As if there were some thought lodged in there that he couldn't bear the contemplation of. "My God," I heard him groan. "My God! Right here and now, in this apartment …."

"Is there something wrong with this apartment?" I asked innocently.

"Not with the apartment, with me," he murmured.

"I won't dispute you there," I said cattishly.

I let go of his arm, and he promptly called it back. I stood up. I got ready to go. I'd been rejected. To have prolonged it would have veered over into buffoonery. I had no self-respect left, but at least I still had my external dignity left. The law of diminishing returns would only have set in from this point on.

I turned and looked at him, still sitting there. "Seduction doesn't agree with you," I let him know. "You look positively harassed."

I saw him wince a little, as though he agreed with me; not only looked it, but felt it. He stood now, to do the polite thing as host.

"I'll get over it," I said, speaking out loud to keep my own courage up. "It doesn't kill you."

He blinked at the word, as though it grated a little.

I was ready to go now. He came closer, to accelerate the process.

"Won't you kiss me good night?" I said.

He did it with his brakes on; used just one arm to support my back. Put his lips to mine, but with a time valve to them. Took them away again as soon as time was up. Mine tried to follow, and lost their way.

We straightened ourselves. "I'll see you out," he said.

"Never mind. Don't rub it in."

He took me at my word, turned back to pour himself another drink. His hand was shaking, and if that's a sign of needing one, he needed one.

I went down the long gallery alone. So safe. Too safe. As safe as when I'd come in. My heart was blushing and my cheeks felt white.

I came opposite that door, the door to his lady-love's room. I stopped and looked at it. And as I did, a creepy feeling all at once came over me. Like a cold, cold wind that comes from nowhere and suddenly knifes you where you stand. As if the room were not empty. As if there were something in there, some terrible revelation, waiting, crying, to be seen. There was almost a pull to it, the feeling was so strong. It seemed to draw me, the way forbidden sights do. Evil sights; sights that are death in themselves and death to behold.

I started to put out my hand toward it. Then I felt his eyes on me, and turned, and saw him standing, watching me, at the end of the gallery, where I'd just come from myself.

"Annie," he said. "Don't." His voice was toneless, strangely quiet. He didn't offer to approach, stayed where he was; but his hands strayed to the cord of his robe and, of their own accord, without his seeming to know what they were doing, fumbled there, until suddenly the knot had disheveled, fallen open. Then each one, holding a loose end of the cord, flicked and played with it, all unconsciously. The way the two ends danced and spun and snaked suggested the tentative twitching of a cat's tail, when it is about to spring.

He was holding it taut across his back, and out at each side, in a sort of elongated bow-shape. It was just a posture, a stance, a vagary of nervous preoccupation, I suppose. An odd one, but meaningless.

I flexed my wrist slightly, as if to complete the touching of the doorknob.

The cord tightened to almost a straight line, stopped moving.

His eyes met mine and mine met his, the length of the gallery.

The impulse to annoy him died.

Indifferently, I desisted. I dropped my hand slowly, and let the door be.

His hands dropped too. The taut pull of the cord slackened, it softened to a dangling loop.

I went on to the outside door and opened it.

"Good night, Dwight," I murmured wanly.

"Good night, Annie," he echoed.

I saw him reach out with one arm and support himself limply against the wall beside him, he was so tired of me by this time.

I closed the outside door.

They tell you wrong when they tell you infatuation dies a sudden death. Infatuation dies a lingering, painful death. Even after all hope is gone the afterglow sometimes stubbornly clings on and on, kidding you, lighting the dark in which you are alone. Infatuation dies as slowly as a slower love; it comes on quicker, that is all.

Twice I went by there in a taxi, in the two weeks following that night. A taxi that didn't have to go by there, that could have taken me another way; but whose way I altered, I interfered with, so that it would take me by there. And each time it stopped a moment at the door. Not of its own accord, either. "Stop here a moment."

But then I didn't get out after all. Just sat there. Perhaps to see if I could sit there like that without getting out, I don't know. Perhaps to see if I was strong enough.

I was. I just barely made it, both times, but I made it.

"Drive on," I said heroically, when the driver turned his head around inquiringly after nothing had happened. It was like leaving your right arm behind, jammed in a door; but I left it.

One of the two times, I had been on my way to a party, and the excuse would have been to ask him if he wanted to come along with me. Had I carried the stop out to its ultimate conclusion. But I don't think we would have gone on to any party, even had I put the invitation to him. It takes two to want to go to any party, when there are two, and one of us wouldn't have wanted to go—even had he said yes.

(I didn't, incidentally, even go on to the party myself, after I drove on from his door; I went home and took off the regalia it had taken me an hour's solid work to array myself in. It hadn't been meant for the general admiration of any party.)

And the second of the two times I stopped, the excuse was even more flimsy. I was supposed to be on my way somewhere else. To friends, I think, for an evening of bridge.

"Drive on," I told the driver.

But I was convalescing; it was only like leaving your hand caught in the door, not your whole arm now.

"Your game isn't what it used to be," my partner told me acidulously later that evening, after we'd gone down for a grand slam.

"No," I agreed, word for word, "my game isn't what it used to be." ("And I'm a dud at the new one," I added to myself.)

But the third time, ah the third time, I stopped down there at the door, there was no excuse at all. None whatever. Not even so fragile a one as a secondhand party or a secondhand, game. I did it as sort of test, and I found out what I wanted to.

I was practically over it. I was cured. I made the discovery for myself sitting there in the taxi, taking my own blood pressure, so to speak, holding my own pulse, listening to my own heart. I could drive away now without a wrench, without feeling that I'd left a part of me behind, caught in his door.

I lighted a cigarette and thought with a sigh of relief: It's passed. It's finished. Now I've got nothing more to worry about.

That was the vaccine of love. Now I'm immune. Now I can go on and just work and live and be placid.

"Y'getting out, lady, or what?" the driver asked fretfully.

"Yes," I said coolly, "I think I will. I want to say good-by to someone in there."

And in perfect safety, in perfect calm, I paid him and got out and went inside to visit my recent, my last, love.

But, as I have often said, they tell you wrong when they tell you infatuation dies a sudden death. It doesn't. *I* know.

I seemed to have picked an inappropriate time for my farewell visit. Or at least, a nonexclusive one.

There'd been somebody else with him. The apartment door was already open, when I stepped off at his foyer, and he was standing there talking to some man in dilatory leave-taking.

The man was heavily built and none too young. In the milder fifties, I should judge. His hair was silvering, his complexion was florid, and there were little skeinlike red blood vessels threading the whites of his eyes. He had a hard-looking face, but he was being excessively amiable at the moment that I came upon the two of them. Almost overdoing it, almost overly amiable, for it didn't blend well with the rest of his characteristics, gave the impression of being a seldom-used, almost rusty attribute; he had to push down hard on the accelerator to get it working at all. And he was keeping his foot pressed down on it for all he was worth so that it couldn't get away from him.

"I hope I haven't troubled you, Mr. Billings," he was apologizing just as the elevator panel opened.

"Not at all," Dwight protested indulgently. There was even something patronizing in his intonation. "I know how those things are. Don't think twice about it. Glad to—" And then they both turned at the slight rustle the panel made, and saw me, and so didn't finish the mutual gallantries they were engaged upon. Or rather, postponed them for a moment.

Dwight's face lighted up at sight of me. I was welcome. There could be no doubt of it. Not like that other night. And yet—How shall I put it? It was not a question of being relieved. I didn't detect that at all. It was rather that he was already so pleased with himself, and with everything else, this evening, that even my arrival pleased him. And I use the adverb "even" advisedly. So that I was welcome by good-humored reflection—anyone would have been at the moment—and not in my own right.

He shook my hand cordially. "Well! Nice of you! Where've you been keeping yourself?" And that sort of thing. But made no move to introduce the departing caller to me.

And his manners were too quick-witted for that to have been an oversight. So what could I infer but that there was a differentiation of status between us that would have made a social introduction inappropriate. In other words, that one call was a personal one and the other was not, so the two were not to be linked.

At the same time, he did not offer to disengage himself from his first caller, conclude the parley, and turn his attention to me. On the contrary, he postponed my playing on his attention and returned to the first matter, as if determined it should run its unhurried course and be completed without any haste, first of all. He even signaled to the car operator not to stand there waiting to take the leavetaker down, as he'd been inclined to do. "We'll ring," he said, and motioned the panel closed with his hand.

And to me: "Go in, Annie. Take your things off. I'll be right with you."

I went in. My last impression of the man standing there with him was that he was slightly ill at ease under my parting scrutiny; call it embarrassed, call it sheepish, call it what you will. He turned his head aside a moment and took a deep draught of an expensive cigar he was holding between his knuckles. As if: Don't look at me so closely. I certainly wasn't staring, so it must have been his own self-consciousness.

I went down the gallery of lost loves. The room door was open now. I went past it without stopping, and down the steps to the drawing-room arena.

I took off my "things," as he'd put it, and primped at my hair, and moved idly around, waiting for him to join me.

I looked at things as I moved. One does, waiting in a room.

He'd left them just as they were, to take his visitor to the door. Probably I hadn't been announced yet, at that moment. I must have been announced after they were both already at the door, and he hadn't come all the way back in here since leaving it the first time.

There were two glasses. Both drained heartily, nothing but ice sweat left in their bottoms; the interview must have been a cordial one.

There were two strips of cellophane shorn from a couple of expensive cigars.

There was a single burned matchstick; one smoker had done that courteous service for both.

His checkbook folder was lying on the corner of the table. He must have taken it out of his pocket at one time, and then forgotten to return it again. Or perhaps thought that could wait until afterward; it was of no moment.

I didn't go near it, or touch it, or examine it in any way. I just saw it lying there.

There was a new blotter lying near it. Almost spotless; it had only been used about once.

That I did pick up, idly, and look at. As if I were a student of Arabic or some other right-to-left scrawl. I looked at it thoughtfully.

He still didn't come in.

Finally I took it over to the mirror with me and fronted it to that, and looked into that.

Part of his signature came out. "-*illings.*" It was the thing he'd written last, so the ink was still freshest when the blotter'd been put to it. Above it were a couple of less distinct tracings, "-*earer.*" And three large circles and two smaller ones. Like this: "OOOoo."

I turned swiftly, as though that had shocked me (but it hadn't; why should it?) and pitched it back onto the table from where I stood. Then I fixed my hair a little more, in places where it didn't need it.

He came in, looking sanguine, looking zestful. I don't remember that he rubbed his hands together, but that was the impression his mood conveyed: of rubbing his hands together.

"Who was that man?" I said indifferently.

"You'll laugh," he said. And he set the example by doing so himself. "That's something for you." Then he waited, as a good raconteur always does. Then he gave me the punch line. "He was a detective. A real, honest-to-goodness, life-sized detective. Badge and everything."

I stopped being indifferent, but I didn't get startled. Only politely incredulous, as a guest should be toward her host's surprise climaxes. "Here? What'd he want with you?"

"Asking if I could give him any information," he said cheerfully. Then in the same tone: "You've heard about Bernette, haven't you?"

I said I hadn't.

"I think you met her up here once."

I visioned a pink brassière and pink drawers. "Yes," I said, "I seem to recall."

"Well, she's disappeared. Hasn't been heard of in weeks."

"Oh," I said. "Is that bad?"

He gave me a wink. "Good," he whispered, as if afraid she'd come in just then and overhear him. And he flung one hand disgustedly toward the doorway, meaning it for her invisible presence. She should stay away.

"Why do they come to you about it?" I asked him.

"Oh," he said impatiently, "some tommyrot or other about her never having been seen again after—after the last time she left here. I dunno, something like that. Just routine. This is the third time this same fellow's been up here. I've been darn good-natured about it." Then he said, more optimistically, "He promised me just now, though, this is the last time; he won't come back any more."

He was fixing two drinks for us, in two fresh glasses. The first two had been shunted aside. The checkbook and the blotter had both vanished, and I'd been facing him in the mirror the whole time; so maybe I'd been mistaken; they hadn't been there in the first place.

"And then there was something about some clothes of hers," he went on offhandedly. "She left some of her things here with me ...." He broke off to ask me: "Are you shocked, Annie?"

"No," I reassured him, "I knew she stopped here now and then."

"I was supposed to send them after her; she said something about letting me know where she could be reached." He shrugged. "But I never heard from her again myself. They're still waiting in there ...."

He finished swirling ice with a neat little tap of the glass mixer against the rim.

"Probably ran off with someone," he said contemptuously.

I nodded dispassionately.

"I know who put him up to it," he went on, with a slight tinge of resentment. I had to take it he meant the detective; he offered no explanation to cover the switch in pronouns. "That dirty little ex-husband of hers."

"Oh, is he ex?" I said. That was another thing I hadn't known.

"Certainly. They were annulled almost as soon as they came back from their wedding trip. I even helped her to do it myself, sent her to my lawyer—"

And paid for it, I knew he'd been about to add; but he didn't.

"I told this fellow tonight," he went on, still with that same tinge of vengefulness, "that they'd better look into his motives, while they were about it. He was only out to get money out of her—"

(And she was only out to get money out of you, I thought, but tactfully didn't say so.)

"Do they think something's happened to her?" I asked.

He didn't answer that directly. "She'll probably turn up someplace. They always do." Then he said grimly, "It won't be here. Now let's have one, you and me." And he came toward me with our drinks.

We sat down on the sofa with them. He didn't need any urging tonight.

We had another pair. Then a third. We let the third pair stand and cool off awhile.

I was the upright arm of the parenthesis tonight, I noticed presently; he was the toppled-over one.

I didn't move my head aside the way he had his; his lips just didn't affect me. It was like being kissed by cardboard.

"I want you to marry me," he said. "I want—what you wanted that night. I want—someone like you."

(That's not good enough, I thought. You should want just me myself, and not someone like me. That leaves it too wide open. This is the rebound. You want the other kind of woman now. Safety, security, tranquillity; not so much fire. Something's shaken you, and you can't stand alone; so if there was a female statue in the room, you'd propose to that.)

"Too late," I said. "I've passed that point, as you arrive at it. You got to it too late. Or I left it too soon."

He wilted and his head went down. He had to go on alone. "I'm sorry," he breathed.

"I am, too." And I was. But it couldn't be helped.

Suddenly I laughed. "Isn't love the damnedest thing?"

He laughed, too, after a moment; ruefully. "A bitch of a thing," he agreed.

And laughing together, we took our leave of each other, parted, never to meet in closeness again. Laughing is a good way to part. As good a way as any.

I read an item about it in the papers a few days afterward, quite by chance. The husband had been picked up and taken in for questioning, in connection with her disappearance. Nothing more than that. There was no other name mentioned.

I read still another item about it in the papers, only a day or two following the first one. The husband had been released again, for lack of evidence.

I never read anything further about it, not another word, from that day on.

The other night at a party I met my last love again. I don't mean my latest; my last, I mean my final one. And he was as taking and as debonair as ever, but not to me any more; a little older maybe; and we said the things you say, holding tall glasses in our hands to keep from feeling lonely, keep from feeling lost.

"Hello, Annie. How've you been?"

"Hello, Dwight. Where've you been keeping yourself lately?"

"I've been around. And you?"

"I've been around, too."

And then when there wasn't anything more to say, we moved on. In opposite directions.

It isn't often that I see him any more. But whenever I do, I still think of her. I wonder what really did become of her.

And just the other night, suddenly, for no reason at all, out of nowhere, the strangest thought entered my head for a moment....

But then I promptly dismissed it again, just as quickly as it had occurred to me, as being too fantastic, too utterly improbable. The people you know never do things like that; the people you *read* about may, but never the people you *know*.

ALL AT ONCE, NO ALICE

All at Once No Alice was originally published in *Argosy* magazine on March of 1940. That year Woolrich released three stories in *Argosy*; this is by far the best one. In 1948, Columbia released *The Return of the Whistler* starring Michael Duane and Lenore Aubert which was entirely based on *All at Once, No Alice*. It is also the first of two great annihilation stories he wrote throughout his career, (the other being *Finger of Doom*) and one of the more powerful premises in noir literature playing out in a living-nightmare situation. This story proves that Woolrich is without equal when it comes to making his readers shudder. A pure gem of noir.

I T WAS OVER so quickly I almost thought something had been left out, but I guess he'd been doing it long enough to know his business. The only way I could tell for sure it was over was when I heard him say: "You may kiss the bride." But then, I'd never gone through it before.

We turned and pecked at each other, a little bashful because they were watching us.

He and the motherly-looking woman who had been a witness—I guess she was his housekeeper—stood there smiling benevolently, and also a little tiredly. The clock said one fifteen. Then he shook hands with the two of us and said, "Good luck to both of you," and she shook with us too and said, "I wish you a lot of happiness."

We shifted from the living room, where it had taken place, out into the front hall, a little awkwardly. Then he held the screen door open and we moved from there out onto the porch.

On the porch step Alice nudged me and whispered, "You forgot something."

I didn't even know how much I was supposed to give him. I took out two singles and held them in one hand, then I took out a five and held that in the other. Then I went back toward him all flustered and said, "I—I guess you thought I was going to leave without remembering this."

I reached my hand down to his and brought it back empty. He kept right on smiling, as if this happened nearly every time too, the bridegroom forgetting like that. It was only after I turned away and rejoined her that I glanced down at my other hand and saw which it was I'd given him. It was the five. That was all right; five thousand of them couldn't have paid him for what he'd done for me, the way I felt about it.

We went down their front walk and got into the car. The lighted doorway outlined them both for a minute. They raised their arms and said, "Good night."

"Good night, and much obliged," I called back. "Wait'll they go in," I said in an undertone to Alice, without starting the engine right away.

As soon as the doorway had blacked out, we turned and melted together 'on the front seat, and this time we made it a real kiss. "Any regrets?" I whispered to her very softly.

"It must have been awful before I was married to you," she whispered back. "How did I ever stand it so long?"

I don't think we said a word all the way in to Michianopolis. We were both too happy. Just the wind and the stars and us. And a couple of cigarettes.

We got to the outskirts around two thirty, and by three were all the way in downtown. We shopped around for a block or two. "This looks like a nice hotel," I said finally. I parked outside and we went in.

I think the first hotel was called the Commander. I noticed that the bellhops let us strictly alone; didn't bustle out to bring in our bags or anything.

I said to the desk man, "We'd like one of your best rooms and bath."

He gave me a sort of rueful smile, as if to say, "You should know better than that." . . . "I only wish I had something to give you," was the way he put it.

"All filled up?" I turned to her and murmured, "Well, we'll have to try someplace else."

He overheard me. "Excuse me, but did you come in without making reservations ahead?"

"Yes, we just drove in now. Why?"

He shook his head compassionately at my ignorance. "I'm afraid you're going to have a hard time finding a room in any of the hotels tonight."

"Why? They can't all be filled up."

"There's a three-day convention of the Knights of Balboa

being held here. All the others started sending their overflow to us as far back as Monday evening, and our own last vacancy went yesterday noon."

The second one was called the Stuyvesant, I think. "There must be something in a city this size," I said when we came out of there. "We'll keep looking until we find it."

I didn't bother noticing the names of the third and fourth. We couldn't turn around and go all the way back to our original point of departure—it would have been midmorning before we reached it—and there was nothing that offered suitable accommodations between; just filling stations, roadside lunch-rooms, and detached farmsteads.

Besides, she was beginning to tire. She refused to admit it, but it was easy to tell. It worried me.

The fifth place was called the Royal. It was already slightly less first-class than the previous ones had been; we were running out of them now. Nothing wrong with it, but just a little seedier and older.

I got the same answer at the desk, but this time I wouldn't take it. The way her face drooped when she heard it was enough to make me persist. I took the night clerk aside out of her hearing.

"Listen, you've got to do something for me, I don't care what it is," I whispered fiercely. "We've just driven all the way from Lake City and my wife's all in. I'm not going to drag her around to another place tonight."

Then as his face continued impassive, "If you can't accommodate both of us, find some way of putting her up at least. I'm willing to take my own chances, go out and sleep in the car or walk around the streets for the night."

"Wait a minute," he said, hooking his chin, "I think I could work out something like that for you. I just thought of something. There's a little bit of a dinky room on the top floor. Ordinarily it's not used as a guest room at all, just as a sort of storeroom. You couldn't possibly both use it, because there's only a single cot in it; but if you don't think your wife would object, I'd be glad to let her have it, and I think you might still be able to find a room for

Cornell Woolrich

yourself at the Y. They don't admit women, and most of these
Knights have brought their wives with them."

I took a look at her pretty, drawn face. "Anything, anything,"
I said gratefully.

He still had his doubts. "You'd better take her up and let her
see it first."

A colored boy came with us, with a passkey. On the way up I
explained it to her. She gave me a rueful look, but I could see she
was too tired even to object as much as she felt she should have.
"Ah, that's mean," she murmured. "Our first night by ourselves."

"It's just for tonight. We'll drive on right after breakfast. It's
important that you get some rest, hon. You can't fool me, you can
hardly keep your eyes open anymore."

She tucked her hand consolingly under my arm. "I don't mind
if you don't. It'll give me something to look forward to, seeing
you in the morning."

The bellboy led us along a quiet, green-carpeted hall, and
around a turn, scanning numbers on the doors. He stopped three
down from the turn, on the right-hand side, put his key in. "This
is it here, sir." The number was 1006.

The man at the desk hadn't exaggerated. The room itself was
little better than an alcove, long and narrow. I suppose two could
have gotten into it; but it would have been a physical
impossibility for two to sleep in it the way it was fitted up. It had
a cot that was little wider than a shelf.

To give you an idea how narrow the room was, the window
was narrower than average, and yet not more than a foot of wall-
strip showed on either side of its frame. In other words it took up
nearly the width of one entire side of the room.

I suppose I could have sat up in the single armchair all night
and slept, or tried to, that way; but as long as there was a chance
of getting a horizontal bed at the Y, why not be sensible about it?
She agreed with me in this.

"Think you can go this, just until the morning?" I asked her,
and the longing way she was eying that miserable cot gave me

the answer. She was so tired, anything would have looked good to her right then.

We went down again and I told him I'd take it. I had the bellboy take her bag out of the car and bring it in, and the desk clerk turned the register around for her to sign.

She poised the inked pen and flashed me a tender look just as she was about to sign. "First time I've used it," she breathed. I looked over her shoulder and watched her trace *Mrs. James Cannon* along the lined space. The last entry above hers was *A. Krumbake, and wife*. I noticed it because it was such a funny name.

The desk clerk had evidently decided by now that we were fairly desirable people. "I'm terribly sorry I couldn't do more for you," he said. "It's just for this one night. By tomorrow morning a lot of them'll be leaving."

I went up with her a second time, to see that she was made as comfortable as she could be under the circumstances. But then there was nothing definitely wrong with the room except its tininess, and the only real hardship was our temporary separation.

I tipped the boy for bringing up her bag, and then I tipped him a second time for going and digging up a nice, fluffy quilt for her at my request—not to spread over her but to spread on top of the mattress and soften it up a little. Those cots aren't as comfortable as regular beds by a darned sight. But she was so tired I was hoping she wouldn't notice the difference.

Then after he'd thanked me for the double header he'd gotten out of it, and left the room, I helped her off with her coat and hung it up for her, and even got down on my heels and undid the straps of her little sandals, so she wouldn't have to bend over and go after them herself. Then we kissed a couple of times and told each other all about it, and I backed out the door.

The last I saw of her that night she was sitting on the edge of that cot in there, her shoeless feet partly tucked under her. She looked just like a little girl. She raised one hand, wriggled the fingers at me in good night as I reluctantly eased the door closed.

"Until tomorrow, sweetheart," she called gently, when there

was a crack of opening left.

"Until tomorrow."

The night was as still around us as if it were holding its breath. The latch went *cluck*, and there we were on opposite sides of it.

The bellboy had taken the car down with him just now after he'd checked her in, and I had to wait out there a minute or two for him to bring it back up again at my ring. I stepped back to the turn in the hall while waiting, to look at the frosted glass transom over her door; and short as the time was, her light was already out. She must have just shrugged off her dress, fallen back flat, and pulled the coverings up over her.

Poor kid, I thought, with a commiserating shake of my head. The glass elevator panel flooded with light and I got in the car. The one bellhop doubled for liftman after twelve.

"I guess she'll be comfortable," he said.

"She was asleep before I left the floor," I told him.

The desk man told me where the nearest branch of the Y was, and I took the car with me as the quickest way of getting over there at that hour. I had no trouble at all getting a room, and not a bad one at that for six bits.

I didn't phone her before going up, to tell her I'd gotten something for myself, because I knew by the way I'd seen that light go out she was fast asleep already, and it would have been unnecessarily cruel to wake her again.

I woke up at eight and again I didn't phone her, to find out how she was, because in the first place I was going right over there myself in a few more minutes, and in the second place I wanted her to get all the sleep she could before I got there.

I even took my time, showered and shaved, and drove over slowly, to make sure of not getting there any earlier than nine.

It was a beautiful day, with the sun as brand-new-looking as if it had never shone before; and I even stopped off and bought a gardenia for her to wear on the shoulder of her dress. I thought: I'll check her out of that depressing dump. We'll drive to the swellest restaurant in town, and she'll sit having orange juice and toast while I sit looking at her face.

I braked in front of the Royal, got out, and went in, lighting up the whole lobby the way I was beaming.

A different man was at the desk now, on the day shift, but I knew the number of her room so I rode right up without stopping. I got out at the tenth, went down the hall the way we'd been led last night—still green-carpeted but a little less quiet now—and around the turn.

When I came to the third door down, on the right-hand side— the door that had 1006 on it—I stopped and listened a minute to see if I could tell whether she was up yet or not. If she wasn't up yet, I was going back downstairs again, hang around in the lobby, and give her another half-hour of badly needed sleep.

But she was up already. I could hear a sound in there as if she were brushing out her dress or coat with a stiff-bristled brush— *skish, skish, skish*—so I knocked, easy and loving, on the door with just three knuckles.

The *skish-skish-skish* broke off a minute, but then went right on again. But the door hadn't been tightly closed into the frame at all, and my knocking sent it drifting inward an inch or two. A whiff of turpentine or something like that nearly threw me over, but without stopping to distinguish what it was, I pushed the door the rest of the way in and walked in.

Then I pulled up short. I saw I had the wrong room.

There wasn't anything in it—no furniture, that is. Just bare floorboards, walls and ceiling. Even the light fixture had been taken down, and two black wires stuck out of a hole, like insect feelers, where it had been.

A man in spotted white overalls and peaked cap was standing on a stepladder slapping a paint brush up and down the walls. *Skish-skish-splop!*

I grunted, "Guess I've got the wrong number," and backed out.

"Guess you must have, bud," he agreed, equally laconic, without even turning his head to see who I was.

I looked up at the door from the outside. Number 1006. But that was the number they'd given her, sure it was. I looked in a second time. Long and narrow, like an alcove. Not more than a foot of wall space on either side of the window frame.

Sure, this was the room, all right. They must have found out they had something better available after all, and changed her after I left last night. I said, "Where'd they put the lady that was in here, you got any idea?"

Skish-skish-skish. "I dunno, bud, you'll have to find out at the desk. It was empty when I come here to work at seven." *Skish-skish-splop!*

I went downstairs to the desk again, and I said, "Excuse me. What room have you got Mrs. Cannon in now?"

He looked up some chart or other they use, behind the scenes, then he came back and said, "We have no Mrs. Cannon here."

I pulled my face back. Then I thrust it forward again. "What's the matter with you?" I said curtly. "I came here with her myself last night. Better take another look."

He did. A longer one. Then he came back and said, "I'm sorry, there's no Mrs. Cannon registered here."

I knew there was nothing to get excited about; it would probably be straightened out in a minute or two; but it was a pain in the neck. I was very patient. After all, this was the first morning of my honeymoon. "Your night man was on duty at the time. It was about three this morning. He gave her 1006."

He looked that up too. "That's not in use," he said. "That's down for redecorating. It's been empty for—"

"I don't care what it is. I tell you they checked my wife in there at three this morning, I went up with her myself! Will you quit arguing and find out what room she's in, for me? I don't want to stand here talking to you all day; I want to be with her."

"But I'm telling you, mister, the chart shows no one by that name."

"Then look in the register if you don't believe me. I watched her sign it myself."

People were standing around the lobby looking at me now, but I didn't care.

"It would be on the chart," he insisted. "It would have been transferred—" He ran the pad of his finger up the register page from bottom to top. Too fast, I couldn't help noticing: without a hitch, as if there were nothing to impede it. Then he went back a page and ran it up that, in the same streamlined way.

"Give it to me," I said impatiently. "I'll find it for you in a minute." I flung it around my way.

A. Krumbake, and wife stared at me. And then under that just a blank space all the way down to the bottom of the page. No more check-ins.

I could feel the pores of my face sort of closing up. That was what it felt like, anyway. Maybe it was just the process of getting pale. "She signed right under that name. It's been rubbed out."

"Oh, no, it hasn't," he told me firmly. "No one tampers with the register like that. People may leave, but their names stay on it."

Dazedly, I traced the ball of my finger back and forth across the white paper under that name, *Krumbake*. Smooth and unrubbed, its semi-glossy finish unimpaired by erasure. I held the page up toward the light and tried to squint through it, to see whether it showed thinner there, either from rubbing or some other means of eradication. It was all of the same even opacity.

I spoke in a lower voice now; I wasn't being impatient anymore. "There's something wrong. Something wrong about this. I can't understand it. I saw her write it. I saw her sign it with my own eyes. I've known it was the right hotel all along, but even if I wasn't sure, this other name, this name above, would prove it to me. Krumbake. I remember it from last night. Maybe they changed her without notifying you down here."

"That wouldn't be possible; it's through me, down here, that all changes are made. It isn't that I don't know what room she's in; it's that there's absolutely no record of any such person ever having been at the hotel, so you see you must be mis—"

"Call the manager for me," I said hoarsely.

I stood there waiting by the onyx-topped desk until he came. I stood there very straight, very impassive, not touching the edge of the counter with my hands in any way, about an inch clear of it.

People were bustling back and forth, casually, normally, cheerily, behind me; plinking their keys down on the onyx; saying, "Any mail for me?"; saying, "I'll be in the coffee shop if I'm called." And something was already trying to make me feel a little cut off from them, a little set apart. As if a shadowy finger had drawn a ring around me where I stood, and mystic vapors were already beginning to rise from it, walling me off from my fellow men.

I wouldn't let the feeling take hold of me—yet—but it was already there, trying to. I'd give an imperceptible shake of my head every once in a while and say to myself, "Things like this don't happen in broad daylight. It's just some kind of misunderstanding; it'll be cleared up presently."

The entrance, the lobby, had seemed so bright when I first came in, but I'd been mistaken. There were shadows lengthening in the far corners that only I could see. The gardenia I had for her was wilting.

The manager was no help at all. He tried to be, listened attentively, but then the most he could do was have the clerk repeat what he'd already done for me, look on the chart and look in the register. After all, details like that were in the hands of the staff. I simply got the same thing as before, only relayed through him now instead of direct from the desk man. "No, there hasn't been any Mrs. Cannon here at any time."

"Your night man will tell you," I finally said in despair, "he'll tell you I brought her here. Get hold of him, ask him. He'll remember us."

"I'll call him down; he rooms right here in the house," he said. But then with his hand on the phone he stopped to ask again, "Are you quite sure it was this hotel, Mr. Cannon? He was on duty until six this morning, and I hate to wake him up unless you—"

"Bring him down," I said. "This is more important to me than his sleep. It's got to be cleared up." I wasn't frightened yet, out-

and-out scared; just baffled, highly worried, and with a peculiar lost feeling.

He came down inside of five minutes. I knew him right away, the minute he stepped out of the car, in spite of the fact that other passengers had come down with him. I was so sure he'd be able to straighten it out that I took a step toward him without waiting for him to join us. If they noticed that, which was a point in favor of my credibility—my knowing him at sight like that—they gave no sign.

I said, "You remember me, don't you? You remember checking my wife into 1006 at three this morning, and telling me I'd have to go elsewhere?"

"No," he said with polite regret. "I'm afraid I don't."

I could feel my face go white as if a soundless bombshell of flour or talcum had just burst all over it. I put one foot behind me and set the heel down and stayed that way.

The manager asked him, "Well, did the gentleman stop at the desk perhaps, just to inquire, and then go elsewhere? Do you remember him at all, Stevens?"

"No, I never saw him until now. It must have been some other hotel."

"But look at me; look at my face," I tried to say. But I guess I didn't put any voice into it, it was just lip motion, because he didn't seem to hear.

The manager shrugged amiably, as if to say, "Well, that's all there is to it, as far as we're concerned."

I was breathing hard, fighting for self-control. "No. No, you can't close this matter. I dem—I ask you to give me one more chance to prove that I—that I—Call the night porter, the night bellboy that carried up her bag for her."

They were giving one another looks by now, as if I were some sort of crank.

"Listen, I'm in the full possession of my faculties, I'm not drunk, I wouldn't come in here like this if I weren't positive—"

The manager was going to try to pacify me and ease me out. "But don't you see you must be mistaken, old man? There's absolutely no record of it. We're very strict about those things. If any of my men checked a guest in without entering it on the chart of available rooms, and in the register, I'd fire him on the spot. Was it the Palace? Was it the Commander, maybe? Try to think now, you'll get it."

And with each soothing syllable, he led me a step nearer the entrance.

I looked up suddenly, saw that the desk had already receded a considerable distance behind us, and balked. "No, don't do this. This is no way to—Will you get that night-to-morning bellhop? Will you do that one more thing for me?"

He sighed, as if I were trying his patience sorely. "He's probably home sleeping. Just a minute; I'll find out."

It turned out he wasn't. They were so overcrowded and undermanned at the moment that instead of being at home he was sleeping right down in the basement, to save time coming and going. He came up in a couple of minutes, still buttoning the collar of his uniform. I knew him right away. He didn't look straight at me at first, but at the manager.

"Do you remember seeing this gentleman come here with a lady, at three this morning? Do you remember carrying her bag up to 1006 for her?"

Then he did look straight at me—and didn't seem to know me. "No, sir, Mr. DeGrasse."

The shock wasn't as great as the first time; it couldn't have been, twice in succession.

"Don't you remember that quilt you got for her, to spread over the mattress, and I gave you a second quarter for bringing it? You must remember that—dark blue, with little white flowers all over it—"

"No, sir, boss."

"But I know your face! I remember that scar just over your eyebrow. And—part your lips a little—that gold cap in front that shows every time you grin."

"No, sir, not me."

My voice was curling up and dying inside my throat. "Then

when you took me down alone with you, the last time, you even said, 'I guess she'll be comfortable'—" I squeezed his upper arm pleadingly. "Don't you remember? Don't you remember?"

"No, sir." This time he said it so low you could hardly hear it, as if his training wouldn't let him contradict me too emphatically, but on the other hand he felt obliged to stick to the facts.

I grabbed at the hem of my coat, bunched it up to emphasize the pattern and the color of the material. "Don't you know me by this?" Then I let my fingers trail helplessly down the line of my jaw. "Don't you know my face?"

He didn't answer anymore, just shook his head each time.

"What're you doing this for? What're you trying to do to me? All of you?" The invisible fumes from that necromancer's ring, that seemed to cut me off from all the world, came swirling up thicker and thicker about me. My voice was strident with a strange new kind of fear, a fear I hadn't known since I was ten.

"You've got me rocky now! You've got me down! Cut it out, I say!"

They were starting to draw back little by little away from me, prudently widen the tight knot they had formed around me. I turned from one to the other, from bellhop to night clerk, night clerk to day clerk, day clerk to manager, and each one as I turned to him retreated slightly.

There was a pause, while I fought against this other, lesser kind of death that was creeping over me—this death called *strangeness*, this snapping of all the customary little threads of cause and effect that are our moorings at other times. Slowly they all drew back from me step by step, until I was left there alone, cut off.

Then the tension exploded. My voice blasted the quiet of the lobby. "I want my wife!" I yelled shatteringly. "Tell me what's become of her. What've you done with her? I came in here with her last night; you can't tell me I didn't. . . ."

They circled, maneuvered around me. I heard the manager say in a hurried undertone, "I knew this was going to happen. I could have told you he was going to end up like this. George! Archer!

Get him out of here fast!"

My arms were suddenly seized from behind and held. I threshed against the constriction, so violently both my legs flung up clear of the floor at one time, dropped back again, but I couldn't break it. There must have been two of them behind me.

The manager had come in close again, now that I was safely pinioned, no doubt hoping that his nearness would succeed in soft-pedaling the disturbance. "Now will you leave here quietly, or do you want us to call the police and turn you over to them?"

"You'd better call them anyway, Mr. DeGrasse," the day clerk put in. "I've run into this mental type before. He'll only come back in again the very minute your back's turned."

"No, I'd rather not, unless he forces me to. It's bad for the hotel. Look at the crowd collecting down here on the main floor already. Tchk! Tchk!"

He tried to reason with me. "Now listen, give me a break, will you? You don't look like the kind of a man who—Won't you please go quietly? If I have you turned loose outside, will you go away and promise not to come in here again?"

"Ali-i-i-i-ice!" I sent it baying harrowingly down the long vista of lobby, lounges, foyers. I'd been gathering it in me the last few seconds while he was speaking to me. I put my heart and soul into it. It should have shaken down the big old-fashioned chandeliers by the vibration it caused alone. My voice broke under the strain. A woman onlooker somewhere in the background bleated at the very intensity of it.

The manager hit himself between the eyes in consternation. "Oh, this is fierce! Hurry up, call an officer quick, get him out of here."

"See, what did I tell you?" the clerk said knowingly.

I got another chestful of air in, tore loose with it. "Somebody help me! You people standing around looking, isn't there one of you will help me? I brought my wife here last night; now she's gone and they're trying to tell me I never—"

A brown hand suddenly sealed my mouth, was as quickly withdrawn again at the manager's panic-stricken admonition.

66

"George! Archer! Don't lay a hand on him. No rough stuff. Make us liable for damages afterwards, y'know."

Then I heard him and the desk man both give a deep breath of relief. "At last!" And I knew a cop must have come in behind me.

The grip on my arms behind my back changed, became single instead of double, one arm instead of two. But I didn't fight against it.

Suddenly I was very passive, unresistant. Because suddenly I had a dread of arrest, confinement. I wanted to preserve my freedom of movement more than all else, to try to find her again. If they threw me in a cell, or put me in a straitjacket, how could I look for her, how could I ever hope to get at the bottom of this mystery?

The police would never believe me. If the very people who had seen her denied her existence, how could I expect those who hadn't to believe in it?

Docile, I let him lead me out to the sidewalk in front of the hotel. The manager came out after us, mopping his forehead, and the desk clerk, and a few of the bolder among the guests who had been watching.

They held a three-cornered consultation in which I took no part. I even let the manager's version of what the trouble was pass unchallenged. Not that he distorted what had actually happened just now, but he made it seem as if I were mistaken about having brought her there last night.

Finally the harness cop asked, "Well, do you want to press charges against him for creating a disturbance in your lobby?"

The manager held his hands palms out, horrified. "I should say not. We're having our biggest rush of the year right now; I can't take time off to run down there and go through all that tommyrot. Just see that he doesn't come in again and create any more scenes."

"I'll see to that, all right," the cop promised truculently.

They went inside again, the manager and the clerk and the gallery that had watched us from the front steps. Inside to the hotel that had swallowed her alive.

The cop read me a lecture, to which I listened in stony silence. Then he gave me a shove that sent me floundering, said, "Keep moving now, hear me?"

I pointed, and said, "That's my car standing there. May I get in it?" He checked first to make sure it was, then he. opened the door, said, "Yeah, get in it and get out of here."

He'd made no slightest attempt to find out what was behind the whole thing, whether there was some truth to my story or not, or whether it was drink, drugs, or mental aberration. But then he was only a harness cop. That's why I hadn't wanted to tangle with him.

This strangeness that had risen up around me was nothing to be fought by an ordinary patrolman. I was going to them—the police—but I was going of my own free will and in my own way, not to be dragged in by the scruff of the neck and then put under observation for the next twenty-four hours.

Ten minutes or so later I got out in front of the first precinct house I came upon, and went in, and said to the desk sergeant, "I want to talk to the lieutenant in charge."

He stared at me coldly.

"What about?"

"About my wife."

I didn't talk to him alone. Three of his men were present. They were just shapes in the background as far as I was concerned, sitting there very quietly, listening.

I told it simply, hoping against hope I could get them to believe me, feeling somehow I couldn't even before I had started.

"I'm Jimmy Cannon, I'm twenty-five years old, and I'm from Lake City. Last evening after dark my girl and I—her name was Alice Brown—we left there in my car, and at 1:15 this morning we were married by a justice of the peace.

"I think his name was Hulskamp—anyway it's a white house with morning glories all over the porch, about fifty miles this side of Lake City.

"We got in here at three, and they gave her a little room at the Royal Hotel. They couldn't put me up, but they put her up alone. The number was 1006. I know that as well as I know I'm sitting here. This morning when I went over there, they were painting the room and I haven't been able to find a trace of her since.

"I saw her sign the register, but her name isn't on it anymore. The night clerk says he never saw her. The bellboy says he never saw her. Now they've got me so I'm scared and shaky, like a little kid is of the dark. I want you men to help me. Won't you men help me?"

"We'll help you"—said the lieutenant in charge. Slowly, awfully slowly; I didn't like that slowness—"if we're able to." And I knew what he meant; if we find any evidence that your story is true.

He turned his head toward one of the three shadowy listeners in the background, at random. The one nearest him. Then he changed his mind, shifted his gaze further along, to the one in the middle. "Ainslie, suppose you take a whack at this. Go over to this hotel and see what you can find out. Take him with you."

So, as he stood up, I separated him from the blurred background for the first time. I was disappointed. He was just another man like me, maybe five years older, maybe an inch or two shorter. He could feel cold and hungry and tired, just as I could. He could believe a lie, just as I could. He couldn't see around corners or through walls, or into hearts any more than I could. What good was he going to be?

He looked as if he'd seen every rotten thing there was in the world. He looked as if he'd once expected to see other things beside that, but didn't anymore. He said, "Yes, sir," and you couldn't tell whether he was bored or interested, or liked the detail or resented it, or gave a rap.

On the way over I said, "You've got to find out what became of her. You've got to make them—"

"I'll do what I can." He couldn't seem to get any emotion into his voice. After all, from his point of view, why should he?

69

"You'll do what you can!" I gasped. "Didn't you ever have a wife?"

He gave me a look, but you couldn't tell what was in it.

We went straight back to the Royal. He was very businesslike, did a streamlined, competent job. Didn't waste a question or a motion, but didn't leave out a single relevant thing either.

I took back what I'd been worried about at first; he was good.

But he wasn't good enough for this, whatever it was.

It went like this: "Let me see your register." He took out a glass, went over the place I pointed out to him where she had signed. Evidently couldn't find any marks of erasure any more than I had with my naked eye.

Then we went up to the room, 1006. The painter was working on the wood trim by now, had all four walls and the ceiling done. It was such a small cubbyhole it wasn't even a half-day's work. He said, "Where was the furniture when you came in here to work this morning? Still in the room, or had the room been cleared?"

"Still in the room; I cleared it myself. There wasn't much; a chair, a scatter rug, a cot."

"Was the cot made or unmade?"

"Made up."

"Was the window opened or closed when you came in?"

"Closed tight."

"Was the air in the room noticeably stale, as if it had been closed up that way all night, or not noticeably so, as if it had only been closed up shortly before?"

"Turrible, like it hadn't been aired for a week. And believe me, when I notice a place is stuffy, you can bet it's stuffy all right."

"Were there any marks on the walls or floor or anywhere around the room that didn't belong there?"

I knew he meant blood, and gnawed the lining of my cheek fearfully.

"Nothing except plain grime, that needed painting bad."

We visited the housekeeper next. She took us to the linen room and showed us. "If there're any dark blue quilts in use in this house, it's the first I know about it. The bellboy *could* have come in here at that hour—but all he would have gotten are maroon ones. And here's my supply list, every quilt accounted for. So it didn't come from here."

We visited the baggage room next. "Look around and see if there's anything in here that resembles that bag of your wife's." I did, and there wasn't. Wherever she had gone, whatever had become of her, her bag had gone with her.

About fifty minutes after we'd first gone in, we were back in my car outside the hotel again. He'd done a good, thorough job; and if I was willing to admit that, it must have been.

We sat there without moving a couple of minutes, me under the wheel. He kept looking at me steadily, sizing me up. I couldn't tell what he was thinking. I threw my head back and started to look up the' face of the building, story by story. I counted as my eyes rose, and when they'd come to the tenth floor I stopped them there, swung them around the corner of the building to the third window from the end, stopped them there for good. It was a skinnier window than the others. So small, so high up, to hold so much mystery. "Alice," I whispered up to it, and it didn't answer, didn't hear.

His voice brought my gaze down from there again. "The burden of the proof has now fallen on you. It's up to you to give me some evidence that she actually went in there. That she actually was with you. That she actually *was*. I wasn't able to find a single person in that building who actually saw her."

I just looked at him, the kind of a look you get from someone right after you stick a knife in his heart. Finally I said with quiet bitterness, "So now I have to prove I had a wife."

The instant, remorseless way he answered that was brutal in itself. "Yes, you do. Can you?"

I pushed my hat off, raked my fingers through my hair, with one and the same gesture. "Could you, if someone asked you in the middle of the street? Could you?"

He peeled out a wallet, flipped it open. A tiny snapshot of a woman's head and shoulders danced in front of my eyes for a split second. He folded it and put it away again. He briefly touched a gold band on his finger, token of that old custom that is starting to revive again, of husbands wearing marriage rings as well as wives.

"And a dozen other ways. You could call Tremont 4102. Or you could call the marriage clerk at the City Hall—"

"But we were just beginning," I said bleakly. "I have no pictures. She was wearing the only ring we had. The certificate was to be mailed to us at Lake City in a few days. You could call this justice of the peace, Hulskamp, out near U.S. 9; he'll tell you—"

"Okay, Cannon, I'll do that. We'll go back to headquarters, I'll tell the lieutenant what I've gotten so far, and I'll do it from there."

Now at last it would be over, now at last it would be straightened out. He left me sitting in the room outside the lieutenant's office, while he was in there reporting to him. He seemed to take a long time, so I knew he must be doing more than just reporting; they must be talking it over.

Finally Ainslie looked out at me, but only to say, "What was the name of that justice you say married you, again?"

"Hulskamp."

He closed the door again. I had another long wait. Finally it opened a second time, he hitched his head at me to come in. The atmosphere, when I got in there, was one of hard, brittle curiosity, without any feeling to it. As when you look at somebody afflicted in a way you never heard of before, and wonder how he got that way.

I got that distinctly. Even from Ainslie, and it was fairly oozing from his lieutenant and the other men in the room. They looked and looked and looked at me.

The lieutenant did the talking. "You say a Justice Hulskamp married you. You still say that?"

"A white house sitting off the road, this side of Lake City, just before you get to U.S. 9—"

"Well, there is a Justice Hulskamp, and he does live out there. We just had him on the phone. He says he never married anyone named James Cannon to anyone named Alice Brown, last night or any other night. He hasn't married anyone who looks like you, recently, to anyone who looks as you say she did. He didn't marry anyone at all at any time last night—"

He was going off someplace while he talked to me, and his voice was going away after him. Ainslie filled a paper cup with water at the cooler in the corner, strewed it deftly across my face, once each way, as if I were some kind of a potted plant, and one of the other guys picked me up from the floor and put me back on the chair again.

The lieutenant's voice came back again stronger, as if he hadn't gone away after all. "Who were her people in Lake City?"

"She was an orphan."

"Well, where did she work there?"

"At the house of a family named Beresford, at 20 New Hampshire Avenue. She was in service there, a maid; she lived with them—"

"Give me long distance. Give me Lake City. This is Michianopolis police headquarters. I want to talk to a party named Beresford, 20 New Hampshire Avenue."

The ring came back fast. "We're holding a man here who claims he married a maid working for you. A girl by the name of Alice Brown."

He'd hung up before I even knew it was over. "There's no maid employed there. They don't know anything about any Alice Brown, never heard of her."

I stayed on the chair this time. I just didn't hear so clearly for a while, everything sort of fuzzy.

". . . Hallucinations . . . And he's in a semi-hysterical condition right now. Notice how jerky his reflexes are?" Someone was chopping the edge of his hand at my kneecaps. "Seems harmless. Let him go. It'll probably wear off. I'll give him a sedative." Someone snapped a bag shut, left the room.

The lieutenant's voice was as flat as it was deadly, and it brooked no argument. "You never had a wife, Cannon!"

I could see only Ainslie's face in the welter before me. "You have, though, haven't you?" I said, so low none of the others could catch it.

The lieutenant was still talking to me. "Now get out of here before we change our minds and call an ambulance to take you away. And don't go back into any more hotels raising a row."

I hung around outside; I wouldn't go away. Where was there to go? One of the others came out, looked at me fleetingly in passing, said with humorous tolerance, "You better get out of here before the lieutenant catches you," and went on about his business.

I waited until I saw Ainslie come out. Then I went up to him. "I've got to talk to you; you've got to listen to me—"

"Why? The matter's closed. You heard the lieutenant."

He went back to some sort of a locker room. I went after him.

"You're not supposed to come back here. Now look, Cannon, I'm telling you for your own good, you're looking for trouble if you keep this up."

"Don't turn me down," I said hoarsely, tugging away at the seam of his sleeve. "Can't you see the state I'm in? I'm like someone in a dark room, crying for a match. I'm like someone drowning, crying for a helping hand. I can't make it alone anymore."

There wasn't anyone in the place but just the two of us. My pawing grip slipped down his sleeve to the hem of his coat, and I was looking up at him from my knees. What did I care? There was no such thing as pride or dignity anymore. I would have crawled flat along the floor on my belly, just to get a word of relief out of anyone.

"Forget you're a detective, and I'm a case. I'm appealing to you as one human being to another. I'm appealing to you as one husband to another. Don't turn your back on me like that, don't pull my hands away from your coat. I don't ask you to do anything for me anymore; you don't have to lift a finger. Just say, 'Yes, you had a wife, Cannon.' Just give me that one glimmer of light in the dark. Say it even if you don't mean it, even if you don't believe it, say it anyway. Oh, say it, will you—"

He drew the back of his hand slowly across his mouth, either in disgust at my abasement or in a sudden access of pity. Maybe a little of both. His voice was hoarse, as if he were sore at the spot I was putting him on.

"Give me anything," he said, shaking me a little and jogging me to my feet, "the slightest thing, to show that she ever existed, to show that there ever was such a person outside of your own mind, and I'll be with you to the bitter end. Give me a pin that she used to fasten her dress with. Give me a grain of powder, a stray hair; but prove that it was hers. But I can't do it unless you do."

"And I have nothing to show you. Not a pin, not a grain of powder."

I took a few dragging steps toward the locker room door. "You're doing something to me that I wouldn't do to a dog," I mumbled. "What you're doing to me is worse than if you were to kill me. You're locking me up in shadows for the rest of my life. You're taking my mind away from me. You're condemning me slowly but surely to madness, to being without a mind. It won't happen right away, but sooner or later, in six months or in a year—Well, I guess that's that."

I fumbled my way out of the locker room and down the passageway outside, guiding myself with one arm along the wall, and past the sergeant's desk and down the steps, and then I was out in the street.

I left my car there where it was. What did I want with it? I started to walk, without knowing where I was going. I walked a long time, and a good long distance.

Then all of a sudden I noticed a lighted drugstore—it was dark by now—across the way. I must have passed others before now, but this was the first one I noticed.

I crossed over and looked in the open doorway. It had telephone booths; I could see them at the back, to one side. I moved on a few steps, stopped, and felt in my pockets. I found a quill toothpick, and I dug the point of it good and hard down the back of my finger, ripped the skin open. Then I threw it away. I wrapped a handkerchief around the finger, and I turned around and went inside.

I said to the clerk, "Give me some iodine. My cat just scratched me and I don't want to take any chances."

He said, "Want me to put it on for you?"

I said, "No, gimme the whole bottle. I'll take it home; we're out of it."

I paid him for it and moved over to one side and started to thumb through one of the directories in the rack. Just as he went back inside the prescription room, I found my number. I went into the end booth and pulled the slide closed. I took off my hat and hung it over the phone mouthpiece, sort of making myself at home.

Then I sat down and started to undo the paper he'd just wrapped around the bottle. When I had it off, I pulled the knot of my tie out a little further to give myself lots of room. Then I took the stopper out of the bottle and tilted my head back and braced myself.

Something that felt like a baseball bat came chopping down on the arm I was bringing up, and nearly broke it in two, and the iodine sprayed all over the side of the booth. Ainslie was standing there in the half-opened slide.

He said, "Come on outta there!" and gave me a pull by the collar of my coat that did it for me. He didn't say anything more until we were out on the sidewalk in front of the place. Then he stopped and looked me over from head to foot as if I were some kind of a microbe. He said, "Well, it was worth coming all this way after you, at that!"

My car was standing there; I must have left the keys in it and he must have tailed me in that. He thumbed it, and I went over and climbed in and sat there limply. He stayed outside.

I said, "I can't live with shadows, Ainslie. I'm frightened, too frightened to go on. You don't know what the nights'll be like from now on. And the days won't be much better. I'd rather go now, fast. Show her to me on a slab at the morgue and I won't whimper. Show her to me all cut up in small pieces and I won't bat an eyelash. But don't say she never was."

"I guessed what was coming from the minute I saw you jab yourself with that toothpick." He watched sardonically while I slowly unwound the handkerchief, that had stayed around my finger all this time. The scratch had hardly bled at all. Just a single hairline of red was on the handkerchief.

We both looked at that.

Then more of the handkerchief came open. We both looked at the initials in the corner. *A.B.* We both, most likely, smelled the faint sweetness that still came from it at the same time. Very faint, for it was such a small handkerchief.

We both looked at each other, and both our minds made the same discovery at the same time. I was the one who spoke it aloud. "It's hers," I said grimly; "the wife that didn't exist."

"This is a fine time to come out with it," he said quietly. "Move over, I'll drive." That was his way of saying, "I'm in."

I said, "I remember now. I got a cinder in my eye, during the drive in, and she lent me her handkerchief to take it out with; I didn't have one of my own on me. I guess I forgot to give it back to her. And this—is it." I looked at him rebukingly. "What a difference a few square inches of linen can make. Without it, I was a madman. With it, I'm a rational being who enlists your co-operation."

"No. You didn't turn it up when it would have done you the most good, back at the station house. You only turned it up several minutes after you were already supposed to have gulped a bottle of iodine. I could tell by your face you'd forgotten about it until then yourself. I think that does make a difference. To me it does, anyway." He meshed gears.

"And what're you going to do about it?"

"Since we don't believe in the supernatural, our only possible premise is that there's been some human agency at work."

I noticed the direction he was taking. "Aren't you going back to the Royal?"

"There's no use bothering with the hotel. D'you see what I mean?"

"No, I don't," I said bluntly. "That was where she disappeared."

"The focus for this wholesale case of astigmatism is elsewhere, outside the hotel. It's true we could try to break them down, there at the hotel. But what about the justice, what about the Beresford house in Lake City? I think it'll be simpler to try to find out the reason rather than the mechanics of the disappearance.

"And the reason lies elsewhere. Because you brought her to the hotel from the justice's. And to the justice's from Lake City. The hotel was the last stage. Find out why the justice denies he married you, and we don't have to find out why the hotel staff denies having seen her. Find out why the Beresford house denies she was a maid there, and we don't have to find out why the justice denies he married you.

"Find out, maybe, something else, and we don't have to find out why the Beresford house denies she was a maid there. The time element keeps moving backward through the whole thing. Now talk to me. How long did you know her? How well? How much did you know about her?"

"Not long. Not well. Practically nothing. It was one of those story-book things. I met her a week ago last night. She was sitting on a bench in the park, as if she were lonely, didn't have a friend in the world. I don't make a habit of accosting girls on park benches, but she looked so dejected it got to me.

"Well, that's how we met. I walked her home afterwards to where she said she lived. But when we got there—holy smoke, it was a mansion! I got nervous, said: 'Gee, this is a pretty swell place for a guy like me to be bringing anyone home to, just a clerk in a store.'

"She laughed and said, 'I'm only the maid. Disappointed?' I said, 'No, I would have been disappointed if you'd been anybody else, because then you wouldn't be in my class.' She seemed relieved after I said that. She said, 'Gee, I've waited so long to find someone who'd like me for myself.'

"Well, to make a long story short, we made an appointment to meet at that same bench the next night. I waited there for two hours and she never showed up. Luckily I went back there the next night again—and there she was. She explained she hadn't been able to get out the night before; the people where she worked were having company or something.

"When I took her home that night I asked her name, which I didn't know yet, and that seemed to scare her. She got sort of flustered, and I saw her look at her handbag. It had the initials A.B. on it; I'd already noticed that the first night I met her. She said, 'Alice Brown.'

"By the third time we met we were already nuts about each other. I asked her whether she'd take a chance and marry me. She said, 'Is it possible someone wants to marry little Alice Brown, who hasn't a friend in the world?' I said yes, and that was all there was to it.

"Only, when I left her that night, she seemed kind of scared. First I thought she was scared I'd change my mind, back out, but it wasn't that. She said, 'Jimmy, let's hurry up and do it, don't let's put it off. Let's do it while—while we have the chance'; and she hung on to my sleeve tight with both hands.

"So the next day I asked for a week off, which I had coming to me from last summer anyway, and I waited for her with the car on the corner three blocks away from the house where she was in service. She came running as if the devil were behind her, but I thought that was because she didn't want to keep me waiting. She just had that one little overnight bag with her.

"She jumped in, and her face looked kind of white, and she said, 'Hurry, Jimmy, hurry!' And away we went. And until we were outside of Lake City, she kept looking back every once in a while, as if she were afraid someone was coming after us."

Ainslie didn't say much after all that rigmarole I'd given him. Just five words, after we'd driven on for about ten minutes or so. "She was afraid of something." And then in another ten minutes, "And whatever it was, it's what's caught up with her now."

We stopped at the filling station where Alice and I had stopped for gas the night before. I looked over the attendants, said: "There's the one serviced us." Ainslie called him over, played a pocket light on my face.

"Do you remember servicing this man last night? This man, and a girl with him?"

"Nope, not me. Maybe one of the oth—"

Neither of us could see his hands at the moment; they were out of range below the car door. I said, "He's got a white scar across the back of his right hand. I saw it last night."

Ainslie said, "Hold it up."

He did, and there was a white cicatrix across it, where stitches had been taken or something. Ainslie said, "Now whaddye say?"

It didn't shake him in the least. "I still say no. Maybe he saw me at one time or another, but I've never seen him, to my knowledge, with or without a girl." He waited a minute, then added: "Why should I deny it, if it was so?"

"We'll be back, in a day or in a week or in a month," Ainslie let him know grimly, "but we'll be back—to find that out."

We drove on. "Those few square inches of linen handkerchief will be wearing pretty thin, if this keeps up," I muttered dejectedly after a while.

"Don't let that worry you," he said, looking straight ahead. "Once I'm sold, I don't unsell easily."

We crossed U.S. 9 a half-hour later. A little white house came skimming along out of the darkness. "This is where I was married to a ghost," I said.

He braked, twisted the grip of the door latch. My hand shot down, stopped his arm.

"Wait; before you go in, listen to this. It may help out that handkerchief. There'll be a round mirror in the hall, to the left of the door, with antlers over it for a hatrack. In their parlor, where he read the service, there'll be an upright piano, with brass candle holders sticking out of the front of it, above the keyboard. It's got a scarf on it that ends in a lot of little plush balls. And on the music rack, the top selection is a copy of *Kiss Me Again*. And on the wall there's a painting of a lot of fruit rolling out of a basket. And this housekeeper, he calls her Dora."

"That's enough," he said in that toneless voice of his. "I told you I was with you anyway, didn't I?" He got out and went over and rang the bell. I went with him, of course.

They must have been asleep; they didn't answer right away. Then the housekeeper opened the door and looked out at us. Before we could say anything, we heard the justice call down the stairs, "Who is it, Dora?"

Ainslie asked if we could come in and talk to him, and straightened his necktie in the round mirror to the left of the door, with antlers over it.

Hulskamp came down in a bathrobe, and Ainslie said: "You married this man to a girl named Alice Brown last night." It wasn't a question.

The justice said, "No. I've already been asked that once, over the phone, and I said I hadn't. I've never seen this young man before." He even put on his glasses to look at me better.

Ainslie didn't argue the matter, almost seemed to take him at his word. "I won't ask you to let me see your records," he said drily, "because they'll undoubtedly—bear out your word."

He strolled as far as the parlor entrance, glanced in idly. I peered over his shoulder. There was an upright piano with brass candle sconces. A copy of *Kiss Me Again* was topmost on its rack. A painting of fruit rolling out of a basket daubed the wall.

"They certainly will!" snapped the justice resentfully.

The housekeeper put her oar in. "I'm a witness at all the marriages the justice performs, and I'm sure the young man's mistaken. I don't ever recall—"

Ainslie steadied me with one hand clasping my arm, and led me out without another word. We got in the car again. Their door closed, somewhat forcefully.

I pounded the rim of the wheel helplessly with my fist. I said, "What is it? Some sort of wholesale conspiracy? But *why*? She's not important; I'm not important."

He threw in the clutch, the little white house ebbed away in the night darkness behind us.

"It's some sort of a conspiracy, all right," he said. "We've got

81

to get the reason for it. That's the quickest, shortest way to clear it up. To take any of the weaker links, the bellboy at the hotel or that filling station attendant, and break them down, would not only take days, but in the end would only get us some anonymous individual who'd either threatened them or paid them to forget having seen your wife, and we wouldn't be much further than before. If we can get the reason behind it all, the source, we don't have to bother with any of these small fry. That's why we're heading back to Lake City instead of just concentrating on that hotel in Michianopolis."

We made Lake City by one a.m. and I showed him the way to New Hampshire Avenue. Number 20 was a massive corner house, and we glided up to it from the back, along the side street; braked across the way from the service entrance I'd always brought her back to. Not a light was showing.

"Don't get out yet," he said. "When you brought her home nights, you brought her to this back door, right?"

"Yes."

"Tell me, did you ever actually see her open it and go in, or did you just leave her here by it and walk off without waiting to see where she went?"

I felt myself get a little frightened again. This was something that hadn't occurred to me until now. "I didn't once actually see the door open and her go inside, now that I come to think of it. She seemed to—to want me to walk off without waiting. She didn't say so, but I could tell. I thought maybe it was because she didn't want her employers to catch on she was going around with anyone. I'd walk off, down that way—"

I pointed to the corner behind us, on the next avenue over. "Then when I got there, I'd look back from there each time. As anyone would. Each time I did, she wasn't there anymore. I thought she'd gone in, but—it's funny, I never saw her go in."

He nodded gloomily. "Just about what I thought. For all you know, she didn't even belong in that house, never went in there at all. A quick little dash, while your back was turned, would have taken her around the corner of the house and out of sight. And the city would have swallowed her up."

"But why?" I said helplessly.

He didn't answer that. We hadn't had a good look at the front of the house yet. As I have said, we had approached from the rear, along the side street. He got out of the car now, and I followed suit. We walked down the few remaining yards to the corner, and turned and looked all up and down the front of it.

It was an expensive limestone building; it spelt real dough, even looking at it in the dark as we were. There was a light showing from the front, through one of the tall ground-floor windows—but a very dim one, almost like a night light. It didn't send any shine outside; just peered wanly around the sides of the blind that had been drawn on the inside.

Something moved close up against the door-facing, stirred a little. If it hadn't been white limestone, it wouldn't have even been noticeable at all. We both saw it at once; I caught instinctively at Ainslie's arm, and a cold knife of dull fear went through me—though why I couldn't tell.

"Crepe on the front door," he whispered. "Somebody's dead in there. Whether she did go in here or didn't, just the same I think we'd better have a look at the inside of this place."

I took a step in the direction of the front door. He recalled me with a curt gesture. "And by that I don't mean march up the front steps, ring the doorbell, and flash my badge."

"Then how?"

Brakes ground somewhere along the side street behind us. We turned our heads and a lacquered sedan-truck had drawn up directly before the service door of 20 New Hampshire Avenue. "Just in time," Ainslie said. "This is how."

We started back toward it. The driver and a helper had gotten down, were unloading batches of camp chairs and stacking them up against the side of the truck, preparatory to taking them in.

"For the services tomorrow, I suppose," Ainslie grunted. He said to the driver: "Who is it that died, bud?"

"Mean to say you ain't heard? It's in alla papers."

"We're from out of town."

"Alma Beresford, the heiress. Richest gal in twenty-four states. She was an orphum, too. Pretty soft for her guardian; not another soul to get the cash but him."

"What was it?" For the first time since I'd known him, you couldn't have called Ainslie's voice toneless; it was sort of springy like a rubber band that's pulled too tight.

"Heart attack, I think." The truckman snapped his fingers. "Like that. Shows you that rich or poor, when you gotta go, you gotta go."

Ainslie asked only one more question. "Why you bringing these setups at an hour like this? They're not going to hold the services in the middle of the night, are they?"

"Nah, but first thing in the morning; so early there wouldn't be a chance to get 'em over here unless we delivered 'em ahead of time." He was suddenly staring fascinatedly at the silvery lining of Ainslie's hand.

Ainslie's voice was toneless again. "Tell you what you fellows are going to do. You're going to save yourselves the trouble of hauling all those camp chairs inside, and you're going to get paid for it in the bargain. Lend us those work aprons y'got on."

He slipped them something apiece; I couldn't see whether it was two dollars or five. "Gimme your delivery ticket; I'll get it receipted for you. You two get back in the truck and lie low."

We both doffed our hats and coats, put them in our own car, rolled our shirt sleeves, put on the work aprons, and rang the service bell. There was a short wait and then a wire-sheathed bulb over the entry glimmered pallidly as an indication someone was coming. The door opened and a gaunt-faced sandy-haired man looked out at us. It was hard to tell just how old he was. He looked like a butler, but he was dressed in a business suit.

"Camp chairs from the Thebes Funerary Chapel," Ainslie said, reading from the delivery ticket.

"Follow me and I'll show you where they're to go," he said in a hushed voice. "Be as quiet as you can. We've only just succeeded in getting Mr. Hastings to lie down and try to rest a little." The guardian, I supposed. In which case this anemic-looking customer would be the guardian's Man Friday.

We each grabbed up a double armful of the camp chairs and went in after him. They were corded together in batches of half a dozen. We could have cleared up the whole consignment at once—they were lightweight—but Ainslie gave me the eye not to; I guess he wanted to have an excuse to prolong our presence as much as possible.

You went down a short delivery passageway, then up a few steps into a brightly lighted kitchen.

A hatchet-faced woman in maid's livery was sitting by a table crying away under one eye-shading hand, a teacup and a tumbler of gin before her. Judging by the redness of her nose, she'd been at it for hours. "My baby," she'd mew every once in a while.

We followed him out at the other side, through a pantry, a gloomy-looking dining room, and finally into a huge cavernous front room, eerily suffused with flickering candlelight that did no more than heighten the shadows in its far corners. It was this wavering pallor that we must have seen from outside of the house.

An open coffin rested on a flower-massed bier at the upper end of the place, a lighted taper glimmering at each corner of it. A violet velvet pall had been spread over the top of it, concealing what lay within.

But a tiny peaked outline, that could have been made by an uptilted nose, was visible in the plush at one extremity of its length. That knife of dread gave an excruciating little twist in me, and again I didn't know why—or refused to admit I did. It was as if I instinctively sensed the nearness of something familiar.

The rest of the room, before this monument to mortality, had been left clear, its original furniture moved aside or taken out. The man who had admitted us gave us our instructions.

"Arrange them in four rows, here in front of the bier. Leave an aisle through them. And be sure and leave enough space up ahead for the divine who will deliver the oration." Then he retreated to the door and stood watching us for a moment.

Ainslie produced a knife from the pocket of his borrowed

apron, began severing the cording that bound the frames of the camp chairs together. I opened them one at a time as he freed them and began setting them up in quadruple rows, being as slow about it as I could.

There was a slight sound and the factotum had tiptoed back toward the kitchen for a moment, perhaps for a sip of the comforting gin. Ainslie raised his head, caught my eye, speared his thumb at the bier imperatively. I was the nearer of us to it at the moment. I knew what he meant: look and see who it was.

I went cold all over, but I put down the camp chair I was fiddling with and edged over toward it on arched feet. The taper flames bent down flat as I approached them, and sort of hissed. Sweat needled out under the roots of my hair. I went around by the head, where that tiny little peak was, reached out, and gingerly took hold of the corners of the velvet pall, which fell loosely over the two sides of the coffin without quite meeting the headboard.

Just as my wrists flexed to tip it back, Ainslie coughed warningly. There was a whispered returning tread from beyond the doorway. I let go, took a quick side-jump back toward where I'd been.

I glanced around and the secretary fellow had come back again, was standing there with his eyes fixed on me. I pretended to be measuring off the distance for the pulpit with my foot.

"You men are rather slow about it," he said, thin-lipped.

"You want 'em just so, don't you?" Ainslie answered. He went out to get the second batch. I pretended one of the stools had jammed and I was having trouble getting it open, as an excuse to linger behind. The secretary was on his guard. He lingered too.

The dick took care of that. He waited until he was halfway back with his load of camp chairs, then dropped them all over the pantry floor with a clatter, to draw the watchdog off.

It worked. He gave a huff of annoyance, turned, and went in to bawl Ainslie out for the noise he had made. The minute the doorway cleared, I gave a catlike spring back toward the velvet mound. This time I made it. I flung the pall back—

Then I let go of it, and the lighted candles started spinning around my head, faster and faster, until they made a comet-like track of fire. The still face staring up at me from the coffin was Alice's.

I felt my knees hit something, and I was swaying back and forth on them there beside the bier. I could hear somebody coming back toward the room, but whether it was Ainslie or the other guy I didn't know and didn't care. Then an arm went around me and steadied me to my feet once more, so I knew it was Ainslie.

"It's her," I said brokenly. "Alice. I can't understand it; she must—have—been this rich girl, Alma Beresford, all the time—"

He let go of me, took a quick step over to the coffin, flung the pall even further back than I had. He dipped his head, as if he were staring nearsightedly. Then he turned and I never felt my shoulder grabbed so hard before, or since. His fingers felt like steel claws that went in, and met in the middle. For a minute I didn't know whether he was attacking me or not; and I was too dazed to care.

He was pointing at the coffin. "Look at that!" he demanded. I didn't know what he meant. He shook me brutally, either to get me to understand or because he was so excited himself. "*She's not dead*. Watch her chest cavern."

I fixed my eyes on it. You could tell only by watching the line where the white satin of her burial gown met the violet quilting of the coffin lining. The white was faintly, but unmistakably and rhythmically, rising and falling.

"They've got her either drugged or in a coma—"

He broke off short, let go of me as if my shoulder were red-hot and burned his fingers. His hand flashed down and up again, and he'd drawn and sighted over my shoulder. "Put it down or I'll let you have it right where you are!" he said.

Something thudded to the carpet. I turned and the secretary was standing there in the doorway, palms out, a fallen revolver lying at his feet.

"Go over and get that, Cannon," Ainslie ordered. "This looks like the finale now. Let's see what we've got."

There was an arched opening behind him, leading out to the front entrance hall, I suppose, and the stairway to the upper floors. We'd come in from the rear, remember. Velvet drapes had been drawn closed over that arch, sealing it up, the whole time we'd been in there.

He must have come in through there. I bent down before the motionless secretary, and, with my fingers an inch away from the fallen gun at his feet, I heard the impact of a head blow and Ainslie gave the peculiar guttural groan of someone going down into unconsciousness.

The secretary's foot snaked out and sped the gun skidding far across to the other side of the room. Then he dropped on my curved back like a dead weight and I went down flat under him, pushing my face into the parquet flooring.

He kept aiming blows at the side of my head from above, but he had only his fists to work with at the moment, and even the ones that landed weren't as effective as whatever it was that had been used on Ainslie. I reached upward and over, caught the secretary by the shoulders of his coat, tugged and at the same time jerked my body out from under him in the opposite direction; and he came flying up in a backward somersault and landed sprawling a few feet away.

I got up and looked. Ainslie lay inert, face down on the floor to one side of the coffin, something gleaming wet down the part of his hair. There was a handsome but vicious-looking gray-haired man in a brocaded dressing gown standing behind him holding a gun on me, trying to cow me with it.

"Get him, Mr. Hastings," panted the one I'd just flung off".

It would have taken more than a gun to hold me, after what I'd been through. I charged at him, around Ainslie's form. He evidently didn't want to fire, didn't want the noise of a shot to be heard there in the house. Instead, he reversed his gun, swung the butt high up over his shoulder; and my own headfirst charge undid me. I couldn't swerve or brake in time, plunged right in under it. A hissing, spark-shedding skyrocket seemed to tear through the top of my head, and I went down into nothingness as Ainslie had.

For an hour after I recovered consciousness I was in complete darkness. Such utter darkness that I couldn't be sure the blow hadn't affected my optic nerve.

I was in a sitting position, on something cold—stone flooring probably—with my hands lashed behind me, around something equally cold and sweating moisture, most likely a water pipe. My feet were tied too, and there was a gag over my mouth. My head blazed with pain.

After what seemed like an age, a smoky gray light began to dilute the blackness; so at least my eyesight wasn't impaired. As the light strengthened it showed me first a barred grate high up on the wall through which the dawn was peering in. Next, a dingy basement around me, presumably that of the same New Hampshire Avenue house we had entered several hours ago.

And finally, if that was any consolation to me, Ainslie sitting facing me from across the way, in about the same fix I was. Hands and feet secured, sitting before another pipe, mouth also gagged. A dark stain down one side of his forehead, long since dried, marked the effect of the blow he had received.

We just stared at each other, unable to communicate. We could turn our heads. He shook his from side to side deprecatingly. I knew what he meant: "Fine spot we ended up in, didn't we?" I nodded, meaning, "You said it."

But we were enjoying perfect comfort and peace of mind, compared to what was to follow. It came within about half an hour at the most. Sounds of activity began to penetrate to where we were. First a desultory moving about sounded over our heads, as if someone were looking things over to make sure everything was in order. Then something heavy was set down: it might have been a table, a desk—or a pulpit.

This cellar compartment we were in seemed to be directly under that large front room where the coffin was and where the obsequies were to be held.

A dawning horror began to percolate through me. I looked at Ainslie and tried to make him understand what I was thinking. I didn't need to, he was thinking the same thing.

She'd been alive when we'd last seen her, last night. Early this same morning, rather. What were they going to do—go ahead with it anyway?

A car door clashed faintly, somewhere off in the distance outside. It must have been at the main entrance of this very house we were in, for within a moment or two new footsteps sounded overhead, picking their way along, as down an aisle under guidance. Then something scraped slightly, like the leg rests of a camp chair straining under the weight of a body.

It repeated itself eight or ten times after that. The impact of a car door outside in the open, then the sedate footsteps over us— some the flat dull ones of men, some the sharp brittle ones of women—then the slight shift and click of the camp chairs. I didn't have to be told its meaning; probably Ainslie didn't either. The mourners were arriving for the services.

It was probably unintentional, our having been placed directly below like this; but it was the most diabolic torture that could ever have been devised. Was she dead yet, or wasn't she? But she had to be before—

They couldn't be that low. Maybe the drug she'd been under last night was timed to take fatal effect between then and now. But suppose it hadn't?

The two of us were writhing there like maimed snakes. Ainslie kept trying to bring his knees up and meet them with his chin, and at first I couldn't understand what his idea was. It was to snag the gag in the cleft between his two tightly pressed knees and pull it down, or at least dislodge it sufficiently to get some sound out. I immediately began trying the same thing myself.

Meanwhile an ominous silence had descended above us. No more car-door thuds, no more footsteps mincing down the aisle to their seats. The services were being held.

The lower half of my face was all numb by now from hitting

my bony up-ended knees so many times. And still I couldn't work it. Neither could he. The rounded structure of the kneecaps kept them from getting close enough to our lips to act as pincers. If only one of us could have made it. If we could hear them that clearly down here, they would have been able to hear us yell up there. And they couldn't all be in on the plot, all those mourners, friends of the family or whoever they were.

Bad as the preliminaries had been, they were as nothing compared to the concluding stages that we now had to endure listening to. There was a sudden concerted mass shifting and scraping above, as if everyone had risen to his feet at one time.

Then a slow, single-file shuffling started in, going in one direction, returning in another. The mourners were filing around the coffin one by one for a last look at the departed. The departed who was still living.

After the last of them had gone out, and while the incessant cracking of car doors was still under way outside, marking the forming of the funeral cortege, there was a quick, businesslike converging of not more than two pairs of feet on one certain place—where the coffin was. A hurried shifting about for a moment or two, then a sharp hammering on wood penetrated to where we were, and nearly drove me crazy; they were fastening down the lid.

After a slight pause that might have been employed in reopening the closed room doors, more feet came in, all male, and moving toward that one certain place where the first two had preceded them. These must be the pallbearers, four or six of them. There was a brief scraping and jockeying about while they lifted the casket to their shoulders, and then the slow, measured tread with which they carried it outside to the waiting hearse.

I let my head fall inertly downward as far over as I could bend it, so Ainslie wouldn't see the tears running out of my eyes.

Motion attracted me and I looked blurredly up again. He was shaking his head steadily back and forth. "Don't give up, keep trying," he meant to say. "It's not too late yet."

About five or ten minutes after the hearse had left, a door opened surreptitiously somewhere close at hand; and a stealthy, frightened tread began to descend toward us, evidently along some steps that were back of me.

Ainslie could see who it was—he was facing that way—but I couldn't until the hatchet-faced maid we had seen crying in the kitchen the night before suddenly sidled out between us. She kept looking back in the direction from which she'd just come, as if scared of her life. She had an ordinary kitchen bread knife in her hand. She wasn't in livery now, but black-hatted, coated and gloved, as if she had started out for the cemetery with the rest and then slipped back unnoticed.

She went for Ainslie's bonds first, cackling terrifiedly the whole time she was sawing away at them. "Oh, if they ever find out I did this, I don't know what they'll do to me! I didn't even know you were down here until I happened to overhear Mr. Hastings whisper to his secretary just now before they left, 'Leave the other two where they are, we can attend to them when we come back.' Which one of you is her Jimmy? She confided in me; I knew about it; I helped her slip in and out of the house that whole week. I took her place under the bedcovers, so that when he'd look in he'd think she was asleep in her room.

"They had no right to do this to you and your friend, Jimmy, even though you were the cause of her death. The excitement was too much for her, she'd been so carefully brought up. She got this heart attack and died. She was already unconscious when they brought her back—from wherever it was you ran off with her to.

"I don't know why I'm helping you. You're a reckless, bad, fortune-hunting scoundrel; Mr. Hastings says so. The marriage wouldn't have been legal anyway; she didn't use her right name. It cost him all kinds of money to hush everyone up about it and destroy the documents, so it wouldn't be found out and you wouldn't have a chance to blackmail her later.

"You killed my baby! But still he should have turned you over to the police, not kept you tied up all ni—"

At this point she finally got through, and Ainslie's gag flew out of his mouth like one of those feathered darts kids shoot through a blow tube. "I *am* the police!" he panted. "And your 'baby' has been murdered, or will be within the next few minutes, by Hastings himself, not this boy here! She was still alive in that coffin at two o'clock this morning."

She gave a scream like the noon whistle of a factory. He kept her from fainting, or at any rate falling in a heap, by pinning her to the wall, took the knife away from her. He freed me in one-tenth of the time it had taken her to rid him of his own bonds. "No," she was groaning hollowly through her hands, "her own family doctor, a lifelong friend of her father and mother, examined her after she was gone, made out the death certificate. He's an honest man, he wouldn't do that—"

"He's old, I take it. Did he see her face?" Ainslie interrupted.

A look of almost stupid consternation froze on her own face. "No. I was at the bedside with him; it was covered. But only a moment before she'd been lying there in full view. The doctor and I both saw her from the door. Then Mr. Hastings had a fainting spell in the other room, and we ran to help him. When the doctor came in again to proceed with his examination, Mr. Olivers had covered her face—to spare Mr. Hastings' feelings.

"Dr. Meade just examined her body. Mr. Hastings pleaded with him not to remove the covering, said he couldn't bear it. And my pet was still wearing the little wrist watch her mother gave her before she died—"

"They substituted another body for hers, that's all; I don't care how many wrist watches it had on it," Ainslie told her brutally. "Stole that of a young girl approximately her own age who had just died from heart failure or some other natural cause, most likely from one of the hospital morgues, and put it over on the doddering family doctor and you both.

"If you look, you'll probably find something in the papers about a vanished corpse. The main thing is to stop that burial; I'm not positive enough on it to take a chance. It may be she in the coffin after all, and not the substitute. Where was the interment to be?"

"In the family plot, at Cypress Hill."

"Come on, Cannon; got your circulation back yet?" He was at the top of the stairs already. "Get the local police and tell them to meet us out there."

Ainslie's badge was all that got us into the cemetery, which was private. The casket had already been lowered out of sight. They were throwing the first shovelsful of earth over it as we burst through the little ring of sedate, bowing mourners.

The last thing I saw was Ainslie snatching an implement from one of the cemetery workers and jumping down bodily into the opening, feet first.

The face of that silver-haired devil, her guardian Hastings, had focused in on my inflamed eyes.

A squad of Lake City police, arriving only minutes after us, were all that saved his life. It took three of them to pull me off him.

Ainslie's voice was what brought me to, more than anything else. "It's all right, Cannon," he was yelling over and over from somewhere behind me. "It's the substitute."

I stumbled over to the lip of the grave between two of the cops and took a look down. It was the face of a stranger that was peering up at me through the shattered coffin lid. I turned away, and they made the mistake of letting go of me.

I went at the secretary this time; Hastings was still stretched out more dead than alive. "What've you done with her? Where've you got her?"

"That ain't the way to make him answer," Ainslie said, and for the second and last time throughout the whole affair his voice wasn't toneless. "*This* is!"

Wham! We had to take about six steps forward to catch up with the secretary where he was now.

Ainslie's method was all right at that. The secretary talked— fast.

Alice was safe; but she wouldn't have been, much longer.

After the mourners had had a last look at her in the coffin, Hastings and the secretary had locked her up for safekeeping—stupefied, of course—and substituted the other body for burial.

And Alice's turn was to come later, when, under cover of night, she was to be spirited away to a hunting lodge in the hills—the lodge that had belonged to her father. There she could have been murdered at leisure.

When we'd flashed back to the New Hampshire Avenue house in a police car, and unlocked the door of the little den where she'd been secreted; and when the police physician who accompanied us brought her out of the opiate they'd kept her under—whose arms were the first to go around her?

"Jimmy"—She sighed a little, after we took time off from the clinches—"he showed up late that night with Chivers, in that dinky little room you left me in.

"They must have been right behind us all the way, paying all those people to say they'd never seen me.

"But he fooled me, pretended he wasn't angry, said he didn't mind if I married and left him. And I was so sleepy and off guard I believed him. Then he handed me a glass of salty-tasting water to drink, and said, 'Come on down to the car. Jimmy's down there waiting for you; we've got him with us.' I staggered down there between them, that's all I remember."

Then she remembered something else and looked at me with fright in her eyes. "Jimmy, you didn't mind marrying little Alice Brown, but I don't suppose Alma Beresford would stand a show with you—?"

"You don't – suppose right," I told her gruffly, "because I'm marrying Alice Brown all over again—even if we've gotta change her name first.

"And this ugly-looking bloke standing up here, name of Ainslie, is going to be best man at our second wedding. Know why? Because he was the only one in the whole world believed there really was a you."

Silent as the Grave

Silent as the Grave was originally published in *Mystery Book Magazine* in November of 1945 and is known to be one of his greatest noir masterpieces. The story made its radio debut in 1946 in an episode of *Molle Mystery Theatre* and its television debut on CBS's *Silver Theatre* in 1949 starring Marsha Hunt and George Reeves (before his days as Superman). Months after *Rear Window* hit international success in 1954, a production company in France (Les Films Gibe) produced a feature entitled *Obsession* which was a combination of two stories: *If the Dead Could Talk* and *Silent as the Grave*. This story was hugely popular because of the thrilling usage of the oscillation motif, the honest portrayal of the economic depression of the thirties, and an almost unbearable build to the climax. In 1979, another French production company, FR3, produced *Foiles Douces* which was a 64 minute teleplay adaptation of the work directed by Maurice Ronet, starring Maurice Ronet and Josephine Charlin.

I T WAS A NIGHT like any other night. The moon was out; and there were stars.

A man and a girl strolling in the dark; the oldest story in the world. The music, mournful, nostalgic on the night air, ebbed away behind them, and the lights of the pavilion went with it. She was glad they were gone; just being with him was entertainment enough. She had her music and her dancing in the sound of his voice, the touch of his hand in hers.

Presently they came to a bench and, without a word, sat down. She knew why they had come out here. She knew what he was going to ask her. She wanted him to ask her. She had her answer ready, before he asked her, and it was "Yes."

His head went back, to look up at the stars. She looked at the turn of his chin, at the gnarled hitch in his throat, those were, for her, the stars. The starlight traced a thin silver line, like frost, along the upturned edge of his profile. That was proportionately all she knew of him, she reflected, that thin, argent, contour line; and the rest was still all in darkness, unknown, unguessed, like a planet already there but not yet emerged.

Her mother said it was risky to love anyone as much as she did him, so soon after meeting him, and knowing so little about him. Her mother said with dark head shakes, "Now don't be in too much of a hurry, young lady!" and "Just be careful what you're doing!" and other things like that your mother says to you. What did her mother know? Her mother's time for love was past.

Three weeks, two days, twelve hours. Yes, it was a short time. Very short for a lifetime.

Mitchell. Kenneth Mitchell. She said it over softly in her mind. Mitchell. Mrs. Frances Mitchell. No, Mrs. Kenneth Mitchell. That was better. She wanted everything to belong to him, even her first name.

"Frances—" His arm slipped around her.

This was it. Here it came now. She nestled closer. "Yes, Ken?"

"I'm in love with you. Would you—you wouldn't marry me, would you?"

"Yes, Ken," she sighed. "I would." She seemed to blend into his arms, almost to lose her own identity, as if she were a part of him, his other self. They didn't stir for awhile, just stayed like that, blindly contented, without need for anything else. All the traffic of courtship—caresses, kisses, words of love—were superfluous. Their oneness was their sole caress.

Then suddenly his arm was gone. She was alone again, there was space between them on the bench.

"I had no right—I didn't mean to ask you that."

"But it's all right, Ken. Can't you tell it's all right?"

"There's something I have to tell you first. Something you've got to know."

Something about some other girl, of course. What else could it be? What else did a man have to tell a girl at a time like this, what else ever mattered between man and girl? All the rest belonged in the man's world, a sphere apart that the girl never entered, that didn't conflict with her.

"But Ken, it doesn't matter. I don't want to know."

"You have to know this. This is something you have to. Before I ask you. Before you answer me."

She edged closer, by way of mute consent. She waited.

"Frances, I killed a man once."

For a minute it was meaningless. All she could feel was a sense of relief. It was almost anticlimax. The threatened impediment had dissolved. She had been afraid of some entanglement barring her way, some undissolved marriage or unsevered amorous connection. But this was from that other sphere, that other plane, the man's world; this had nothing to do with her, this didn't conflict with her in any way. This wasn't anything that could affect their love.

This was almost as if a small boy were to come to you and

say, "I threw a rock through somebody's window and broke it." He shouldn't have, it was wrong of him, the policeman down on the corner mightn't approve—but that didn't lessen your own affection for him in any way; how could it?

She breathed deeply, in lightened tension. "I thought it was— that there was somebody else." Then almost in parenthesis, "What was it, an accident?"

He shook his head doggedly. "It was no accident. It was what they call—murder. I went looking for him, and I found him, and—I did it."

Their oneness persisted; the thing had no power to divide them, every pore in her body was conscious of that fact. "What did they do to you, Ken?"

He said it lower than before. "They never found out it was me. They don't know to this day. I never gave myself up, because— well, he had it coming to him, he deserved it. He'd done me an injury. And I never forgive an injury."

An old rancor came up in him. She could feel the stiffening, the anger, from somewhere out of his past.

"It happened in St. Louis, long ago. Ten years ago. His name was Joseph Bailey, and he—"

Her hand flew up against his mouth, sealing it. "No more. I don't want to know any more."

They sat like that for a few minutes. Then, finally, her hand dropped. She had made her decision.

"Ask me what you were going to," she whispered. "Ask me. Nothing makes any difference. Nothing could change the way I feel about you. Nothing you could tell me."

His eyes kept pleading with her in the starlight. "But maybe later you won't feel the same. That's what I'm afraid of. Promise me you won't change. Promise me you won't throw it up to me, some day, if we should quarrel, like people do. I couldn't stand that, Frances. Promise me you'll never mention it, never remind me, in days to come."

She tilted her face to look up into his eyes. "I'll do more than promise. I swear it to you. I take a sacred vow, here and now.

You'll never hear me speak of it again. It'll be just as though you never told me. It'll never pass my lips. *I'll be as silent as the grave, dear heart. As silent as the grave, forever."*

He made a sudden little move, and her arms, outstretched to poise protestingly against his shoulders, seemed to cave in across the little dimpled hollows opposite their elbows, and the span between the two of them had vanished, they were together again for good.

It was a night like any other night. The moon was out; and there were stars.

That this state of chronic happiness could keep on like that for three years after was no surprise to her, for she had expected it to. She had known it would, she had been sure it would, but still she could not have explained why it should. How was it that it lasted with them, when others seemed to lose it so slowly but nevertheless so surely? Was she different from others? Was he?

She knew they weren't. She knew it wasn't that. They were as hemmed-into a tiny cubicle of two rooms and bath, ceilings low over their heads, as any other city dwellers. They were stripped of all artifices, all privacy, all mystery, before one another. There would be nothing, soon, that they could say to one another they had not said before; nothing they could do they had not seen one another do already. Almost, nothing they could think, the other did not guess that they were thinking.

He came home as pinched and chilled in the winter, as frayed and tired in the summer, as any other man, as all other men. His feet sometimes would hurt and he would take his shoes off. On Sundays he didn't shave, and the rim of his jaw would look shadowed and soiled. Her hair could grow as dank hovering over the torrid steaming stewpans, of a blazing July evening, as any other woman's; her nose could grow as blue and she could sniffle just as inelegantly through it, on arising before him at the crack of a bitter winter dawn to close the windows and turn the heat valves, as any other woman's.

And still, whatever this magic was that filled their hearts with content, it survived all that. It survived without a necktie at the table, without cosmetics at the night table, without the utterance of any startlingly original remark any longer, without the belated revelation of any new quality, any unguessed facet to the personality, kept hidden until now.

Why was this? No one could know. If they could not know themselves, how could anyone else know?

It wasn't one of these gusty, flaring things that quickly exhausts itself and dies out again, leaving an ash of bitterness and cold. It reminded her of the pilot light on the gas stove in her kitchen. Not very bright, not very noticeable, but always there, burning steady, burning low, at the center of its little world.

A doctor once, whom they had gone to consult about some minor matter—a boil on Ken's neck that required lancing—came as close, perhaps, to putting his finger on it as anyone could have, though even his interpretation may have veered too closely to the clinical. Looking them over in shrewd appraisal, as they sat there before him side by side after the trivial operation, he asked with kindly interest, "About how long are you two married, six months or so?"

"Three years last May," she answered, with a smile that had in it both vainglory and humility.

It apparently startled him somewhat. She saw him shake his head slightly, in admiring approval. "You seem to be very well-mated," he murmured thoughtfully. Then added, "Both mentally and physically."

She looked down at the floor for a moment, and could feel her face grow warm. It was a little bit like—being disrobed for an examination. Neither she nor Ken referred to it between themselves afterward, on leaving.

They were so content, so at peace with one another and hence with the world, they didn't even want much more than they had in a material way. Ambition is a plant that sprouts best in the loam of discontent. Certainly they didn't crave great wealth. For what purpose? Clothes? In the darkness of the picture theater they went to once a week, who could tell whether she had on a fifty-dollar or a five-dollar dress? Better furniture, a roomier apartment? They'd have that some day, maybe in a year, or two, or three; it wasn't urgent. What difference did your surroundings make, when all you saw, all you cared about, all you were aware of, was that other face before you? When it wasn't there, the walls were barren; when it was, they were lighted, radiant, warm. A car? They could have that, too, in a little while; only a very small down payment was required. But what real need was there for one, when the subway kiosk was only down at the next corner?

Even children—She didn't really miss them, and when her mother, once or twice, slyly asked her if she were avoiding having any, her answer was: "No, but it's just as well we haven't had any. It's Ken I love; I haven't room for anything else."

The job he had, fit him like a comfortable pair of old shoes. He'd grown into it. He'd already had it for two years before their marriage, five in all now. It had become a part of the very warp and woof of his existence, as closely knitted to him as she was. It was not a job, that designation was incorrect, not just an offhand way of earning a living. It was that part of his life that was spent away from her, from morning until early evening each day, and just as cherished, just as dear to him in another way, as the part spent with her.

The man over him was lenient, friendly, understanding. Hallett was his name, and he had made an invisible third at the table with them so many nights that she felt she knew him well, though she had never met him.

He'd say, "Hallett came back from his vacation today, and you wouldn't know him. He's put on fifteen pounds in the two weeks."

"I'm glad he picked up a little, he was looking all in before he went away," she would say, although she'd never seen him. But Ken had said he was.

Or, "Hallett's kid is coming out with a new tooth. I wish you could have seen him. He was sitting there proud as a peacock all day."

"My, but it's forward!" she'd marvel. "That's the second one, already, in no time at all."

Nearly every night he sat there with them at the table like that, an invisible but welcome third.

Once, around the time the dying decade was merging unnoticeably into the strange new times ahead, Ken received an offer of another job, at better pay.

"Did you tell Hallett about it?" she asked him.

"Sure. I wouldn't do anything behind his back. He's been too regular to me."

"What did he say?"

"He said much as he'd hate to see me go, he didn't want to stand in my way. He gave it to me fair and square. He said he couldn't give me any more than I'm getting now. He said the bottom's starting to drop out of everything; what happened in Wall Street is starting to spread around now, and it'll take a good six months, maybe more, before it wears off again. But on the other hand, he told me, as long as he's with the outfit, I haven't got a thing to worry about, he'll see that I'm treated fair and square. I can consider myself set for life."

And in a day or two, when she asked him, "Have you decided what you'll do about that?"

"I've turned the offer down; I'm staying with Hallett."

She'd known he would. She was glad he had. She wanted him happy. Or rather, she wanted the two of them to be happy; his happiness was hers.

And then suddenly there was no Hallett any more. He was gone overnight, and a stranger had taken his place at their supper table. It was almost like a personal bereavement to the two of them, that first night when he came home and told her. Her face even paled for a moment or two, as his must have when he'd first learned it earlier in the day. He couldn't eat very much.

"What's he like, this new man, this Parker?"

"I can't tell yet, I only saw him today for the first time." He tried to be fair to him. "I suppose he's all right. He's sort of lost, hasn't got the hang of things yet." He turned his fork over a few times, without lifting it from the table.

"You'll get used to him," she tried to console him. And then with an odd little burst of commiseration, "That poor woman! Hallett's wife. Just think what she must be going through tonight!"

She had a rather strongly developed fellow-feeling for other women, not a very commonly met with trait.

"He doesn't like me," he blurted out one night a few weeks later.

"Maybe you just imagine that." She wondered, privately, how anyone could possibly not like Ken.

"I can tell. He knows I'm one of Hallett's old men, of course, and he's got it in for me. I can tell by the way he looks at me."

"Well, don't give him an opening, don't give him a chance to show it."

"I'm not. I'm minding my own business, and doing my job, like I've always done."

They were selling apples and tangerines on the street corners now. That is to say, peddling them out of sheer destitution, in a city that had never known emergency beggary before, only the professional kind. These vendors were men in their prime, able-bodied. Then abruptly within a month or two, the phenomenon had vanished again, as if already the proportion of those reduced to such straits, as over against those remaining still above it, had increased too greatly to permit any further profit to be derived from it. The ratio of the needy to the prospering had reversed itself.

Parker cut his wages in half. His bitterness, brought home to smoulder there in worried sight of her, was not due so much to that in itself as to the fact that others, there a shorter time than he, had not been similarly reduced. "Parker's own men," as he expressed it.

"But are you sure?"

"I asked a couple of them. They wouldn't admit it, but I could tell by the look on their faces when they heard it that they hadn't been cut themselves."

"But that's not fair."

His mouth twisted into an ugly shape. "You bet it isn't. I'm taking the cut, so that some of his men don't have to be let out."

"Maybe if you went to him and—"

"That's just what he'd like me to do, so that he could chuck me out altogether. You should have seen his face when I stepped away from the cashier's window and opened my envelope. I caught him looking at me with a smirking expression all over his face."

"But why, Ken? You haven't done anything to him."

"He's got it in for me, that's all. And that's something you can't buck. You can't buck that on any job, when the guy over you has it in for you. He's got you, and you know it, and he knows it."

"Maybe things'll begin to clear up, and you can go somewhere else. The President says by next spring—"

"Does he work at my job?" he said glumly. Then after a while he added, "I'm only hanging on because I have to. I've got to get out of there, the minute I can. It's gotten so that just looking at the guy does something to me, inside. Every time he even passes in back of me while I'm busy at my layouts, I can feel something—"

She could sense that tightening-up again come over him that she had noticed one night long ago. Long ago, on a bench, beneath the stars.

"I don't hate easy, Frances," he muttered, "but once I start in, I don't quit easy either. I never forget an injury."

She dropped her eyelids for a moment, raised them again. A forbidding memory had crossed her mind just then. "Sh!" she urged, "Sh-h-h," and pressed her hand soothingly to his forehead, as if to cool it.

It was a night like any other night. There was no moon, but there were stars.

She was already badly frightened by then, it was so late and she had stood so long watching for him from the window. Then when she finally saw his figure approaching below in the dark, she knew by his walk something was the matter. He didn't even remember the right door, went on past their own house entrance almost to the next one down, then just as she was about to fling up the window and call out to him, he turned abruptly, retraced his steps, and came in where he belonged.

She left the window, and in the moment or two it took her to reach their flat door, wrung her hands close before her face in flurried, unseen appeal, to whom or what she did not know herself.

He came up the stairs quietly and slowly, to where she was waiting. His face was white with spent emotion, but composed. There was a big rent in his shirt, up near the collar, and two of the buttons on his coat were gone. Then when he'd gone in past her, wordlessly, and raised his hands to remove his hat, she saw that his hair was disordered, and there was a faint trace of orange across his knuckles that must have been left there by shed blood.

He sat down heavily and blew breath between his cupped hands, as though to warm them, although it wasn't cold out.

She drew up a kitchen chair and sat down across the table from him. He didn't seem to want to say anything, and she was afraid to for awhile. Presently she reached over toward him timidly, as if afraid of being rebuffed, and drew the knot of his necktie out from under his rumpled collar, where it had become wedged, and around toward the front where it belonged.

"Parker, Ken?" she asked finally.

He began to speak as though his silence had been an oversight, he had simply been waiting to have it called to his attention. His voice was husky from recent stress. "They took me to the police station, that's why I got back so late."

She started using the tips of her fingers for the teeth of a comb, raking his hair back with them, very softly, very persuasively. She didn't say anything.

He smiled at nothing she could see there on the floor. "I hit him *good*," he said with grim satisfaction. "Boy, what a slam I gave him! That one sock alone was worth everything I've had to take from him all these months. He went all the way back across his own desk and then down to the floor on the other side of it, and all the stuff he had on it went down on top of him. Just like you see in the pictures."

They were just like little boys, she thought. Only, the consequences of their acts could be so much graver when their bodies had become those of men.

"If they hadn't grabbed me and held me back, I think while I was at it I would have—"

She tried to ward the word off by quickly shuttering her eyes. He didn't say it anyway.

"So then he called in a cop. You know—trying to throw a scare into me. They held me over there for awhile. Finally he phoned in that he didn't intend lodging any complaint, they could let me go if they wanted to. Bighearted." He almost spat the word. "So I'm through there," he said finally.

"Never mind, maybe it's better so. I'm glad it's over. It was starting to get you, Ken. I could see it more and more every day."

"I'll get another job," he said. "Watch me."

She waited a moment or two. Then she asked timidly, "But what about references, Ken? They'll want them everywhere, no matter where you go; these days especially, when there are a dozen and one applicants for every job. And as long as he's down there in charge, even if someone just phones in to ask anything about you, he'd be just mean enough to—"

He didn't answer for some time, as though that had only now occurred to him—for the first time. Then finally he said, "If I ever find that out—" And didn't finish it.

Their money came to an end on a crisp fall morning in the third year of the bad new times, the Election Year, that was. They went together to the bank to draw it out, although the account was in his name alone. The way a couple feel obliged to attend some solemn formal occasion together, a deathbed or a funeral, when the presence of one without the other would be unthinkable.

"This closes the account," the teller reminded them gratuitously.

It was only a matter of four-dollars-fifty-cents, that was all that was left by then; but somehow when the leaves of the passbook had been perforated to form the letters "Closed" and it had been returned to them worthless, it did make a difference, a vast difference. She could feel it herself; a psychological difference. There was a horrid nightmare-feeling to it of going down over their heads into black, bottomless depths of water, never to rise again.

He walked out of the bank dazed, staring down at the little booklet, frittering its pages back and forth under his thumb endlessly. She had to guide him, unnoticeably, with her arm under his to keep him from jostling into people. Outside on the sidewalk he came to a halt, as though not knowing which way to go. "There goes—security," he said finally. "There go—three years of our lives."

"Don't, Ken," she pleaded. "Don't take it like that." She freed the booklet gently from his hands and shied it into a refuse can. "Come on. Come on home now."

He only said one thing more, very quietly, almost stonily. But she didn't like the sound of it. "I have Garrett Parker to thank for this."

He got something to do several weeks later, but it wasn't a job any more. He was paid by the hour, twenty-five cents an hour. Demonstrating in a drugstore window. Some impulse made her follow him there later in the day; he had told her where it was.

She saw this small crowd collected in front of the place, and she crept up behind them, rose on tiptoes, looked fearfully over their shoulders. He was within the lighted showcase, stripped to his undershirt and trousers. He had always had powerful shoulders and biceps, they showed up well. He was holding up a small patent-medicine, pointing to it, then flexing his arms so that his muscles swelled, striking himself on the chest like Tarzan in the movies. At twenty-five cents an hour. For anyone who came along the street to stand and gape at.

She would have died rather than let him see her looking at him; his crucifixion was complete enough without that. She turned and fled all the way home, her arms protectively clasped around her own form as though she had been suddenly stripped naked. She couldn't forget that telltale pulsing she had noted at his temple, that betrayed how he had been steeling himself.

She didn't say anything when he came home at last, only tried not to look at the seventy-five cents he put down on the edge of the table. She didn't tell him that she'd seen him, that she knew what it was for.

He toppled into a chair and hung his head.

"I'm ashamed," he breathed stifledly. "Frances, I'm so ashamed."

"Don't go back there again, Ken," she said. "I won't let you."

His attitude of humiliation, of self-reproach, was much harder to bear than the conditions that had brought them to this pass. "I shouldn't have met you, married you. I'm not even able to give you food for your mouth, I'm no good."

She dropped to her knees beside him. "I don't know what words to say, to tell you what you mean to me. I'm as proud of you now as if you had all kinds of money, and were on top of the world. I don't know how not to be proud of you."

From his hidden face and concave middle, arched over the table-top, came those peculiar, wrenching guttural sounds of male grief she had never heard before and never wanted to hear again. And through the subsiding sobs, at last, a still, cold voice filtered. "One man did this to me. One man."

Then a ray of brightness, when night was at its darkest. A beam of hope. He went to look up Hallett in his despair; his former boss, the one before.

"Oh, Ken! Can he do something for you—?"

He couldn't bring it out coherently at first. But the mere fact that he wanted to so bad, was so pitifully anxious to tell it, showed her in a flash that it must be good. "Wait'll you hear—My own line of work, France! He's going to talk to them right tomorrow. I'm to go down there. He's not in the business himself any more, but he knows these people, and he thinks he can swing it for me. He says with my previous experience there shouldn't be any reason—And what do you think he tried to do? I caught him trying to slip something into my pocket when I wasn't looking. A five-dollar bill. Didn't want to hurt my feelings by asking me openly if I—"

His face was a poem of gratitude. He said with husky, feigned censure that was meant for the deepest admiration, "The old son-of-a-gun. What can you do with a guy like that?"

He couldn't sleep all night, that night. But there was a difference. He didn't lie there growling surreptitiously deep inside his throat, hissing maledictions through his clenched teeth. He lay there wide-eyed, breathlessly hopeful. She knew, because she couldn't sleep either. They both got up much earlier than they needed to, red-eyed, haggard, supremely happy. She walked with him as far as the corner to see him off. She wished him luck. Long after he had disappeared from sight she stood there looking after him. Praying.

But when he came back there was something wrong. Her own face dimmed to the lacklustre of his.

"Ken, didn't they—? Did Hallett forget to talk to them?"

"References," he said tersely. He swallowed before he could bring himself to pronounce the name. "Parker."

She just looked at him, caught her underlip with her teeth in foreboding.

"He was my last boss, after Hallett. Hallett's recommendation wasn't enough by itself."

He dropped heavily into a chair, shaded his eyes. "They'll let me know tomorrow. It's still this way." He seesawed his hand uncertainly, to show her. "I think I still have a chance."

She knew what he was thinking, though. "Don't be afraid. No one could be that inhuman. What can he truthfully say against your ability? Nothing. Only that you lost your temper once and went for him."

She could see his cigarette all night in the dark, glowing and then dimming again, over there by the window. Like a pulsing ember of frustration.

When he was leaving the next day, she said : "Ken, I know it's extravagant, but would you phone me as soon as you find out? I'll wait downstairs in the candy store, right by their phone. Just so I'll—I'll know sooner."

He didn't say anything, but he kissed her affirmatively.

She waited there from ten on. She sat perched on one of the high stools before the soft-drink counter. She chatted with the proprietor's wife. She sat on, waiting, long after they'd stopped chatting for lack of anything further to talk about. She was glad when three o'clock came, and the woman changed places with her high-school-age daughter, and was no longer there to be a witness to her misery.

Four o'clock came, and five, and the new place would be closing soon. All business places closed around five or so.

She stood up abruptly, and put a nickel in the phone, and called it herself; he'd given her its name.

Timidly she asked, "Has there—has there been a new man taken on today?"

The girl said, "Yes, I believe there has."

Her heart soared, and all the wait was nothing. "Could you— would you give me his name, please?"

The girl looked it up, or got it from someone.

"Howard Ellson," she said.

She felt her way along the soft-drink counter, and out the door, and upstairs to their flat. He was sitting there, with the lights unlit. He must have come back long ago, hours ago, while she stayed on waiting in the candy store below.

He just looked up at her, then looked down again. She would have read that look anyway, even if she hadn't already known. She didn't go to him and put her hands on him. His grief needed elbowroom.

"*He* did it," he said after a long time.

He took a long breath, seemed to draw air slowly into his lungs, for a whole minute or two, and never let it out again. "I ought to kill him," he said almost inaudibly.

"Ken," she moaned. "Ken."

"It was my one chance, and it won't come again. I had it, and I lost it—thanks to him. Someone else has the job now, and people hang onto their jobs these days. I can't asked Hallett to go around acting as an employment agent for me. Months more of misery now for the two of us. On *his* account. Maybe years. Do you know what that means?" He pulled his shirt open and ground his fist against his bared chest. "Do you know what it does to you, in *here*, when you can blame that all on one man? Not Fate, not Conditions, not Bad Luck or Coincidence—but one man, walking around on the very same streets you are, not very far from where you are."

"Ken, don't. Think of me. I can't stand it when I hear you talk like that."

And then he said again, more softly than the first time, almost in a baleful whisper, "I'd like to kill him." And she saw his hands close up and freeze.

She got him to eat a little, after awhile. She thought the worst of it was over by then. And then later, he was sitting there in the kitchen, directly behind her, while she washed the dishes.

There wasn't a sound from him. She turned her head suddenly and looked, and the chair was empty. The wet plate dropped and shattered into the spokes of a wheel, and she ran to the door and looked out.

Hours later she was waiting down on the corner for him, when he finally came along. He was drunk, she could tell by his walk. But that didn't matter, nothing mattered; only that he came along. She ran to him and put her arm about his waist, and they went wavering back toward the house together.

"Ken, why did you do this to me, why did you frighten me this way? You left without a word, without saying goodbye. Ken, I thought such awful things."

He knew what she was saying, could understand. "Poor France," he said. "I'm drunk. It didn't do any good. I didn't forget once, the whole time I was doing it."

They went up the inside stairs slowly, side by side, reeling as though they were both drunk and not just one of them. "I'm drunk, France. You never saw me that way before, did you? You don't want to kiss me now, do you? But I still want to kiss you. More than ever."

"I do. Look. I do."

When they got inside their own flat, he toppled heavily into a chair, almost pulling her down with him.

"Shall I help you off with your shoes?"

He shook his head, smiled wanly. "I'm not that drunk." His hands went up.

"Let me see your face. Why are you covering your face like that?"

"What is there to see?"

There was nothing. It was just his face, as it had always been. His hands, released, went up to it again and covered it once more.

Just before their evening meal, something happened to change him. She couldn't tell exactly what it was, at first. He'd still seemed all right when he came in with the paper and sat down to read it. Then by the time she'd called him to eat, there was already something different about him, some alteration had taken place. It had none of the symptoms she was so familiar with by now. She couldn't tell what it was. She could discern something utterly new in it, constraint, furtiveness; and could only ascribe it to remorse for last night's drunkenness. But if he was ashamed, why so belatedly ashamed, at the end of the day? Why not immediately on getting up and facing her this morning? He hadn't been then.

She saw him looking at her closely several times, as if wondering how to forestall some discovery she was bound to make eventually herself. Abruptly, he said, "Did you see that, in the paper?"

"What?" she asked.

"Turn toward the back. No, the page after that."

Parker had been found dead on the street near his house. The details didn't matter. Scarcely any were given, anyway. Only that he had met death by violence at somebody's hands. "Some person unknown," the paper said.

She peered at him through the mist of stupefaction that the

item had created in her mind. She saw him drop his eyes, then raise them again with an effort, to meet hers.

"Why didn't you tell me right away? As soon as you first read it?"

"I felt funny about it," he admitted with a defensive shrug.

At first she couldn't understand what he meant by that. "But why, Ken? Why should you feel funny about it?"

He looked away, sidewise, down at the floor. "Because I've been talking about him like I have; knocking him so."

It sounded lame, it didn't ring true somehow. She felt his real reason went deeper than that. But for once her understanding of him failed her, she couldn't imagine what it was.

Presently, as they sat there discussing the event, she murmured, with that characteristic compassion of hers toward other women: "I feel sorry for his poor wife. What she must have felt, when he didn't come home, and then finally a stranger rang the doorbell to tell her—"

"It was a good job!" he blurted out savagely. "He had it coming to him, if anyone ever did!"

She sat in stunned silence after that. Not because of what he'd just said, but because of a discovery that what he had just said had brought about. The discovery was this : his recent self-consciousness about the item being in the paper was not due to the way he had reviled Parker, as he had said it was. It could not be. For here he was doing it again. He'd contradicted himself, without realizing it.

It must have been due to something else.

It only came to her that night, in a flash, as she lay awake in the dark, thinking. A flash that seemed to light up the whole room, with a horrid ruddy glow. She had been thinking: It may be better, for Ken's sake, that this has happened to Parker, that he's out of the way now. It's like a load off my mind. Because I've been dreading for weeks and months past now, that this very thing *might* happen some day. Only it would be Ken who—

And then the flash came.

Why should he be self-conscious in front of me when he first read it tonight?

Why should he take such a long time to show it to me? Why not instantly?

He told me once he never forgives an injury.

He's done it once already, *there*, before we were married.

Even to herself she never said "St. Louis."

She propped herself up on her elbow, turned toward him. She stretched out her hand to touch him, but something seemed to hold it back, she couldn't make it go all the way. "Ken," she whispered fearfully.

He was either fast asleep or he didn't hear the faint breathing of his name.

No, I'd better not ask him, she thought. How can I ask him? To ask him about this would be like reproaching him for that other time. I've made my vow, and I must keep it. Never to speak of it, never.

She forced herself to lie back again. She pressed her hand tightly to her mouth, held it that way, as if to smother the horrid question that kept trying to force its way out.

"It isn't so," she said to herself over and over again. "It can't be. He was out drinking that night. Only out drinking."

And then an insidious afterthought, as if malignantly hovering about waiting its opportunity, forced its way in.

"But *where* was he out drinking that night? Where did he go?"

The next night he was sitting there in the room with her reading the paper.

She spoke at last. For five whole minutes she'd been trying to. "Ken. Where—what bar did you go to, that night you—came home like that?"

He took a minute's time. "I don't remember," he said, through the newspaper like a screen.

"Quinn's, down by the corner?"

"No," he said. "Further away. Some bar or other. I don't remember." He gave the newspaper a shake, as if to say: Stop this.

She daren't go any farther. Why should he go farther away than Quinn's? In Quinn's they'd trust him for a drink or two. Elsewhere they wouldn't. And he must have had quite a few that night.

"Did they get him yet?" she asked presently.

"Who?"

"Whoever did that. You know, Parker." She turned to look at him as she asked it, drying a dish with its rim held pressed into her midriff. She could only see the top of his forehead, the paper hid his face from there down.

"No," he said tonelessly. "Not as far as I see."

"They will in a day or two, I suppose?" she suggested. "They always do."

"Not always," he said curtly. Neither forehead nor paper moved. He must have stopped reading, or the one would have slowly climbed above the other as his eyes went down the page.

She turned away again, put the dried plate down atop the others. They didn't once, she agreed silently. In St. Louis.

He roamed restlessly about for awhile, stood here, stood there. Finally he said, "Think I'll take a little walk, get some air."

"You'd better cover up good," she warned. "It's ice-cold out. Your coat is like tissue paper. Put your sweater on underneath."

But when he'd done so, he complained, "I can't wear both things. Too bulky." And he took the coat off, and left just the sweater on. He went out, and it stayed there where he'd flung it, carelessly rumpled on a chair.

She got a clothesbrush, and drew the coat across her lap, and started to dust it off a little. She turned the linings of the pockets out, to rid them of the debris, the tobacco grains and clotted bits of wool that she knew by experience were likely to adhere along their seams. A crumpled scrap of pale-green paper clung to one of them even after it had been reversed, and she plucked it off. It was nothing, only a trolley-car ticket.

Her clothesbrush halted again after a single upward stroke. Funny he should take a trolley, when the subway was so much more accessible to where they lived, and so much faster. She picked it up again from where she had discarded it, and straightened out the creases so that it expanded to twice its length.

Why, this wasn't even a downtown line, she could tell by the list of transfer points running down one side of it, under the heading "Not Good if Detached."

> "Canton Boulevard, South.
> Macomber Avenue, South.
> Fillmore Avenue, South."

The coat fell off her lap and she stepped over it in moving across the room, forgetful of the fact that she had just been about to brush it. The newspaper was on the table where he'd thrown it when he finished with it, but she didn't want that one, she wanted the previous night's. She found it thrust away in a receptacle with paper bags and things.

Two words out of all the hundreds it contained were all she wanted, and she found them quickly, for she knew which text they were imbedded in. ". . . Garrett Parker, of 25 Fillmore Avenue, South . . ."

The ticket's date, printed in red, was that of two nights ago, the night he had been out drinking. It had a double row of little boxes, each with a numeral in it, to mark the exact hour of issuance. The upper ones were for A.M., the lower for P.M. The "10" of the bottom row had been neatly punched through with a little round hole. She wouldn't have known which it was, only the "9" was still there on one side of it, the "11" on the other. The time of Parker's death had been between ten and half-past.

A blind interval, during which movement became automatic, unrecorded, followed. She was standing before the stove, holding the pilot key out so that the light flared wide, thrusting the pale-green ticket into it. Her face was that of a desperately sick woman.

"Now I know," she kept saying to herself over and over. "Now I know."

She put out the lights and raised the window shade.

It was a night like any other night. There was no moon, but there were stars.

Two nights later she saw *the name* for the first time, this stranger's name that meant nothing to her. Pulled out of thin air.

"They got him," Ken said abruptly. And she thought she heard him give a long sigh.

She ran over quickly beside him, to read. They had arrested a man named Considine, on the accusation of having killed Parker. He'd worked for Parker; not in Ken's time, but more recently, a few short weeks ago. He'd been unjustly discharged. He'd borne a grudge. It was Ken's case all over again, almost terrifyingly so. Just with a change of names. He couldn't prove where he'd been that night, around ten to half-past. He said he'd gone out and had a few drinks, and couldn't remember. She was almost terrified by the similarity.

That was about all there was to it. It was only a small item at the foot of a back page. But it meant so much in someone's life. In theirs too, for that matter. Immunity from now on. She could see him go out on the streets now without that cold terror in her heart. She could hear a knock at their door, or a heavy tread coming up the stairs, without dying a little.

"He denies he did it, Ken," she said mournfully, without meeting his eyes.

"They all do," he said callousedly. "You don't expect him to admit it, do you?" He put the paper aside, stood up. "Let's go out to a movie," he said. "I—I feel a lot better tonight."

It came creeping back that night in the dark, the banished named. Considine. Just an abstract name in a newspaper. Jones, Smith, Brown, Considine. She said to herself, "I must forget this name. I must say, 'It doesn't belong to anyone real. There is no such man.'"

She tossed and turned restlessly in the bed.

There is no such man, there is no such man, there is no such—

But it kept pounding at her mercilessly, like the throbbing of a drum. "Considine. Considine. Considine."

He was working again. They'd taken him back at his old place, now that Parker was out of the way. His wages were exactly two-thirds of what they had been when he was with the concern the time before. But the world about them, beginning to struggle painfully up out of the depths, had found new standards of contentment, frugality, simplicity. Safety, security, came drifting back within sight on the troubled waters, but never again the old expansiveness.

They discontinued accepting relief almost with his first pay check. They were compelled to, under penalty of prosecution, but thousands postponed doing so as long as they could. But with him it was almost a physical restorative, an aid to convalescence. His step became firmer, quicker. The old, open untroubled width of eye returned. Slowly the soreness of spirit was eased, the bitterness was mellowed, as he basked in the renewed illusion of being of some use in the world, as under therapeutic rays.

Even heartiness, gayety, began to peer tentatively forth again at intermittent times, as when he brought her home his pay envelopes on alternate Saturdays. What they contained stood for so much more than the intrinsic value of the money they held.

"Why can't I get you to smile any more?" he asked wistfully, as she looked down at it in her lap where he'd dropped it.

"I do smile—look—I do. I smile whenever you do, like I always did."

"But it doesn't go in. It doesn't go inside."

("*He* had a job too, poor soul," she thought.)

The name had vanished again from the newspapers, after that first brief mention—it seemed like months ago, or was it only weeks? It was such a minor, unimportant case after all. She never went near the papers any more while he was present. But once or twice, when they were preparing for bed, she made some excuse to go back into the other room in her nightgown, stand hurriedly searching through them for a moment before putting the light out. There was never any mention of it that she could find. But still he's real, she told herself, returning wraith-like to where her own husband lay safe in the darkness; he's real, he's somewhere.

One night she asked, "Whatever became of that man they arrested—on account of Parker? Are they still holding him?"

"They must be. I haven't read of his being released."

"All this time in jail," she thought, "while we—"

And suddenly within a week, as if her question had been ill-omened, had released pent-up evil forces held in abeyance all the while, they read of his being brought to trial. It wasn't a celebrated crime, it wasn't given much space. Things like that were happening all the time in a big city such as theirs, people charged with murder being tried for their lives. In the standard-sized paper that he habitually brought home there were never any pictures, as least not of that sort of thing. But once he happened to bring a tabloid in addition; not that he had bought it, but someone had left it on the subway seat next to him and it was practically uncreased. And this was two-thirds pictures and very little text, and all of that very sort of thing.

Leafing unsuspectingly through it, she looked up, stunned.

"What's the matter?"

"He has a wife," she said aghast, as though she'd seen a ghost. "I didn't know that until now."

"Who? Oh, Considine. What made you think he hadn't?" And after a moment he added, "Even murderers have wives."

Ah yes, she agreed to herself, with poignant bitterness. Yes, Kenneth Mitchell, you're right, even murderers have wives.

That night she had a terrifying dream, in which a stranger's face hovered over her as she lay there. The face of a strange woman, stricken with grief. It bent low above her own. "You have your husband," it whispered balefully. "Where is mine?"

She turned her face feverishly, to try to avoid the accusing sight.

"Murderess!" hissed the phantom. "Murderess!"

"I didn't do it," she breathed tormentedly. "*He* did."

"*He* killed Parker. But you are the one who is killing my husband. By remaining silent. *You*, not he! Murderess,

murderess!"

She awoke with a stifled scream, and fled from the bed, and ran to the window and stood there looking out.

Her breast was rising and falling convulsively, and there was cold moisture on her face. She'd always had such a strongly developed feeling of sympathy for other women.

It was a night like any other night. Without a moon, and without stars.

She found herself looking at the house from the opposite side of the street. Its cracker-box outline, its canary-brick facing, dim with soot, looked so prosaic, so matter-of-fact. It was just a flat like thousands of others, all over the city. On nearly every street you could see one just like it.

She tried to tear herself away, and she couldn't. She wondered: behind which one of those windows is she sitting, agonized, stifling her pain? Waiting for the night to come. He dies tonight; tonight is his last night.

I'm the only one can save him. If I go on my way now, if I go home, nothing can save him; he'll surely die tonight. If I come back tomorrow, it'll be too late. He'll be gone, then, and nothing can bring him back.

She crossed the street, against the traffic, dazedly, like a sleepwalker. She went up to the door, pulled it open, went inside. She was in a grubby hallway that smelled of dust and stale cooking. She went over to the letter boxes and lowered her head, scanning the names.

A janitress came out from behind the stairs carrying a pail of water. "Who did you wish to see, Missus?"

"Considine. Are they—is she still living here?"

"Sure. She's up on the third. You know her?"

"No," Frances said simply. "I felt I—had to see her. I feel sorry for people in trouble."

The janitress nodded. "Yes, that's trouble, all right."

"What's she like?" Frances asked.

"Like you. About your age. Nice little body. She was so happy with him before it happened. She had another baby since they took him to jail."

"She's taking it hard, I suppose?"

Again the janitress' choice of an illustration was deadly. "Wouldn't you? He was all she had."

She had once been about Frances' own age. She was a crazed automaton now, beyond calculations of age or personality. She seemed unable to stand entirely straight, even in the narrow door opening. She stood bowed forward, as if a heavy lodestone were suspended from her neck.

"You don't know me," Frances said. "I'd like to talk to you. Please let me come in. I'd like to talk to you."

The woman in the doorway said listlessly, "Come in." Her dazed mind evidently couldn't grasp the fact that Frances was a complete stranger to her.

She began to cry again as soon as the door was closed. It had become so continuous by now there was scarcely any facial change went with it; just a renewed dimming of the puffy eyes and then a glistening track down the cheek. She said, as though she had known Frances a long time, "My sister is coming over to take the children and me back with her later, but she didn't get here yet. But *tonight!* Oh, how am I going to stand it *tonight?"*

There was a little boy standing there, staring up at Frances. The mother patted the top of his head absently. "No, you go inside. Don't come in here. Stay inside and play with the baby like I told you."

She turned to Frances when he had gone. "He doesn't know," she choked. "How can I tell him? He keeps *asking*. He keeps asking all the time where he is."

Frances kept opening and closing the frame of her handbag. Over and over, incessantly, without looking at it.

The other woman's voice rose, strangulated. "What harm has that child done? I'm not asking anything for myself, but is it right to take that child's father away from him? Is that what the Law is for, to punish innocent children?"

"Don't," Frances breathed expiringly, and covered her ears. "I can't stand it."

The woman turned toward the window. It looked out on a whitewashed brick shaft. The wall was blue with shade now nearly all the way up, only at the very top was their still a triangular wedge of crimson sunlight, shaped like a guillotine blade. She pointed to it, held her shaking arm extended full-length. "Look how fast it goes, that sun," she groaned. "Why doesn't somebody stop it? Oh, why doesn't somebody make it stay *still?*"

Frances impulsively stepped close to her, took her shoulders, gently tried to turn her away. She resisted passively. Her waist and shoulders turned under the coaxing pressure, but her face remained stubbornly fixed on the evaporating patch of sunlight out there. "That's his last sun," she whimpered. "That's the last time he'll ever see it. Don't let them take the sun away from him. Oh, miss, whoever you are, don't let them!"

Frances drew her to a chair, sat her down in it. She stroked her disheveled hair back from her brow. She brought a little water in a glass, held it for her to drink. "Sh-h-h-h," she whispered on a long-drawn breath. "Sh-h-h-h."

"I was up to see him Sunday," Mrs. Considine murmured presently, quieting a little. "I said goodbye Sunday. I don't know how I got back here. If I hadn't known my children were here waiting for me, if my brother-in-law hadn't been with me on the train—Oh, that awful train ride! The wheels kept going around in my head. They kept saying, 'Goodbye forever, goodbye, goodbye, goodbye—' "

Frances winced, and, bending down over her from behind the chair, tilted her own face for a moment, ceilingward, as if in supplication of some sort of guidance neither one of them could see.

"Did he—" She could barely make herself heard. "Did he—say it wasn't he—he didn't?"

"He told me again, like he's told me from the beginning. He swore it to me by our two children. He didn't, he didn't; he never went near that man. I *know* he's telling the truth. You'd have to know my Al like I do. He wouldn't lie to me, my Al wouldn't lie to me. It isn't in him to do that to anyone; I know him too well. He only went out for a few beers that night; is there any harm in that? Just that night he had to go. I even said to him, 'Al, don't go tonight.' Never *dreaming*. You know, just because I wanted him to stay around, I was lonely. But he went to look up his friend Nick Mano. That's a friend of his, Nick Mano. And just that night Nick had to be out. If he'd only been with him, they wouldn't have been able to say—but he waited around for him. And that's when it happened." The figure in the chair rocked desolately to and fro. "But who is there will listen? Who is there will help me? Who *can* help me?"

I can, Frances thought. I can, I alone. Only I. It was as though a bright, cold light had suddenly been turned on. Everything, the outlines of things, the room about her, the woman in the chair immediately below her, suddenly seemed so clear, crystal-clear, diamond-clear, where until now they had been hazy, blurred by her own turmoil. Everything seemed so lucid, so logical, so— inevitable.

The other woman's voice droned on, in its litany of misery. "The last words he said to me Sunday, his very last words when they were making me leave, were, 'I didn't do it, Frances. They're taking me away from you for something I didn't do.'"

"Is that your name?" Frances shuddered violently. "My God!" she moaned low.

The woman's sobbing singsong continued. Suddenly she turned her head questioningly toward the back of the chair. "Miss—?" she called out wonderingly. "Miss—?"

There was no one standing there any longer. The room was empty. The door hung cryptically open.

Suddenly she found herself in a phone booth. Somewhere, she didn't know where. It seemed so simple, so easy. A little light went on, to see by. She found a nickel and she dropped it in. Just like when you wanted to phone the grocer or the butcher. No different. So easy, so simple, so compulsory.

A voice said, "Police Department, good evening."

She said, "I want to talk to someone about that Parker case. What they're killing that man for tonight. I don't know how to go about it—"

"Just a moment." Another voice got on. It wasn't a frightening voice. It was impersonal, but it wasn't severe, or bullying, or anything. It was just like—well, once she'd had to call up one of the department stores about making an exchange; it took patience, but she'd finally succeeded in making herself understood. "Yes, ma'm. Now, what is it?"

She said, "It's about that Parker case. He didn't do it. That man they're—putting away tonight. Considine. He didn't do it. You *must* believe me—"

The voice was calmingly reasonable. First things first. "Would you give me your name please?"

You had to give your name when you were asked it by a police official, even over the telephone wire. It never occurred to you not to. The habit of being law-abiding, of never having anything to hide or fear, saw to that. "I'm Mrs. Kenneth Mitchell."

The voice showed approving consideration. "And what is your address, please, Mrs. Mitchell?"

"Forty Forthway." Then she added, gratuitously, "Apartment C." The stores always liked that, when you gave the exact flat number. It made it easier for them to deliver. It seemed to add plausibility now.

"Yes, Mrs. Mitchell. And now you say—?"

"He didn't do it. Considine. I know it, oh, I know it! You've *got* to listen to me. I wouldn't have done this, if I weren't sure—"

"What makes you think that, Mrs. Mitchell?"

"Because—because—" She floundered, helpless. "Because I *know* he didn't. I *know.*"

The voice was considerate, patient, willing to give her a fair hearing to almost any lengths. "But you must have some reason for such a belief, Mrs. Mitchell."

"I have," she protested tearfully. "I have."

"Then what is it, Mrs. Mitchell?"

Somehow she found herself in a verbal corner. She couldn't seem to extricate herself, go back along the way she'd entered and thus get out again. She hadn't thought this far ahead. There were two parts to the act of vindication. Exoneration. And then substitution. But she only realized that now. She hadn't taken the second one into her calculation, visualized it. And they were indivisible, the two.

The voice persisted, nudging her, nudging her ever so gently. Not allowing her to stand still in her cul-de-sac. "But what is your reason for thinking Considine didn't do it, Mrs. Mitchell? How can you be so sure?"

"Because—Because—" There wasn't any other way. It had to be one or the other. To be believed at all. And to be believed was uppermost in her tormented mind just then. Overshadowing every other consideration. "Because my own husband did it."

The voice showed no dramatic alteration whatever. It continued on its even tenor. It still seemed reluctant to believe her. Perhaps having found this attitude to be the most profitable up to now, it shrewdly continued with it, "Are you sure of what you're saying, Mrs. Mitchell?"

It was easier from there on. She began speaking more volubly, in the effort to convince him. "Yes! Yes! I am. Oh, I am. He worked for Parker for years. He was unjustly discharged; we've been through a lot of hardship on Parker's account. He often said he would, and I know he meant it. Oh, I can't remember every little thing now any more—I found a trolley-car ticket in his pocket that he used that night—"

"Have you kept this?"

"No, I didn't. I did away with it."

The voice said, almost skeptically, "You haven't anything more conclusive than that, then?"

"No. But I *know* he did it. I know what I'm saying. Oh, don't let them kill that man! You've got to stop them." She had to beat down his disbelief, his obtuseness; why didn't his voice change, why didn't he get excited, interested? Didn't they *care?* "Don't you believe me? I *know*!" she kept repeating.

"Yes, but how? Why?"

"Because he did it once before."

"How do you know that?"

"Because he told me!" She was almost beside herself. "He told me the night we became engaged. They never found out, but he *told* me about it. That's why I know he did it this time too."

"And how long ago was this, this first time?"

Oh, why was he so thick, so stupid? What difference did *time* make? "Ten years before we were married. In St. Louis."

"And you've been married?"

"Three years."

"Thirteen years ago, in St. Louis," the voice said with judicial impartiality. She could somehow sense that a pencil point was moving over paper; some slightly absent inflection of the voice gave her that. "But you have no way of knowing whether that's true, either; simply that he told you that. Is that right?"

"But he wouldn't have *told* me, if it weren't. Why would he have *told* me that? The man's name was Joe Bailey; I've never forgotten the name."

"Joe Bailey," the voice repeated mechanically.

"Don't you see?" she pleaded tearfully. "All I'm trying to get you to do is have them stop that thing tonight! It mustn't be carried out. Even if it's only a postponement—Oh, please; I don't know the man, I've never even seen him. But I can't sleep thinking about it—"

But to the end his voice never changed, woke up; she couldn't seem to impress it on him that she was telling him the truth. "I understand, Mrs. Mitchell, I don't know whether there's anything I can do, but I'll see. But you haven't given us very much to go by." It pondered briefly. "Perhaps it might be better if you'd come, down here. If you'd care to give us your statement personally—"

Suddenly she was frightened. In a new way. You didn't just step into a booth on your homeward way, put through a call, and secure the reprieve of a condemned man. There was more to it than that. You became involved, tangled up; your own life interfered with. Worst of all, *he'd* find out about it. It was like a dash of cold water full in the face. The clear white flame of altruism was quenched, went out with a hiss of sudden personal fear. The old blurredness came back, of before her visit to the Considine flat.

"Oh, no, I can't!" she gasped. "I can't make it. I—I have to go home and fix supper—he's waiting for me—I'm late—"

She hung up. She came out of the booth, staggering a little. Almost at once a telephone started ringing behind her, where she'd just come from. It frightened her all the more, and she started to run. She ran all the way. She ran until her hat fell off, and she left it there behind her. She ran, and a sobbing voice kept saying over and over somewhere inside her, "I didn't mean it! I didn't mean it!" She ran until the night around her had fogged with her own exhausted exertion, and she couldn't see which way she was going any more.

Then suddenly he had stopped her, on the sidewalk out in front of their home. She ran straight into his arms, without seeing him.

He said, "Frances!" and his arms were around her and the whole thing vanished. The whole thing she'd been fleeing from.

"I didn't mean it, Ken!" she panted distraught. "Ken, I didn't mean it!"

"Why, because you're late? What's so terrible, what's the difference? Don't take it like that. As long as you're here now." He took her upstairs with him, carrying her, holding her feet off the ground. "I didn't know what happened to you. I was starting to get uneasy. But it's all right now."

And there was the lamplight of home around her, and the whole thing—back there—was just like a bad dream.

"Let me fix your supper. No, I've got to fix your supper. They can't take this away from me." She went into the kitchen, and squatted on her heels before the stove, and thrust the broiler-pan with meat on it into its proper rack.

He followed her and looked at her searchingly. "Something's the matter. You're not well."

"They can't take this away from me," she kept repeating. Then she said, "She's happy now. I gave all this back to her. She'll have this again now, herself."

"Who's happy?" He put his hand across her forehead, as if to test its temperature. "Frances," he pleaded. "Don't frighten me like this. Something's happened to you. You're hysterical. Won't you tell me what it is? You saw a bad picture. You were nearly run down on the street. Won't you tell me?"

She tried to struggle to her feet, and he tried to help her. Suddenly she sagged limply backward into his arms, and he caught her and kept her from falling. "I've given it back to her," she breathed. "Oh, Ken," she whispered, "Ken, I dreamed I did a terrible thing." Her eyes dropped closed, and she lay inert, pressed against him.

He had her on the sofa when she opened them again. She was lying on the sofa, and he was crouched there beside her, holding her hand between his, his face anguished.

"Ken—"

"Sh, lie quiet now. Don't talk. The doctor'll be here soon. I phoned him to come over."

"They can't take this away from me," she breathed. She tried to turn her head a little and look out past the obtruding sofa arm. "Ken, your supper—The table, not set yet—The meat, it's been in too long—Ken, I've never been so late with you before—"

She tried to struggle upright, and he pressed her gently back. "No, never mind now. Just lie still, lie quiet—"

"Ken—"

"He'll be here soon. What is it? What hurts you?"

"The whole world, Ken," she whispered. "The whole world hurts me,"

Suddenly recollection, like a galvanic electric shock, coursed through her. He couldn't hold her prone any more. She jolted upright, fastened her hands to the revers of his coat, shook him imploringly. "Ken, it wasn't a dream—! It happened! Quick, the valise—!"

He tried to restrain her, while she struggled, strove against him.

"Our valise—the big one—where is it? Get it out. No, you've got to listen to me! Bring the valise in here. Hurry, Ken. Get out your things. And mine—"

The sudden pounding was like surf breaking against a rocky shore, and coming back again and back and back.

Her arms whipped inextricably around his neck like a knot. Like the knot of a hangman's noose.

He tried to regain his feet. "It's only the doctor. But why does he make so much noise—?"

"No!" she screamed. "Don't go! Don't go near it!"

"I've got to let him in. I sent for him."

"No," she groaned, in an access of disemboweling terror. "Don't go!" She wouldn't loosen her arms. She held him down there by her, in a headlock, with convulsive strength. "Stay here with me like this. Let me hold you tight like this. Oh, make it *last*, I want it to *last*—"

He had to exert all his strength to pry her grip loose. And then he burst the embrace and left her fallen draggingly, from sofa seat to floor, one arm still extended after him in futile desperation. And he was gone.

She couldn't call out, she couldn't speak. She couldn't even see any more. She could only listen. As to the resonance of a knell.

A door opened. "You're under arrest for the murder of Joseph Bailey, in St. Louis, Missouri, thirteen years ago." And then, "Your own wife."

She tottered to her feet, and staggered after him, arms feeling the way for her blinded eyes. She came up against the front of someone's gray suit—but Ken's was a blue one—and someone held her, propping her like a sort of spindly, life-sized doll without any bones in it.

And then that voice, tomblike, guttural with all the pain and all the dismay and all the heartbreak there have ever been in the whole world, since the first man loved the first woman. And the first woman loved the first man.

"Frances, Frances, what have you done to me?"

Calling out to her, calling, in haunting supplication, as it receded from the room, from her life, from her love, forever.

"Fran-ces, Fran-ces, what have you done to me—?"

Fading away at last into the irretrievable distance.

Somebody kept holding her up, somebody anonymous, somebody in a gray suit.

"But have they saved Considine at least? At least have I done that much?"

"Considine was executed half an hour ago. He made a full confession of guilt fifteen minutes before he went to the Chair."

She was slipping down the front of the gray suit, it seemed to go rushing up past her. Her thoughts exploded into white-hot particles of agony, that slowly cooled and went out one by one.

"I will be silent as the grave, dear heart. Silent as the grave forever. For now indeed I am one."

It was a night like any other night. There was no moon; there were no stars.

AFTER DINNER STORY

After Dinner Story was originally published in *Black Mask* in January of 1938. Due to its popularity, it was later the title of a collection of short stories (*The After Dinner Story Collection*) published by Lippincott in 1944 under his writing pseudonym William Irish. This story saw great succes in radio (NBC Radio's *Molle Mystery Theatre*, 1939) and television (CBS's *Suspense*, 1949, starring Otto Kruger.) Woolrich creates a small, simple world full of many options and secrets, leaving the readers, listeners and viewers playing the role of detective trapped in an epic whodunit scenario that has lasted the test of time.

MACKENZIE GOT ON the elevator at the thirteenth floor. He was a water-filter salesman and had stopped in at his home-office to make out his accounts before going home for the day. Later on that night he told his wife, half-laughingly, that that must have been why it happened to *him*, his getting on at the thirteenth floor. A lot of buildings omit them.

The red bulb bloomed and the car stopped for him. It was an express, omitting all floors, both coming and going, below the tenth. There were two other men in it already when he got on, not counting the operator. It was late in the day, and most of the offices had already emptied themselves. One of the passengers was a scholarly looking man with rimless glasses, tall and slightly stooped. The time came when MacKenzie learned all their names. This was Kenshaw. The other was stout and cherubic looking, one of two partners in a struggling concern that was trying to market fountain-pens with tiny light bulbs in their barrels— without much success. He was fiddling with one of his own samples on the way down, clicking it on and off with an air of proud ownership. He turned out to be named Lambert.

The car was very efficient looking, very smooth running, sleek with bronze and chromium. It appeared very safe. It stopped at the next floor down, the twelfth, and a surly looking individual with bushy brows stepped in, Prendergast. Then the number 11 on the operator's call-board lit up, and it stopped there, too. A man about MacKenzie's own age and an older man with a trim white mustache were standing there side by side when the door opened. Only the young man, however, got on; the elder man gripped him by the arm in parting and turned away remarking loudly, "Tell Elinor I was asking for her." The younger answered, " 'By, Dad," and stepped in. Hardecker was his name. Almost at

137

the same time 10 was flashing.

The entry from 11 had turned to face the door, as all passengers are supposed to do in an elevator for their own safety. MacKenzie happened to glance at the sour-pussed man with the bushy brows at that moment; the latter was directly behind the newest arrival. He was glaring at the back of Hardecker's head with baleful intensity; in fact MacKenzie had never seen such a hundred-watt glower anywhere before except on a movie "heavy." The man's features, it must be admitted, lent themselves to just such an expression admirably; he had a swell headstart even when his face was in repose.

MacKenzie imagined this little by-play was due to the newcomer's having inadvertently trodden on the other's toe in turning to face forward. As a matter of fact, he himself was hardly conscious of analyzing the whole thing thus thoroughly; these were all just disconnected thoughts.

Ten was still another single passenger, a bill collector judging by the sheaf of pink, green, and canary slips he kept riffling through. He hadn't, by the gloomy look he wore, been having much luck today; or maybe his feet hurt him. This one was Megaffin.

There were now seven people in the car, counting the operator, standing in a compact little group facing the door, and no more stops due until it reached street level. Not a very great crowd; certainly far from the maximum the mechanism was able to hold. The framed notice, tacked to the panel just before MacKenzie's eyes, showed that it had been last inspected barely ten days before.

It never stopped at the street floor.

MacKenzie, trying to reconstruct the sequence of events for his wife that night, said that the operator seemed to put on added speed as soon as they had left the tenth floor behind. It was an express, so he didn't think anything of it. He remembered noticing at this point that the operator had a boil on the back of his neck, just above his uniform collar, with a Maltese cross of adhesive over it. He got that peculiar sinking sensation at the pit of his

138

stomach many people get from a too-precipitate drop. The man near him, the young fellow from the eleventh, turned and gave him a half-humorous, half-pained look, so he knew that he must be feeling it too. Somebody farther back whistled slightly to show his discomfort.

The car was a closed one, all metal, so you couldn't see the shaft doors flashing up. They must have been ticking off at a furious rate, just the same. MacKenzie began to get a peculiar ringing in his ears, like when he took the subway under the East River, and his knee-joints seemed to loosen up, trying to buckle under him.

But what really first told him—and all of them—that something had gone wrong and this was not a normal descent, was the sudden, futile, jerky way the operator was wangling the control-lever to and fro. It traveled the short arc of its orbit readily enough, but the car refused to answer to it. He kept slamming it into the socket at one end of the groove, marked Stop for all eyes to read, and nothing happened. Fractions of seconds, not minutes, were going by.

They heard him say in a muffled voice, "Look out! We're going to hit!" And that was all there was time for.

The whole thing was a matter of instants. The click of a camera-shutter. The velocity of the descent became sickening; MacKenzie felt as if he were going to throw up. Then there was a tremendous bang like a cannon, an explosion of blackness, and of bulb-glass showering down as the light went out.

They all toppled together in a heap, like a bunch of nine-pins. MacKenzie, who had gone over backwards, was the luckiest of the lot; he could feel squirming bodies bedded under him, didn't touch the hard-rubber floor of the car at all. However, his hip and shoulder got a bad wrench, and the sole of his foot went numb, through shoe and all, from the stinging impact it got flying up and slapping the bronze wall of the car.

There was no opportunity to extricate one's self, try to regain one's feet. They were going up again—on springs or something. It was a little sickening too, but not as bad as the coming down had been. It slackened, reversed into a drop, and they banged a second time. Not with the terrific impact of the first, but a sort of cushioned bang that scrambled them up even more than they were already. Somebody's shoe grazed MacKenzie's skull. He couldn't see it but quickly caught it and warded it aside before it kicked him and gave him a fracture.

A voice near him was yelling, "Stop it! Cut it out!" half-hysterically, as though the jockeying up and down could be controlled. Even MacKenzie, badly frightened and shaken up as he was, hadn't lost his head to that extent.

The car finally settled, after a second slight bounce that barely cleared the springs under it at all, and a third and almost unnoticeable jolt. The rest was pitch darkness, a sense of suffocation, a commingling of threshing bodies like an ant-heap, groans from the badly hurt and an ominous sigh or two from those even beyond groaning.

Somebody directly under MacKenzie was not moving at all. He put his hand on him, felt an upright, stiff collar, and just above it a small swelling, criss-crossed by plaster. The operator was dead. There was an inertness that told MacKenzie, and the rubber matting beneath the operator's skull was sticky.

He felt then for the sleek metal wall of the enclosure that had buried them all alive, reached up it like a fly struggling up glass, with the heels of his hands and the points of his elbows. He squirmed the rest of his body up after these precarious grips. Upright again, he leaned against cold bronze.

The voice, there's always one in every catastrophe or panic, that had been pleading to "Cut it out!" was now begging with childish vehemence: "Get me outa here! For the love of Mike, I've got a wife and kids. Get me outa here!"

MacKenzie had the impression it was the surly looking fellow with the bushy eyebrows. The probabilities, he felt, were all for it. Such visible truculence and toughness are usually all hollow inside, a mask of weakness.

"Shut up," he said, "I've got a wife too. What's that got to do with it?"

The important thing, he recognized, was not the darkness, nor their trapped position at the bottom of a sealed-up shaft, nor even any possible injuries any of them had received. But the least noticeable of all the many corollaries of their predicament was the most dangerous. It was that vague sense of stuffiness, of suffocation. Something had to be done about that at once. The operator had opened the front panel of the car at each floor, simply by latch-motion. There was no reason why that could not be repeated down here, even though there was no accompanying opening in the shaft-wall facing it. Enough air would filter down the crack between the jammed-in car and the wall, narrow though it was, to keep them breathing until help came. They were going to need that air before this was over.

MacKenzie's arms executed interlocking circles against the satiny metal face of the car, groping for the indented grip used to unlatch it. "Match," he ordered. "Somebody light a match, I'm trying to get this thing open. We're practically airtight in here."

The immediate, and expected, reaction was a howl of dismay from the tough-looking bird, like a dog's craven yelp.

Another voice, more self-controlled, said, "Wait a minute." Then nothing happened.

"Here I am; here, hand 'em to me," said MacKenzie, shovelling his upturned hand in and out through the velvety darkness.

"They won't strike, got all wet. Glass must have cut me." And then an alarmed "My shirt's all covered with blood!"

"All right, it mayn't be yours," said MacKenzie steadyingly. "Feel yourself before you let loose. If it is, hold a handkerchief to it. That bulb glass isn't strong enough to pierce very deep." And then in exasperation he hollered out, "For the love of—! Six men! Haven't any of you got a match to give me?" Which was unfair, considering that he himself had run short just before he left his office, had been meaning to get a folder at the cigar-store when he got off the car. "Hey, you, the guy that was fiddling with that trick fountain-pen coming down, how about that gadget of yours?"

A new voice unfrightened but infinitely crestfallen answered disappointedly: "It—it broke." And then with a sadness that betokened there were other, greater tragedies than what had happened to the car: "It shows you can't drop it without breakage. And that was the chief point of our whole advertising campaign." Then an indistinct mumble: "Fifteen hundred dollars capital! Wait'll Belman hears what a white elephant we've got on our hands." Which, under the circumstances, was far funnier than it was intended.

At least he's not yellow, whoever he is, thought MacKenzie. "Never mind," he exclaimed suddenly. "I've got it." His fingertips had found the slot at the far end of the seamless cast-bronze panel. The thing didn't feel buckled in any way but if the concussion had done that to it, if it refused to open. . . .

He pulled back the latch, leaning over the operator's lifeless body to do so, tugged at the slide. It gave, fell back about a third of its usual orbit along the groove, then stalled unmanageably. That was sufficient for their present needs; there was no question of egress through it. The rough-edged bricks of the shaft-wall were a finger's width beyond the lips of the car's orifice; not even a venturesome cat could have got a paw between without jamming it. What mattered was that they wouldn't asphyxiate now, no matter how long it took to free the mechanism, raise it.

"It's all right, fellows," he called reassuringly to those behind him, "I've got some air into the thing now."

If there was light farther up the shaft, it didn't reach down this far. The shaft wall opposite the opening was as black as the inside of the car itself.

He said, "They've heard us. They know what's happened. No use yelling at the top of your voice like that, only makes it tougher for the rest of us. They'll get an emergency crew on the job. We'll just have to sit and wait, that's all."

The nerve-tingling bellows for help, probably the tough guy again, were silenced shamefacedly. A groaning still kept up intermittently from someone else. "My arm, Oh, Gawd, it hurts!" The sighing, from an injury that had gone deeper still, had suspiciously quieted some time before. Either the man had fainted, or he, too, was dead.

MacKenzie, matter-of-factly but not callously, reached down for the operator's outflung form, shifted it into the angle between two of the walls, and propped it upright there. Then he sat down himself in the clear floor space provided, tucked up his legs, wrapped his arms around them. He wouldn't have called himself a brave man; he was just a realist.

There was a momentary silence from all of them at once, one of those pauses. Then, because there was also, or seemed to be, a complete stillness from overhead in the shaft, panic stabbed at the tough guy again. "They gonna leave us here all night?" he whimpered. "What you guys sit there like that for? Don't you wanna get out?"

"For Pete's sake, somebody clip that loud-mouth on the chin!" urged MacKenzie truculently.

There was a soundless indrawn whistle. "My arm! Oh, my arm!"

"Must be busted," suggested MacKenzie sympathetically. "Try wrapping your shirt tight around it to kill the pain."

Time seemed to stand still, jog forward a few notches at a time every so often, like something on a belt. The rustle of a restless body, a groan, an exhalation of impatience, an occasional cry from the craven in their midst, whom MacKenzie sat on each time with increasing acidity as his own nerves slowly frayed.

The waiting, the sense of trapped helplessness, began to tell on them, far more than the accident had.

"They may think we're all dead and take their time," someone said.

"They never do in a case like this," MacKenzie answered shortly. "They're doing whatever they're doing as fast as they can. Give 'em time."

A new voice, that he hadn't heard until then, said to no one in particular, "I'm glad my father didn't get on here with me."

Somebody chimed in, "I wish I hadn't gone back after that

damn phone call. It was a wrong number, and I coulda ridden down the trip before this."

MacKenzie sneered, "Ah, you talk like a bunch of ten-year-olds! It's happened; what's the good of wishing about it?"

He had a watch on his wrist with a luminous dial. He wished that he hadn't had, or that it had gone out of commission like the other man's trick fountain-pen. It was too nerve-racking; every minute his eyes sought it, and when it seemed like half-an-hour had gone by, it was only five minutes. He wisely refrained from mentioning it to any of the others; they would have kept asking him, "How long is it now?" until he went screwy.

When they'd been down twenty-two and one-half minutes from the time he'd first looked at it, and were all in a state of nervous instability bordering on frenzy, including himself, there was a sudden unexpected, unannounced thump directly overhead, as though something heavy had landed on the roof of the car.

This time it was MacKenzie who leaped up, pressed his cheek flat against the brick-work outside the open panel, and funnelled up the paper-thin gap: "Hello! Hello!"

"Yeah," a voice came down "we're coming to you, take it easy!"

More thumping for a while, as though somebody were jigging over their heads. Then a sudden metallic din, like a boiler factory going full blast. The whole car seemed to vibrate with it, it became numbing to touch it for long at any one point. The confined space of the shaft magnified the noise into a torrent of sound, drowning out all their remarks. MacKenzie couldn't stand it, finally had to stick his palms up flat against his ears. A blue electric spark shot down the narrow crevice outside the door from above. Then another, then a third. They all went out too quickly to cast any light inside.

Acetylene torches! They were having to cut a hole through the car-roof to get at them. If there was a basement opening in the shaft, and there must have been, the car must have plunged down even beyond that, to sub-basement level, wound up in a dead-end cul-de sac at pit-bottom. There was apparently no other way.

A spark materialized eerily through the ceiling. Then another, then a semi-circular gush of them. A curtain of fire descended half-way into their midst, illuminating their faces wanly for a minute. Luckily it went out before it touched the car floor.

The noise broke off short and the silence in its wake was deafening. A voice shouted just above them: "Look out for sparks, you guys below, we're coming through. Keep your eyes closed, get back against the walls!"

The noise came on again, nearer at hand, louder than before. MacKenzie's teeth were on edge from the incessant vibration. Being rescued was worse than being stuck down there. He wondered how the others were standing it, especially that poor guy with the broken wing. He thought he heard a voice scream: "Elinor! Elinor!" twice, like that, but you couldn't be sure of anything in that infernal din.

The sparks kept coming down like a dripping waterfall; MacKenzie squinted his eyes cagily, kept one hand shielded up over them to protect his eyesight. He thought he saw one spark shoot across horizontal, instead of down vertical like all the others; it was a different color too, more orange. He thought it must be an optical illusion produced by the alternating glare and darkness they were all being subjected to; either that, or a detached splinter of combusted metal from the roof, ricocheting off the wall. He closed his eyes all the way, just to play safe.

There wasn't much more to it after that. The noise and sparks stopped abruptly. They pried up the crescent-shape flap they had cut in the roof with crowbars, to keep it from toppling inward and crushing those below. The cool, icy beams of torches flickered through. A cop jumped down into their midst and ropes were sent snaking down after him. He said in a brisk, matter-of-fact way: "All right, who's first now? Who's the worst hurt of yez all?"

His torch showed three forms motionless at the feet of the others in the confined space. The operator, huddled in the corner where MacKenzie had propped him; the scholarly looking man with the rimless glasses (minus them now, and a deep gash under one eye to show what had become of them) lying senseless on his side; and the young fellow who had got on at the eleventh, tumbled partly across him, face down.

"The operator's dead," MacKenzie answered as spokesman for the rest, "and these two're out of their pain just now. There's a guy with a busted arm here, take him first."

The cop deftly looped the rope under the armpits of the ashen-faced bill collector, who was knotting the slack of one sleeve tightly in his other hand and sweating away like a fish in the torchlight.

"Haul away!" the cop shouted toward the opening. "And take your time, the guy's hurt."

The bill collector went up through the ceiling, groaning, legs drawn up under him like a trussed-up fowl.

The scholarly looking man went next, head bobbing down in unconsciousness. When the noose came down empty, the cop bent over to fasten it around the young fellow still on the floor.

MacKenzie saw him change his mind, pry open one eyelid, pass the rope on to the tough-looking mugg who had been such a cry-baby, and who was shaking all over from the nervous reaction to the fright he'd had.

"What's the matter with him?" MacKenzie butted in, pointing to the floor.

"He's dead," the cop answered briefly. "He can wait, the living come first."

"Dead! Why, I heard him say he was glad his father didn't get on with him, long after we hit!"

"I don't care what you heard him say!" the cop answered. "He coulda said it, and still be dead now! Nuts. Are you telling me my business? You seem to be pretty chipper for a guy that's just come through an experience like this!"

"Skip it," said MacKenzie placatingly. He figured it was no business of his anyway, if the guy had seemed all right at first and now was dead. He might have had a weak heart.

He and the disheartened fountain-pen entrepreneur seemed to be the only two out of the lot who were totally unharmed. The latter, however, was so broken-hearted over the failure of his appliance to stand up under an emergency, that he seemed hardly to care whether he went up or stayed down or what became of him. He kept examining the defective gadget even on his way up through the aperture in the car-roof, with the expression of a man who has just bitten into a very sour lemon.

MacKenzie was the last one up the shaft, except the two fatalities. He was pulled in over the lip of the basement opening, from which the sliding doors had been taken down bodily. It was a bare four feet above the roof of the car; in other words the shaft continued on down past it for little more than the height of the car. He couldn't understand why it had been built that way, and not ended flush with the basement, in which case their long imprisonment could have been avoided. It was explained to him later, by the building superintendent, that it was necessary to give the car additional clearance underneath, or else it would have run the risk of jamming each time it came down to the basement.

There were stretchers there in the basement passageway, and the bill collector and the studious looking man were being given first-aid by a pair of internes. The hard-looking egg was gulping down a large glass of spirits of ammonia between clicking teeth. MacKenzie let one of the internes look him over, at the latter's insistence; was told what he knew already, that he was O.K. He gave his name and address to the lieutenant of police in charge, and walked up a flight of stairs to the street level, thinking, "The old-fashioned way's the best after all."

He found the lobby of the building choked with a milling crowd, warded off a number of ambulance chasers who tried to tell him how badly hurt he was. "There's money in it, buddy, don't be a sucker!" MacKenzie phoned his wife from a near-by booth to shorten her anxiety, then he left the scene for home.

His last fleeting impression was of a forlorn figure standing there in the lobby, a man with a trim white mustache, the father of the young fellow lying dead below, buttonholing every cop within reach, asking over and over again, "Where's my son? Why haven't they brought my son up yet?" And not getting any answer from any of them—which was an answer in itself. MacKenzie pushed out into the street.

Friday, that was four days later, the doorbell rang right after supper and he had a visitor. "MacKenzie? You were in that elevator Monday night, weren't you, sir?"

"Yes," MacKenzie grinned, he sure was.

"I'm from Police Headquarters. Mind if I ask you a few questions? I've been going around to all of 'em checking up."

"Come in and sit down," said MacKenzie interestedly. His first guess was that they were trying to track down labor sabotage, or some violation of the building laws. "Matter, anything phony about it?"

"Not for our money," said the dick, evidently because this was the last leg of what was simply a routine questioning of all the survivors, and he refused to differ from his superiors. "The young fellow that was lying dead there in the bottom of the car—not the operator but young Wesley Hardecker—was found by the examiner to have a bullet imbedded in his heart."

MacKenzie jolted, gave a long-drawn whistle that brought his Scotty to the door questioningly. "Whew! You mean somebody shot him while we were all cooped up down there in that two-by-four?"

The dick showed, without being too pugnacious about it, that he was there to ask the questions, not answer them. "Did you know him at all?"

"Never saw him in my life before, until he got on the car that night. I know his name by now, because I read it in the papers next day; I didn't at the time."

The visitor nodded, as though this was the answer he'd got from all the others too. "Well, did you hear anything like a shot while you were down there?"

"No, not before they started the blow-torches. And after that, you couldn't have heard one anyway. Matter of fact, I had my hands over my ears at one time. I did see a flash, though," he went on eagerly. "Or at least, I remember seeing one of the sparks shoot *across* instead of dropping down, and it was more orange in color."

Again the dick nodded. "Yeah, a couple of others saw that too. That was probably it, right there. Did it light up anyone's face behind it, anything like that?"

"No," MacKenzie admitted, "my eyes were all pinwheels, between the coal-blackness and these flashing sparks coming down through the roof; we'd been warned, anyway, to keep them shut a minute before." He paused thoughtfully, went on: "It doesn't seem to hang together, does it? Why should anyone pick such a time and place to—"

"It hangs together beautifully,"' contradicted the dick. "It's his old man, the elder Hardecker, that's raising a stink, trying to read something phony into it. It's suicide while of unsound mind, and has been all along; and that's what the findings of the coroner's inquest are going to be too. We haven't turned up anything that throws a doubt on that. Old man Hardecker himself hasn't been able to identify a single one of you as having ever known or seen his son—or himself—before six o'clock last Monday evening. The gun was the fellow's own, and he had a license for it. He had it with him when he got in the car. It was under his body when it was picked up. The only fingerprints brought out on it were his. The examiner finds the wound a contact wound, powder burns all around it."

"The way we were crowded together down there, any kind of a shot at anyone would have been a contact," MacKenzie tried to object.

The dick waved this aside. "The nitrate test shows that his fingers fired the shot. It's true that we neglected to give it to anyone else at the time, but since there'd been only one shot fired out of the gun, and no other gun was found, that don't stack up to much. The bullet, of course, was from that gun and no other, ballistics has told us. The guy was a nervous, high-strung young fellow. He went hysterical down there, cracked up, and when he couldn't stand it any more, took himself out of it. And against this, his old man is beefing that he was happy, he had a lovely wife, they were expecting a kid and he had everything to live for.

"Well, all right," objected MacKenzie mildly, "but why should he do it when they were already working on the roof over us, and it was just a matter of minutes before they got to us. Why not before? That don't sound logical. Matter of fact, his voice sounded calm and unfrightened enough while we were waiting."

The detective got up, as though the discussion were ended, but condescended to enlighten him, on his way to the door: "People don't crack up at a minute's notice; it was after he'd been down there twenty minutes, half an hour, it got him. When you heard him say that, he was probably trying to hold himself together, kid himself he was brave or something. Any psychiatrist will tell you what noise'll do to someone already under a strain or tension. The noise of the blow-torches gave him the finishing touch; that's why he did it then, couldn't think straight any more. As far as having a wife and expecting a kid is concerned, that would only make him lose his head all the quicker. A man without ties. or responsibilities is always more cold-blooded in an emergency."

"It's a new one on me, but maybe you're right. I only know water-filters."

"It's my job to be right about things like that. Good-night, Mr. MacKenzie."

The voice on the wire said, "Mr. MacKenzie? Is this the Mr. Stephen MacKenzie who was in an elevator accident a year ago last August? The newspapers gave—"

"Yes, I was."

"Well, I'd like you to come to dinner at my house next Saturday evening, at exactly seven o'clock."

MacKenzie cocked his brows at himself in the wall mirror. "Hadn't you better tell me who you are, first?"

"Sorry," said the voice crisply. "I thought I had. I've been doing this for the past hour or so, and it's beginning to tell on me. This is Harold Hardecker; I'm head of the Hardecker Import and Export Company."

"Well, I still don't place you, Mr. Hardecker," MacKenzie said levelly. "Are you one of the men who was on that elevator with me?"

"No, my son was. He lost his life."

"Oh," said MacKenzie. He remembered now. A man with a trim white mustache, standing in the milling crowd, buttonholing the cops as they hurried by. . . .

"Can I expect you then at seven next Saturday, Mr. MacKenzie? I'm at— Park Avenue."

"Frankly," said MacKenzie, who was a plain soul not much given to social hypocrisy, "I don't see any point to it. I don't believe we've ever spoken to one another before. Why do you single me out?"

Hardecker explained patiently, even good-naturedly, "I'm not singling you out, Mr. MacKenzie. I've already contacted each of the others who were on the car that night with my son, and they've all agreed to be there. I don't wish to disclose what I have in mind beforehand; I'm giving this dinner for that purpose. However, I might mention that my son died intestate, and his poor wife passed away in childbirth in the early hours of the following morning. His estate reverted to me, and I am a lonely old man, without friends or relatives, and with more money already than I know what to do with. It occurred to me to bring together five perfect strangers, who shared a common hazard with my son, who were with him during the last few moments of his life." The voice paused insinuatingly, to let this sink in. Then it resumed, "If you'll be at my house for dinner Saturday at seven, I'll have an announcement of considerable importance to make. It's to your interest to be present when I do."

MacKenzie scanned his water-filter-salesman's salary with his mind's eye, and found it altogether unsatisfactory, as he had done not once but many times before. "All right," he agreed, after a moment's consideration. . . .

Saturday at six he was still saying, "You can't tell me. The guy isn't in his right mind, to do a thing like this. Five people that he don't know from Adam, and that don't know each other. I wonder if it's a practical joke?"

"Well, if you feel that way, why didn't you refuse him?" said his wife, brushing out his dark blue coat.

"I'm curious to find out what it's all about. I want to see what the gag is." Curiosity is one of the strongest human traits. It's almost irresistible. The expectation of getting something for nothing is no slouch either. MacKenzie was a good guy, but he was a guy after all, not an image on a stained-glass window.

At the door she said with belated anxiety, "Steve, I know you can take care of yourself and all that, but if you don't like the looks of things, I mean if none of the others show up, don't stay there alone."

He laughed. He'd made up his mind by now, had even spent the windfall ahead of time, already. "You make me feel like one of those innocents in the old silent pictures, that were always being invited to a big blow-out and when they got there they were alone with the villain and just supper for two. Don't worry, Toots, if there's no one else there, I turn around and come back."

The building had a Park Avenue address, but was actually on one of the exclusive side-streets just off that thoroughfare. A small ultra-ultra cooperative, with only one apartment to a floor. "Mr. Harold Hardecker?" asked Mr. MacKenzie in the lobby. "Stephen MacKenzie."

He saw the hallman take out a small typed list of five names, four of which had already been penciled out; cross out the last one. "Go right up, Mr. MacKenzie. Third floor."

A butler opened the single door in the elevator foyer for him, greeted him by name and took his hat. A single glance at the money this place spelled would have been enough to restore anyone's confidence. People that lived like this were perfectly capable of having five strangers in to dinner, subdividing a dead son's estate among them, and chalking it off as just that evening's little whimsey. The sense of proportion alters above a certain yearly income.

He remembered Hardecker readily enough as soon as he saw him coming toward him along the central gallery that seemed to bisect the place like a bowling-alley. It took him about three and a half minutes to get up to him, at that. The man had aged appreciably from the visual snapshot that was all he'd had of him at the scene of the accident. He was slightly stooped, very thin at the waist, looked as though he'd suffered. But the white mustache was as trim and needle-pointed as ever, and he had on one of the new turned-over soft collars under his dinner jacket, which gave him a peculiarly boyish look in spite of the almost blinding white of his undiminished hair, cropped close as a Prussian's.

Hardecker held out his hand, said with just the right mixture of dignity and warmth, "How do you do, Mr. MacKenzie, I'm very glad to know you. Come in and meet the others and have a pick-up."

There were no women present in the living-room, just the four men sitting around at ease. There was no sense of strain, of stiffness; an advantage that stag gatherings are apt to have over mixed parties anyway, not through the fault of women, but through men's consciousness of them.

Kenshaw, the scholarly looking man, had a white scar still visible under his left eye where his glasses had broken. The cherubic Lambert had deserted the illuminated fountain-pen business, he hurriedly confided unasked to MacKenzie, for the ladies' foundation-girdle business. No more mechanical gadgets for him. Or as he put it, unarguably, "A brassiere they gotta have, or else. But who needs a fountain-pen?" The hard-bitten mugg was introduced as Prendergast, occupation undisclosed. Megaffin, the bill collector, was no longer a bill collector. "I send out my own now," he explained, swiveling a synthetic diamond around on his pinky.

MacKenzie selected Scotch, and when he'd caught up with the rest, the butler came to the door, almost as though he'd been timing him through a knot-hole. He just looked in, then went away again.

"Let's go and get down to business now, gentlemen, shall we?" Hardecker grinned. He had the happy faculty, MacKenzie said to himself, of making you feel perfectly at home, without overdoing it, getting in your hair. Which looks easier than it is.

No flowers, candles, fripperies like that were on the table set for six; just a good substantial man's board. Hardecker said, "Just sit down anywhere you choose, only keep the head for me." Lambert and Kenshaw took one side, Prendergast and Megaffin on the other. MacKenzie sat down at the foot. It was obvious that whatever announcement their host intended making was being kept for the end of the meal, as was only fitting.

The butler had closed a pair of sliding doors beyond them after they were all in, and he stayed outside. The waiting was done by a man. It was a typical bachelor's repast, plain, marvelously cooked, without dainty or frivolous accessories to detract from it, salads, vegetables, things like that. Each course had its vintage corollary. And at the end no cloying sweets. Roquefort cheese, coffee with the blue flame of Courvoisier flickering above each glass. It was a masterpiece. And each one, as it ended, relaxed in his chair in a haze of golden day-dreams. They anticipated coming into money, money they hadn't had to work for, maybe more money than they'd ever had before. It wasn't such a bad world after all.

One thing had struck MacKenzie, but since he'd never been waited on by servants in a private home before, only in restaurants, he couldn't determine whether it was unusual or customary. There was an expensive mahogany buffet running across one side of the dining-room, but the waiter had done no serving or carving on it, had brought in each portion separately, always individually. Even the roast. The coffee and the wines, too, had been poured behind the scenes, the glasses and the cups brought in already filled. It gave the man a lot more work and slowed the meal somewhat, but if that was the way it was done in Hardecker's house, that was the way it was done.

When they were already luxuriating with their cigars and cigarettes, and the cloth had been cleared of all but the emptied coffee cups, an additional dish was brought in. It was a silver chalice, a sort of stemmed bowl, holding a thick yellowish substance that looked like mayonnaise. The waiter placed it in the exact geometrical center of the table, even measuring with his eye its distance from both sides, and from the head and foot, and shifting its position to conform. Then he took the lid off and left it open. Threads of steam rose sluggishly from it. Every eye was on it interestedly.

"Is it well mixed?" they heard Hardecker ask.

"Yes sir," said the waiter.

"That will be all; don't come in again."

The man left by the pantry door he had been using, and it clicked slightly after it had closed behind him.

Somebody—Megaffin—asked cozily: "What's *that* got in it?" evidently on the look-out for still more treats.

"Oh, quite a number of things," Hardecker answered carelessly, "whites of eggs, mustard, as well as certain other ingredients all beaten up together."

MacKenzie, trying to be funny, said, "Sounds like an antidote."

"It is an antidote," Hardecker answered, looking steadily down the table at him. He must have pushed a call button or something under the table. The butler opened the sliding doors and stood between them, without coming in.

Hardecker didn't turn his head. "You have that gun I gave you? Stand there, please, on the other side of those doors and see that no one comes out of here. If they try it, you know what to do."

The doors slipped to again, effaced him, but not before MacKenzie, facing that way, had seen something glimmer in his hand.

Tension was slow in coming on, the change was too abrupt, they had been too steeped in the rosy afterglow of the meal and their own imminent good fortune. Then too, not all of them were equally alert mentally—particularly Megaffin, who had been on such a fourth dimensional plane of unaccustomedness all evening he couldn't tell menace from hospitality, even when a gun was mentioned.

Its first focal point was Hardecker's own face—that went slowly white, grim, remorseless. From there it darted out to MacKenzie and Lambert, caught at them, paled them too. The rest grew allergic to it one by one, until there was complete silence at the table.

Hardecker spoke. Not loudly, not angrily, but in a steely, pitiless voice. "Gentlemen, there's a murderer in our midst."

Five breaths were sharply indrawn together, making a fearful "Ffff!" sound around the table. Not so much aghast at the statement itself, as aghast at the implication of retribution that lurked just behind it. And behind that was the shadowy suspicion that it had already been exacted.

No one said anything.

The hard, remorseless cores of Hardecker's eyes shot from face to face. He was smoking a long slim cigar, cigarette-thin. He pointed it straight out before him, indicated them all with it without moving it much, like a dark finger of doom. "Gentlemen, one of you killed my son." Pause. "On August 30, 1936." Pause. "And hasn't paid for it yet."

The words were like a stone going down into a deep pool of transparent water, and the ripples spreading out from them spelled fear.

MacKenzie said slowly, "You setting yourself above the properly constituted authorities? The findings of the coroner's inquest were suicide while of unsound mind. Why do you hold them incompe—"

Hardecker cut him short like a whip. "This isn't a discussion. It's—" a long pause, then very low but very audible: "an execution."

There was another of those strangling silences. They took it in a variety of ways, each according to his temperament. MacKenzie just kept staring at him, startled, apprehensive. Apprehensive, but not inordinately frightened, any more than he had been that night on the elevator. The scholarly-looking Kenshaw had a rebuking look on his face, that of a teacher for an unruly pupil, and the scar on his cheek stood out whitely. Megaffin looked shifty, like some small weasel at bay, planning its next move. The pugnacious-looking guy was going to cave in again in a minute, judging by the wavering of his facial lines. Lambert pinched the bridge of his nose momentarily, dropped his hand, mumbled something that sounded like, "*Oy*, I give up my pinochle club to come here, yet!"

Hardecker resumed, as though he hadn't said anything unusual just now. "I know who the man is. I know which one among you the man is. It's taken me a year to find out, but now I know, beyond the shadow of a doubt." He was looking at his cigar now, watching the ash drop off of its own weight onto his coffee saucer. "The police wouldn't listen to me, they insisted it was suicide. The evidence was insufficient to convince them the first time, and for all I know it still may be." He raised his eyes. "But I demand justice for the taking of my son's life." He took an expensive, dime-thin, octagonal watch out of his pocket, placed it face up on the table before him. "Gentlemen, it's now nine o'clock. In half an hour, at the most, one of you will be dead. Did you notice that you were all served separately just now? One dish, and one alone out of all of them, was deadly. It's putting in its slow, sure work right as we sit here." He pointed to the silver tureen, equi-distant from all of them. "There's the answer. There's the antidote. I have no wish to set myself up as executioner above the law. Let the murderer be the chooser. Let him reach out and save his life and stand convicted before all of you. Or let him keep silent and go down to his death without confessing, privately executed for what can't be publicly proved. In twenty-five minutes collapse will come without warning. Then it will be too late."

It was Lambert who voiced the question in all their minds. "But are you sure you did this to the right—"

"I haven't made any mistake, the waiter was carefully rehearsed, you are all perfectly unharmed but the killer."

Lambert didn't seem to derive much consolation from this.

"Now he tells us! A fine way to digest a meal," he brooded aloud. "Why didn't you serve the murderer first, so then the rest of us could eat in peace at least?"

"Shut up," somebody said terrifiedly.

"Twenty minutes to go," Hardecker said, tonelessly as a chime signal over the radio.

MacKenzie said, without heat, "You can't be sane, you know, to do a thing like this."

"Did you ever have a son?" was the answer.

Something seemed to snap in Megaffin. His chair jolted back. "I'm gettin' out of here," he said hoarsely.

The doors parted about two inches, silently as water, and a black metal cylinder peered through. "That man there," directed Hardecker. "Shoot him where he stands if he doesn't sit down."

Megaffin shrank down in his seat again like a whipped cur, tried to shelter himself behind Prendergast's shoulder. The doors slipped together again into a hair-line crack.

"I couldn't," sighed the cherubic-faced Lambert, "feel more at home if I was in the Brown House at Munich!"

"Eighteen minutes," was the comment from the head of the table.

Prendergast suddenly grimaced uncontrollably, flattened his forearms on the table, and ducked his head onto them. He sniveled aloud. "I can't stand it! Lemme out of here! *I* didn't do it!"

A wave of revulsion went around the table. It was not because he'd broken down, analyzed MacKenzie, it was just that he didn't have the face for it. It should have been Lambert with his kewpie physiognomy, if anyone. The latter, however, was having other troubles. He touched the side of his head, tapped himself on the chest. "Whoof!" he murmured, "What heartburn! He should live so long, I don't take this up with my lawyer!"

"This is no way," said MacKenzie surlily. "If you had any kind of a case—"

"This is my way," was Hardecker's crackling answer. "I've given the man his choice. He needn't have it this way; he has his alternative. Fourteen minutes. Let me remind you, the longer the antidote's delayed, the more doubtful its efficiency will be. If it's postponed too long, it may miss altogether."

Conscious of a sticking sensation in his stomach, as though a mass of concrete had lodged there, MacKenzie felt a burning sensation shoot out from it. There is such a thing as nervous indigestion, he knew, but. . . . He eyed the silver goblet reflectively.

But they were all doing that almost incessantly. Prendergast had raised his head again, but it remained a woebegone mask of infantile fretfulness. Megaffin was green in the face and kept moistening his lips. Kenshaw was the most self-controlled of the lot; he had folded his arms and just sat there, as though waiting to see which one of the others would reach for the salvation in the silver container.

MacKenzie could feel a painful pulsing under his solar plexus now, he was in acute discomfort that verged on cramp. The thought of what this might be was bringing out sweat on his forehead.

Lambert reached out abruptly, and they all quit breathing for a minute. But his hand dodged the silver tureen, plunged into a box of perfectos to one side of it. He grabbed up two, stuck one in his breast-pocket, the other between his teeth. "On you," he remarked resentfully to Hardecker.

Somebody gave a strained laugh at the fase alarm they had all had. Kenshaw took off his glasses, wiped them ruefully, as though disappointed it hadn't been the pay-off after all.

MacKenzie said, "You're alienating whatever sympathy's due you, by pulling a stunt like this."

"I'm not asking for sympathy," was Hardecker's coldly ferocious answer. "It's atonement I want. Three lives were taken from me: My only son, my daughter-in-law, their prematurely born child. I demand payment for that!"

Lambert said aloud, for his own benefit, "Jennie wouldn't believe this when I tell her."

Prendergast clutched his throat all at once, whimpered: "I can't breathe! He's done it to *me*, so help me!"

MacKenzie, hostile now to Hardecker, tried to steady him just on general principle. "Gas around the heart, maybe. Don't fall for it if you're not sure."

"Don't fall for it," was the ungrateful yelp, "and if I drop dead are *you* gonna bring me back?"

"He ought to be arrested for this," said Kenshaw, displaying emotion for the first time. His glasses had clouded over, giving him a peculiar sightless look.

"Arrested?" snapped Lambert. He wagged his head from side to side. "He's going to be sued like no one was ever sued before! When I get through with him he'll go on relief."

Hardecker threw him a contemptuous look. "About ten minutes," he said. "He seems to prefer the more certain way. Stubborn, eh? He'd rather die than admit it."

MacKenzie gripped the seat of his chair, his churning insides heaved. He thought, "If this is the McCoy that I'm feeling now, I'm going to bash his head in with a chair before I go. I'll give him something to poison innocent people about!"

Megaffin was starting to swear at their tormentor, in a whining, guttery sing-song.

"*Mazzeltov*," seconded Lambert, with a formal nod of approval. "Your breath, but my ideas."

"Five minutes. It will almost certainly fail if it's not downed within the next thirty seconds." Hardecker pocketed his watch, as though there were no further need for consulting it.

MacKenzie gagged, hauled at the knot of his tie, undid his collar-button. A needle of suffocating pain had just splintered into his heart.

Only the whites of Prendergast's eyes showed, he was going off into some fit or fainting spell. Even Lambert quit pulling at his cigar, as though it sickened him. Kenshaw took off his glasses for the third time in five minutes, to clear them.

A pair of arms suddenly shot out, grasped the silver bowl, swung it. It was uptilted over someone's face and there was a hollow, metallic groaning coming from behind it, infinitely gruesome to hear. It had happened so quickly, MacKenzie couldn't be sure who it was for a minute, long as he had been sitting at the macabre table with all of them. He had to do it by a quick process of elimination. Man sitting beside Lambert—Kenshaw, the scholarly-looking one, the man who had had least to say since the ordeal had begun! He was gulping with a convulsive rising and falling of his Adam's apple, visible in the shadow just below the lower rim of the bowl.

Then suddenly he flung it aside, his face was visible again, the drained receptacle clanged against the wall where he'd cast it, dropped heavily to the floor. He couldn't talk for a minute or two, and neither could anyone else, except possibly Hardecker, and he didn't. Just sat staring at the self-confessed culprit with pitiless eyes.

Finally Kenshaw panted, cheeks twitching, "Will it—will it—save me?"

Hardecker folded his arms, said to the others, but without taking his eyes off Kenshaw: "So now you know. So now you see whether I was right or not."

Kenshaw was holding his hands pressed tightly to the sides of his head. A sudden flood of words was unloosed from him, as though he found it a relief to talk now, after the long unbearable tension he'd been through. "Sure you were right, and I'd do it over again! I'm glad he's gone. The rich man's son, that had everything. But that wasn't enough for him, was it? He had to show off how good he was—Horatio Alger stuff, paddle your own canoe from riches to more riches! He couldn't take a job with your own firm, could he? No, people might say you were helping him. He had to come to the place *I* worked and ask for a job. Not just anonymously. No, he had to mention whose son he was, to swing the scales in his favor! They were afraid to offend you, they thought maybe they'd get a pull with you, through him. It didn't count that I'd been with them all the best years of my life, that I had someone home too, just like he had, that I couldn't go

161

anywhere else and mention the name of an influential father! They fired me."

His voice rose shrilly. "D'you know what happened to me? D'you know or care how I tramped the streets in the rain, at my age, looking for work? D'you know my wife had to get down on her knees and scrub dirty office corridors? D'you know how I washed dishes, carried sandwich-boards through the streets, slept on park benches, all on account of a smart-aleck with Rover Boy ideas? Yes, it preyed on my mind, why wouldn't it? I suppose you found the threatening letters I wrote him, that's how you knew."

Hardecker just shook his head slightly in denial.

"Then he got on the elevator that day. He didn't see me, probably wouldn't have known me if he had, but I saw him. I knew him. Then we fell—and I hoped he was dead, I hoped he was dead! But he wasn't. The idea took hold of me slowly, waiting down there in the dark. The torches started making noise, and I grabbed him, I was going to choke him. But he wrenched himself free and took out his gun to defend himself against what I guess he thought was a fear-crazed man. I wasn't fear-crazed, I was revenge-crazed, I knew what I was doing!

"I grabbed his hand. Not the gun, but the hand that was holding it. I turned it around the other way, into his own heart. He said 'Elinor, Elinor!' but that didn't save him; that was the wrong name, that was *his* wife not mine. I squeezed the finger he had on the trigger with my own, and he fired his own weapon. So the police were right, it was suicide in a way.

"He leaned against me, there wasn't room enough in there to fall. I flung myself down first under him, so they'd find us that way, and eased him down on top of me. He bled on me a little while and then he quit. And when they came through I pretended I'd fainted."

Hardecker said, "Murderer. Murderer." Like drops of ice-water. "He didn't *know* he'd done all that to you; oh, why didn't you give him a chance at least, why weren't you a man? Murderer! Murderer!"

Kenshaw started reaching downward to the floor, where he'd

dropped his glasses when he had seized the antidote. His face was on a level with the table-top. He scowled: "No matter what they've all heard me say just now, you'll never be able to prove I did it. Nobody saw me. Only the dark."

A whisper sounded: "And that's where you're going. Into the dark."

Kenshaw's head vanished suddenly below the table. The empty back of his chair whirled over sidewise, cracked against the floor.

They were all on their feet now, bending over him. All but Hardecker. MacKenzie got up from his knees. "He's dead!" he said. "The antidote didn't work in time!"

Hardecker said, "That wasn't the antidote, that was the poison itself. He hadn't been given any until he gulped that down. He convicted himself and carried out sentence upon himself with one and the same gesture. I hadn't known which one of you it was until then. I'd only known it hadn't been my son's own doing, because, you see, the noise of those torches wouldn't have affected him much, he was partly deaf from birth."

He pushed his chair back and stood up. "I didn't summon you here under false pretenses; his estate will be divided in equal parts among the four of you that are left. And now I'm ready to take my own medicine. Call the police, let them and their prosecutors and their courts of law decide whether I killed him or his own guilty conscience did!"

DEATH AT THE BURLESQUE

Death at the Burlesque was originally published in *Detective Fiction Weekly* in June of 1941. Not unlike the gilded starlets of this story, this title went through many costume changes; it was originally submitted as *Gilt Edged Murder*, published as *The Fatal Footlights* and later re-published as the story included within this volume: *Death at the Burlesque*. This tale is known for being one of his most chilling noir-cop thrillers and later came to the attention of Ian Fleming who used the "guilded death" motif in his classic James Bond novel *Goldfinger* in 1959.

E SAW VILMA FIRST. She was the dark one. Then he saw Gilda. She was the golden one. He didn't see the man at all, that first night. He didn't know any of their names. He didn't want to. He'd just gone to a show on his night off.

He had an aisle seat, alongside the runway. He'd told the ticket seller he wanted to see more than just their baby-blue eyes. The ticket seller had said, "You will." He'd been right, it turned out.

It was, of course, simply burlesque under a different name, to evade the licensing restrictions of the last few years. But at the moment Benson took his seat, there wasn't anything going on that a fourteen-year-old schoolgirl couldn't have watched with perfect propriety. A black-haired singer in a flowing, full-length dress was rendering *Mighty Lak a Rose*. And she was good, too.

But this was his night off and he felt kind of cheated. "Did I walk in on a funeral?" he asked himself. He shouldn't have asked that, maybe. The mocking little gods of circumstances were only too willing to arrange it for him.

The singer walked off, the orchestra gave out with an introductory flourish, and the proceedings snapped back into character. The curtains parted to reveal a "living statue" group— five or six nymphs enameled a chalky white, their torsos veiled by wisps of cheesecloth, presided over by a central "statue" poised on a pedestal in their midst. This was Gilda, the main attraction.

Gilda stood there, head thrown back, seemingly in the act of nibbling at a dangling cluster of grapes. Whether she was as innocent of vesture as she seemed was beside the point; her body was coated with a thick layer of scintillant golden paint which was certainly far more protective than any ordinary clothes would have been. But that didn't dampen the general enthusiasm any. It

167

was just the principle of the thing that mattered. Good clean fun, so to speak. She got a tremendous hand without doing a thing— just for art's sake.

The curtains coyly came together again, veiling the tableau. There was a teasing pause, maintained just long enough to whet the audience's appetite for more, then they parted once more and the "statuary" had assumed a different position. Gilda was now shading her eyes with one hand, one leg poised behind her, and staring yearningly toward the horizon—or more strictly speaking, a fire door at the side of the auditorium.

Benson caught the spirit of the thing along with everyone else and whacked his hands. The curtains met, parted once more, and again the tableau had altered. This time Gilda was up on tiptoes on her pedestal, her body arched over as though she was looking at her own reflection in a pool.

Just before the curtains obliterated her, Benson thought he saw her waver a little, as if having difficulty maintaining her balance. Or maybe it was simply faulty timing. She had prepared to change positions a little too soon, before the curtains entirely concealed her from view. That slight flaw didn't discourage the applause any. It had reached the pitch of a bombardment. The audience wasn't a critical one; it didn't care about complete muscular control as long as it got complete undress. Or the illusion of it, through gold-plating.

The pause was a little longer this time, as though there had been a slight hitch. Benson wondered where the dancing came in. They had billed her out front as "The Golden Dancer," he remembered, and he wanted his money's worth. He didn't have long to wait. The footlights along the runway, unused until now, gushed up, the curtains parted, and Gilda was down on the stage floor now, and in motion.

She was coming out on the runway to dance over their heads. For this additional intimacy, she had provided herself with a protective mantle of gauzy black—just in case some of the Commissioner's men happened to be in the audience.

She wasn't any great shakes as a dancer; nobody expected her to be, nobody cared. It was mostly a matter of waving her arms, turning this way and that, and flourishing the mantle around her, a little bit like a bullfighter does his cape. She managed, while continually promising revealing gaps in it, to keep it all around her at all times, in a sort of black haze, like smoke. It was simply the striptease in a newer variation.

But indifferent as her dancing ability was to begin with, a noticeable hesitation began to creep into its posturing after she had been on the runway a few moments. She seemed to keep forgetting what to do next.

"They hardly have time to rehearse at all," Benson thought leniently.

Her motions had slowed down like a clock that needs winding. He saw her cast a look over her shoulders at the unoccupied main stage, as if in search of help. The lesser nymphs hadn't come out with her this last time, were probably doing a quick change for the next number.

For a moment she stood there perfectly still, no longer moving a muscle. The swirling black gauze deflated about her, fell limp. Benson's grin of approval dimmed and died while he craned his neck up at her. Suddenly she started to go off-balance, to fall.

He only had time to throw up his arms instinctively, half to ward her off, half to catch her and break her fall. Her looming body blurred the runway lights for an instant, and then she had landed across him, one foot still up there on the runway behind her. The black stuff of her mantle came down after her, like a parachute, and half-smothered him. He had to claw at it to free his head.

Those in the rows farther back, who hadn't been close enough to notice the break in her performance that had come just before the fall, started to applaud and even laugh. They seemed to think it was still part of her routine, or that she had actually missed her footing and tumbled down on him, and either way it struck them as the funniest thing they had ever seen.

Benson already knew better, by the inert way her head and shoulders lay across his knees. "Take it easy. I've got you," he whispered reassuringly, trying to hold her as she started to slide to the floor between the rows of seats.

Her eyes rolled unseeingly up at him, showing all whites, but some memory of where she was and what she had been doing still lingered in the darkness rolling over her.

"I'm so sorry. Did I hurt you, mister?" she breathed. "Guess I've spoiled the show—" It ended with a long-drawn sigh—and she was still.

The laughter and handclapping was dying down, because her head didn't bob up again at the place where she had disappeared from view, and they were catching on that something was wrong. A hairy-armed man in rolled blue shirt-sleeves popped partly out of the wings, not caring if he was seen or not, and wigwagged frantically to the band leader, then jumped back again where he'd come from. The droopy music they'd been playing for her broke off short and a rackety rumba took its place. A long line of chorus girls came spilling out on the stage, most of them out of step and desperately working to get their shoulder straps adjusted.

Benson was already struggling up the aisle with his inert golden burden. A couple of ushers came hustling down to help him, but he elbowed them aside. "You quiet the house down. I can get her back there by myself,"

A man with a cigar sticking flat out of his mouth like a tusk met him at the back, threw open a door marked *Manager*. "Bring her in here to my office, until I can send for a doctor—" Before closing it after the three of them, he stopped to scan the subsiding ripples of excitement in the audience. "How they taking it? All right, keep 'em down in their seats, usher. No refunds, understand?" He closed the door and came in.

Benson had to put her in the manager's swivel chair; there wasn't even a couch or sofa in the place. Even with the shaded desk light on, the place stayed dim and shadowy. Her body gleamed weirdly in the gloom, like a shiny mermaid.

"Thanks a lot, bud," the manager said to him crisply. "You don't have to wait; the doctor'll be here in a minute—"

"The tin says stick around." Benson reburied the badge in his pocket.

The manager widened his eyes. "That's a hot one. You're probably the only headquarters man out there tonight, and she keels over into your lap."

"That's the kind of luck I always have," Benson said, bending over the girl. "I can't even see a show once a year, without my job horning in."

The manager took another squint outside the door to see how his house was getting along. "Forgotten all about it already," he reported contentedly. He turned back. "How's she coming?"

" She's dead, " Benson said muffledly, from below one arm, ear to the girl's gold brassière.

The manager gave a sharp intake of breath, but his reaction was a purely professional one. "Gee, who'll I get to fill in for her on such short notice? What the hell happened to her? She was all right at the matinee!"

"What'd you expect her do do," Benson said short-temperedly, "come and inform you she was going to die in the middle of her act tonight, so you'd have time to get a substitute?" He lifted one of the golden eyelids to try for optical reflex; there wasn't any.

The hastily summoned doctor had paused outside the door, trying to take in as much of the show free as he could before he had to attend to business. He came in still looking fascinatedly behind him. "You're too late," the manager scowled. "This headquarters man says she's dead already."

Benson was on the desk phone by now with his back to the two of them. A big belly-laugh rolled in from outside before they could get the door closed, and drowned out what he was saying. He covered the mouthpiece until he could go ahead. "Forty-second Street, just off Broadway, Okay." He hung up. "The examiner's office is sending a man over. We'll hear what he says."

The doctor smiled. "Well, he can't say any more than I can. She's dead and that's that."

"He can say why," Benson countered, dipping four fingers of each hand into his coat pockets and wiggling his thumbs.

The doctor closed the door after him.

"Now he's going to stand and chisel the rest of the show free, just because he was called in," the manager predicted sourly.

"He can have my seat," Benson remarked. "I won't be using it any more tonight."

He brushed a fleck of gold paint off the front of his coat, then another off the cuff of his coat sleeve. "Let's get the arithmetic down." He took out a black notebook, poised a worn-down pencil stub over the topmost ruled line of a blank page. The pages that had gone before—and many had gone before—were all closely scrawled over with names, addresses, and other data. Then, one by one, wavy downward lines were scored through them. That meant: case closed.

The manager opened a drawer in his desk, took out a ledger, sought a pertinent page, traced a sausage-like thumb down a list of payroll names. "Here she is. Real name, Annie Willis, 'Gilda' was just her—"

Benson jotted. "I know."

He gave the address on West 135th. "There's a phone number to go with it, too."

Benson jotted. He looked up, said, "Oh, hello, Jacobson," as the man from the examiner's office came in, went back to his note-taking again.

Outside, 300-odd people sat watching a line-up of girls dance. Inside, the business of documenting a human death went on, with low-voiced diligence.

Benson repeated: "Nearest of kin, Frank Willis, husband—"

The examining assistant groused softly to. himself: "I can't get anything out of it at all, especially through all this gilt. It mighta been a heart attack; it mighta been acute indigestion. All I can give you for sure, until we get downtown, is she's dead, good and dead—"

The manager was getting peevish at this protracted invasion of his privacy. "That makes three times she's been dead, already. I'm willing to believe it, if no one else is."

Benson murmured, "This is the part I hate worst," and began

to dial with his pencil stub.

An usher sidled in, asked: "What'll we do about the marquee, boss? She's still up on it, and it's gotta be changed now for tomorrow's matinee."

"Just take down the 'G' from 'Gilda', see? Then stick in an 'H' instead, make it 'Hilda.' That saves the trouble of changing the whole—"

"But who's Hilda, boss?"

"I don't know myself! If the customers don't see anyone called Hilda, that'll teach them not to believe in signs!"

Benson was saying quietly: "Is this Frank Willis? Are you the husband of Annie Willis, working at the New Rotterdam Theater?...All right, now take it easy. She died during the performance this evening...Yeah, onstage about half an hour ago...No, you won't find her here by the time you get down. You'll be notified when the body's released by the medical examiner's office. They want to perform an autopsy...Now don't get frightened, that's just a matter of form, they always do that. It just means an examination...You can claim her at the city morgue when they're through with her."

He hung up, murmured under his breath: "Funny how a strange word they don't understand, like 'autopsy,' always throws a scare into them when they first hear it." He eyed the manager's swivel chair. It was empty now, except for a swath of gold-paint flecks down the middle of the back, like a sunset reflection. He grimaced discontentedly. "I shoulda stayed home tonight altogether. Then somebody else would have had to handle the blamed thing! Never saw it to fail yet. Every time I try to see a show—"

Next day at 11 a cop handed Benson a typewritten autopsy report.

Benson didn't place the name for a minute. Then: "Oh yeah, that girl in the show last night—Gilda." He glanced down at his own form with rueful recollection. "It's going to cost me two bucks to have the front of that other suit dry-cleaned. Okay, thanks. I'll take it into the lieutenant."

He scanned it cursorily himself first, before doing so. Then he stopped short, frowned, went back and read one or two of the passages more carefully.

"...Death caused by sealing of the pores over nearly the entire body surface for a protracted period. This substance is deleterious when kept on for longer than an hour or two at the most. It is composed of infinitesimal particles of gold leaf which adhere to the pores, blocking them. This produces a form of bodily suffocation, as fatal in the end, if less immediate than stoppage of the breathing passage. The symptoms are delayed, then strike with cumulative suddenness, resulting in weakness, dizziness, collapse, and finally death. Otherwise the subject was perfectly sound organically in every way. There can be no doubt that this application of theatrical pigment and failure to remove it in time was the sole cause of mortality—"

He tapped a couple of nails on the desk undecidedly a minute or two. Finally he picked up the phone and got the manager of the New Rotterdam Theater. He hadn't come in yet, but they switched the call to his home. "This is Benson, headquarters man that was in your office last night. How long had this Gilda— Annie Willis, you know—been doing this gilt act?"

"Oh, quite some time—five or six months now."

"Then she wasn't green at it; she wasn't just breaking it in."

"No, no, she was an old hand at it."

He hung up, tapped his nails some more. "Funny she didn't know enough by this time to take it off before it had a chance to smother her," he murmured half under his breath.

The report should have gone into his lieutenant, and that should have ended it. Accidental death due to carelessness, that was all. She'd been too lazy or too rushed to remove the harmful substance between shows, and had paid the penalty.

But a good detective is five-sixths hard work and one-sixth blind, spontaneous "hunches." Benson wasn't a bad detective, And his one-sixth had come uppermost just then. He folded the examiner's report, put it in his pocket, and didn't take it into his lieutenant. He went back to the New Rotterdam Theater on 42nd Street, instead.

It was open even this early, although the stage show didn't go on yet. A handful of sidewalk beachcombers were drifting in, to get in out of the sun. The manager had evidently thought better of his marquee short-change of the night before. The canopy still misleadingly proclaimed "Gilda, the Golden Dancer," but below it there was now affixed a small placard, so tiny it was invisible unless you got up on a ladder to scan it: "Next Week."

The manager acted anything but glad to see him back so soon. "I knew that wasn't the end of it! With you fellows these things go on forever. Listen, she keeled over in front of everybody in the theater. People are dropping dead on the streets like that every minute of the day, here, there, everywhere. What's there to find out about? Something gave out inside. It was her time to go, and there you are."

Benson wasn't an argumentative sort of person. "Sure," he agreed unruffledly, "And now it's my time to come nosing around about it—and there *you* are. Who shared her dressing room with her—or did she have one to herself?"

The manager shrugged disdainfully. "These aren't the days when the Ziegfeld Follies played this house. She split it with Vilma Lyons—that's the show's ballad singer, you know, the only full-dressed girl in the company—and June McKee. She leads the chorus in a couple of numbers."

"Are her belongings still in it?"

"They must be. Nobody's called for them yet, as far as I know."

"Let's go back there," Benson suggested.

"Listen, the show's cooking to go on—"

"I won't get in its way," Benson assured him.

They came out of the office, went down a side aisle skirting the orchestra, with scattered spectators already lounging here and there. A seven-year-old talking picture, with Morse Code dots and dashes running up it all the time, was clouding the screen at the moment. They climbed onto the stage at the side, went in behind the screen, through the wings, and down a short, damp, feebly lighted passage, humming with feminine voices coming from behind doors that kept opening and closing as girls came in from the alley at the other end of the passage, in twos and threes.

The manager thumped one of the doors, turned the knob, and opened it with one and the same gesture—and a perfect indifference to the consequences. "Put on something, kids. There's a detective coming in."

"What's the matter, isn't he over twenty-one?" one of them jeered.

The manager stood aside to let Benson pass, then went back along the passageway toward his office with the warning: "Don't gum them up now. This show hits fast once it gets going."

There were two girls in there, working away at opposite ends of a three-paneled mirror. The middle space and chair were vacant. Benson's face appeared in all three of the mirrors at once, as he came in and closed the door after him. One girl clutched at a wrapper, flung it around her shoulders. The other calmly went ahead applying make-up, leaving her undraped backbone exposed to view down to her waist.

"You two have been sharing the same dressing room with Annie Willis," he said. "Did she usually leave this shiny junk on between shows, or take it off each time?"

The chorus leader, the one the manager had called June McKee, answered, in high-pitched derogation at such denseness. "Whadd'ye think, she could go out and eat between shows with her face all gold like that? She woulda had a crowd following her along the street! Sure she took it off."

They looked at one another with a sudden flash of enlightened curiosity. The McKee girl, a strawberry blonde, turned around toward him. "Sa-ay, is that what killed her, that gold stuff?" she asked in a husky whisper.

Benson overrode that. "Did she take it off yesterday or did she leave it on?"

"She left it on." She turned to her bench mate, the brunette ballad singer, for corroboration. "Didn't she, Vilma?

Remember?"

"Where is this gold stuff? I'd like to see it."

"It must be here with the rest of her stuff." The McKee girl reached over, pulled out the middle of the three table drawers, left it open for him to help himself. "Look in there."

It was in pulverized form, in a small jar. It had a greenish tinge to it that way. He read the label. It was put up by a reputable cosmetic manufacturing company. There were directions for application and removal, and then an explicit warning: "Do not allow to remain on any longer than necessary after each performance." She must have read that a dozen times in the course of using the stuff. She couldn't have failed to see it.

"You say she left it on yesterday. Why? Have you any idea?"

Again it was the McKee girl who answered, spading her palms at him. "Because she mislaid the cleanser, the stuff that came with it to remove it. They both come together. You can't buy one without the other. It's a special preparation that sort of curls it up and *peels* it off clean and even. Nothing else works as well or as quick. You can't use cold cream, and even alcohol isn't much good. You can scrub your head off and it just makes a mess of your skin—"

"And yesterday it disappeared?"

"Right after the finale, she started to holler: 'Who took my paint remover? Anybody seen my paint remover?' Well, between the three of us, we turned the room inside out, and no sign of it. She emptied her whole drawer out. Everything else was there but that. She even went into a couple of the other dressing rooms to find out if anybody had it in there. I told her nobody else would want it. She was the only one in the company who used that gilt junk. It wouldn't have been any good to anyone else. It never turned up."

"Finish telling me."

"Finally Vilma and me had to go out and eat. Time was getting short. Other nights, the three of us always ate together. We told her if she found it in time to hurry up after us. We'd keep a place for her at our table. She never showed up. When we got back for the night show, sure enough, she was still in her electroplating. She told us she'd had to send Jimmy the handyman out for something and had eaten right in the dressing room,"

Benson cocked his head slightly, as when one looks downward into a narrow space. "Are you sure this bottle of remover couldn't have been in the drawer and she missed seeing it?"

"That was the first place we cased. We had everything out. I remember holding it up in my hand empty and thumping the bottom of it just for luck!"

His wrist shot out of his cuff, hitched back into it again, like some sort of a hydraulic brake. "Then what's it doing in there now?" He was holding a small bottle, mate to the first, except that its contents were liquid and there was a small sponge attached to its neck.

It got quiet in the dressing room, deathly quiet. So quiet you could even hear the sound track from the screen out front.

The McKee girl's lower lip was trembling. "It was put back—*after!* Somebody *wanted* her to die like that! With us right here in the same room with her!" She took a deep breath, threw open her own drawer, and with a defiant look at Benson, as if to say, "Try and stop me," tilted a small, flat gin bottle to her mouth.

The ballet singer, Vilma Lyons, suddenly dropped her head into her folded arms on the littered dressing table and began to sob.

The stage manager bopped a fist on the door and called in: "The customers are waiting to see your operations. If that dick's still questioning you in there, tell him to put on a girdle and follow you out on the runway!"

"Yes, sir, boss, I'm Jimmy, the handyman." He put down his bucket, followed Benson out into the alley, where they wouldn't be in the way of the girls hustling in and out on quick changes. "Yes, sir, Miss Gilda sent me out last night between shows to try to get her another bottle of that there stuff, which took off the gold paint."

"Why didn't you get it?"

"I couldn't! I went to the big theatrical drugstore on Eighth where she told me. It's the only place around here where you can get it and even there they don't keep much on hand, never get much call for it. The drugstore man told me somebody else just beat me to it. He told me he just got through selling the last bottle he had in stock, before I got there."

"Keep on," Benson said curtly.

"That's about all. The drugstore man promised to order another bottle for her right away from his company's warehouse or the wholesaler that puts it up, and see that it's in first thing in the morning. So I went back and told her. Then she sent me across the street to the cafeteria to bring her a sandwich. When I came back the second time, she was sitting there acting kind of low, holding her head. She said, 'Jimmy, I'm sorry I ordered that bite, after all. I don't feel well. I hope nothing happens to me from leaving this stuff on too long.'"

All Benson said was: "You come along and point out that druggist to me."

"Come in, Benson."

"Lieutenant, I've got a problem. I've got a report here from Jacobson that I haven't turned in to you yet. I've been keeping it until I know what to do about it."

"What's the hitch?"

"Lieutenant, is there such a thing as a *negative* murder? By that I mean, when not a finger is lifted against the victim, not a hair of her head is actually touched. But the murder is accomplished by *withholding* something, so that death is caused by an absence or lack."

The lieutenant was quick on the trigger. "Certainly! If a man locks another man up in a room, and withholds food from him until the guy has starved to death, you'd call that murder, wouldn't you? Even though the guy that caused his death never touched him with a ten-foot pole, never stepped in past the locked door at all."

Benson plucked doubtfully at the cord of skin between his throat and chin. "But what do you do when you have no proof of *intention?* I mean, when you've got evidence that the act of withholding or removal was committed, but no proof that the intention was murderous. And how you gonna get proof of intention, anyway? It's something inside the mind, isn't it?"

The lieutenant glowered, said: "What do you do? I'll tell you what you do. You bring your bird in and you keep him until you get the intention *out* of his mind and down in typewriting! That's what you do!"

The man was alone when he started down the three flights of stairs in the shoddy walk-up apartment on West 135th. He was still alone when he got down to the bottom of them. And then somehow, between the foot of the stairs and the street door, he wasn't alone any more. Benson was walking along beside him, as soundlessly as though his own shadow had crept forward and overtaken him along the poorly lit passage.

He shied sideways and came to a dead stop against the wall, the apparition was so unexpected.

Benson said quietly: "Come on, what're you stopping for? You were leaving the house, weren't you, Willis? Well, you're still leaving the house, what's the difference?"

They walked on as far as the street entrance. Benson just kept one fingertip touching the other's elbow, in a sort of mockery of guidance. Willis said, "What am I pinched for?"

"Who said you were pinched? Do *you* know of anything you should be pinched for?"

"No, I don't."

"Then you're not pinched. Simple enough, isn't it?"

Willis didn't say another word after that. Benson only said two things more himself, one to his charge, the other to a cab driver. He remarked: "Come on, we'll ride it. I'm no piker." And when a cab had sidled up to his signal, he named a precinct police station.

They rode the whole way in stony silence, Willis staring straight ahead in morbid reverie, Benson with his eyes toward the cab window—but on the shadowy reflection of Willis's face given back by the glass, not the street outside.

They got out and Benson took him in and left him waiting in a room at the back for a few minutes, while he went off to attend to something else. This wasn't accidental; it was the psychological build-up—or rather, breakdown—preceding the grill. It had been known to work wonders.

It didn't this time. Willis didn't break. A sense of innocence can sometimes lend moral support; but so can a sense of having outwitted justice.

"The guy must be innocent," another dick remarked.

"He knows we can't get him. There's nothing more in his actions to be uncovered, don't you see? We've got everything there is to get on him, and it isn't enough. And we can't get at his intentions. They got to come out through his own mouth. All he has to do is hold out. It's easy to keep a single, simple idea like that in your mind.

"What breaks down most of them is the uncertainty of something they did wrong, something they didn't cover up right, something cropping up and tripping them—an exploded alibi, a surprise identification by a material witness. He has none of that uncertainty to buck. All he has to do is to sit tight inside his own skin."

To his lieutenant, the next day, Benson said, "I'm morally certain he killed her. What are the three things that count in every crime? Motive, opportunity, and method. He rings the bell on each count. Motive? Well, the oldest one in the world between men and women. He'd lost his head about someone else, and didn't know how else to get rid of her. She was in the way in more than just one sense. She was a deterrent, because of the other woman's sense of loyalty. It wouldn't have done any good if he walked out on her or divorced her; the other woman wouldn't have had him unless he was free, and he knew it.

"It so happens the other woman was a lifelong friend of the wife. She even lived with them, up at the 135th Street place, for a while after they were first married. Then she got out, maybe because she realized a set-up like that was only asking for trouble."

"Have you found out who this other woman is?"

"Sure. Vilma Lyons, the ballad singer in the same show with the wife. I went up to the theater yesterday afternoon. I questioned the two girls who shared Annie Willis's dressing room with her. One of them talked a blue streak. The other one didn't open her mouth; I don't recall her making a single remark during the entire interview. She was too busy *thinking back*. She knew; her intuition must have already told her who had done it. At the end, she suddenly buried her face in her arms and cried. I didn't say a word. I let her take her own time. I let her think it over. I knew she'd come to me of her own accord sooner or later. She did, after curtain time last night, down here at the station house. Weren't we going to *get* the person who had done that to her friend, she wanted to know? Wasn't he going to be punished for it? Was he going to get away with it scot-free?"

"Did she accuse him?"

"She had nothing to accuse him of. He hadn't said anything to her. He hadn't even shown her by the look on his face. And then little by little I caught on, by reading between the lines of what she said, that he'd liked her a little too well."

He shrugged. "She can't help us—she admitted it herself. Because he started giving her these long, haunting looks when he thought she wasn't noticing, and acting discontented and restless, that isn't evidence he killed his wife. But she *knows*, in her own mind, just as I *know* in mine, who hid that remover from Annie Willis, and with what object, and why. She hates him like poison now. I could read it on her face. He's taken her friend from her. They'd chummed together since they were both in pigtails, at the same orphanage."

"All right. What about Opportunity, your second factor?"

"He rings the bell there, too. And again it doesn't do us any good. Sure, he admits he was sitting out front at the matinee day before yesterday. But so was he a dozen times before. Sure, he admits he went backstage to her dressing room, after she'd gone back to it alone and while the other two were still onstage. But so had he a dozen times before. He claims it was already missing then. She told him so, and asked him to go out and get her another bottle. But who's to prove that? She's not alive, and neither of the two other girls had come off the stage yet."

"Well, what happened to the second bottle that would have saved her life?"

"He paid for it. The clerk wrapped it for him. He started out holding it in his hand. And at the drug store entrance he collided with someone coming in. It was jarred out of his hand and shattered on the floor!"

And as if he could sense what the lieutenant was going to say, he hurriedly added: "There were witnesses galore to the incident; the clerk himself, the soda jerk, the cashier, I questioned every one of them. Not one could say for sure that it wasn't a genuine accident. Not one could swear that he'd seen Willis actually relax his hand and let it fall, or deliberately get in this other party's way."

"Then why didn't he go back and tell her? Why did he leave her there like that with this stuff killing her, so that she had to send the handyman out to see if he could get hold of any for her?"

"We can't get anything on him for that, either. He did the natural thing; he went scouting around for it in other places—the way a man would, who was ashamed to come back and tell her he'd just smashed the one bottle they had left in stock." And through thinned lips he added acidly, "Everything he did was so natural. That's why we can't get him!"

The lieutenant said, "There's an important little point in that smashed-bottle angle. Did he know it was the last bottle on hand *before* he dropped it, or did he only find out after he stepped back to the counter and tried to get another?"

Benson nodded. "I bore down heavy on that with the drug clerk. Unless Willis was deaf, dumb, and blind, he knew that that was the last bottle in the store before he started away from the counter with it. The clerk not only had a hard time finding it, but when he finally located it, he remarked, " 'This is the last one we've got left.'"

"Then that accident was no accident."

"Can you *prove* it?" was all Benson said.

The lieutenant answered that by discarding it. "Go ahead," he said sourly.

"I checked with every one of the other places he told me he'd been to after leaving there, and he *had* asked for it in each one. They corroborated him. He wasn't in much danger of coming across it anywhere else and he knew it! The drug clerk had not only forewarned him that he didn't think he'd find it anywhere else, but his wife must have told him the same thing before she sent him out." And screwing his mouth up, Benson said, "But it looked good for the record, and it kept him away from the theater—while she was dying by inches from cellular asphyxiation!"

"Didn't he go back at all? Did he stay out from then on?"

"No one saw him come back, not a soul, I made sure of that before I put it up to him." Benson smiled bleakly. "I know what you're thinking, and I thought of that, too. If he didn't go back at all, then he wasn't responsible for making the remover disappear in the first place. Because it was back in the drawer before the next matinee—I found it there myself.

"Now get the point involved: He had a choice between the natural thing and the completely exonerating thing. But the exonerating thing would have meant behaving a little oddly. The natural thing for a man sent out on an errand by his wife is to return eventually, even it it's an hour later, even if it's only to report that he was unsuccessful. The exonerating thing, in this case, was for him to stay out for good. All he had to do was claim he never went back, and he was absolutely in the clear, absolutely eliminated."

"Well?" The lieutenant could hardly wait for the answer.

"He played it straight all the way through. He admitted, of his own accord and without having been seen by anybody, that he stopped back for a minute to tell her he hadn't been able to get it, after chasing all over the Forties for the stuff. And that, of course, is when the missing bottle got back into the drawer."

The lieutenant was almost goggle-eyed. "Well I'll be—! She was still alive, the murder hadn't even been completed yet, and he was already removing the traces of it by replacing the bottle!"

"The timing of her act guaranteed that she was already as good as dead, even with the bottle back within her reach. She couldn't take the gilt off now for another three hours. Using it continuously had already lowered her resistance. That brief breathing spell she should have had between shows spelled the difference between life and death. In other words, Lieutenant, he left her alive, with fifty people around her who talked to her, rubbed shoulders with her in the wings, after he'd gone. And later she even danced onstage before a couple hundred more. *But he'd already murdered her!"*

"But you say he didn't have to admit he stopped back at the theater, and yet he did."

"Sure, but to me that doesn't prove his innocence, that only proves his guilt and infernal cleverness. By avoiding the slightest lie, the slightest deviation in his account of his actual movements, he's much safer than by grasping at a chance of automatic, complete vindication. Somebody just *might* have seen him come back; he couldn't be sure."

Benson took a deep breath. "There it all is, Lieutenant; motive, opportunity, and method. And it don't do us much good, does it? There isn't any more evidence to be had. There never will be. There's nothing more to uncover—because it all *is* uncovered already. We couldn't get him on a disorderly conduct charge on all of it put together, much less for murder. What do I do with him now?"

The lieutenant took a long time answering, as though he hated to have to. Finally he did. "We'll have to turn him loose; we can't hold him indefinitely."

"I hate to see him walk out of here free," Benson said.

"There's no use busting your brains about it. It's a freak that only happens maybe once in a thousand times—but it happened this time."

Later that same morning Benson walked out to the entrance of the precinct house with Willis, after the formalities of release had been gone through. Benson stopped short at the top of the entrance steps, marking the end of his authority. He smiled. "Well, if we couldn't get anything out of you in there last night, I didn't expect to get anything out of you out here right now." His mouth thinned. "Here's the street. Beat it."

Willis went down the steps, walked on a short distance alone and unhindered. Then he decided to cross over to the opposite side of the street. When he had reached it, he stopped a minute and looked back.

Benson was still standing there on the police station steps, looking after him. Their stares met. Benson couldn't read his look, whether it conveyed mockery or relief or just casual indifference. But for that matter, Willis couldn't read Benson's either; whether it conveyed regret or philosophic acceptance of defeat or held a vague promise that things between them weren't over yet. And it wasn't because of the distance that separated them; it was because the thoughts of both were locked up in their minds.

There was a brittle quality of long-smoldering rancor about her, even when she first opened the door, even before she'd had time to see who was standing there. She must have just got home from the show. She still had her coat and hat on. But she was already holding a little jigger glass of colorless liquid between two of her fingers, as if trying to cauterize the inner resentment that was continually gnawing at her. Her eyes traveled over his form from head to foot and back again.

"Been letting any more killers go since I saw you last?" she said sultrily.

"You've taken that pretty much to heart, haven't you?" Benson answered levelly.

"Why wouldn't I? Her ghost powders its nose on the bench next to me twice a day! A couple performances ago I caught myself turning around and saying: 'Did you get paid this week—' before I stopped to think." She emptied the jigger. "And do you know what keeps the soreness from healing? Because the person that did it is still around, untouched, unpunished. Because he got away with it. You know who I mean or do I have to break out with a name?"

"You can't prove it, any more than we could, so why bring up a name?"

"Prove it! *Prove* it! You make me sick." She refilled the jigger. "You're the police! Why weren't you able to get him?"

"You talk like a fool," he said patiently. "You talk like we let him go purposely. D'you think I enjoyed watching him walk out scot-free under my nose? And that ain't all. I've been passed over on the promotion list, on account of it. They didn't *say* it was that; they didn't say it was anything. They didn't have to. I can figure it out for myself. It's the first blank I've drawn in six years. It's eating at my insides, too, like yours."

She relented at the sign of a bitterness that matched her own. "Misery likes company, I guess. Come on in, as long as you're here. Have a stab," she said grudgingly, and pushed the gin slightly toward him.

They sat in brooding silence for several minutes, two frustrated people. Finally she spoke again. "He had the nerve to put *his* flowers on her grave! Imagine, flowers from the killer to the one he killed! I found them there when I went there myself, before the matinee today, to leave some roses of my own. The caretaker told me whose they were. I tore them in a thousand pieces when he wasn't looking."

"I know," he said. "He goes up twice a week, leaves fresh flowers each time. I've been casing him night and day. The hypocritical rat! All the way through from the beginning, he's done the natural thing. He does it whether he thinks anyone's watching or not, and that's the safe way for him to do it."

He refilled his own jigger without asking permission. He laughed harshly. "But he's not pining away. I cased his flat while he was out today, and I found enough evidence to show there's some blonde been hanging around to console him. Gilt hairpins on the kitchen floor, a double set of dirty dishes—two of everything—in the sink."

She lidded her eyes, touched a hand to her own jet-black hair. "I'm not surprised," she said huskily. "That would be about his speed. Maybe you can still get something on him through her."

He shook his head. "He can go around with ten blondes if he feels like it. He's within his rights. We can't hold him just for that—"

"What's the matter with the laws these days?" she said almost savagely. "Here we are, you and I, sitting here in this room. We both know he killed Annie Willis. You're drawing pay from the police department, and he's moving around fancy-free only a couple of blocks away from us!"

He nodded as though he agreed with her. "They fail you every once in a while," he admitted gloomily, "the statutes as they are written down on the books. They slip a cog and let someone fall through—" Then he went on: "But there's an older law than the statutes we work under. I don't know if you ever heard of it or not. It's called the Mosaic Law. 'An eye for an eye, and a tooth for a tooth.' And when the modern set-up goes back on you, that one never does. It's short and sweet, got no amendments, dodges, or habeas corpuses to clutter it up. 'An eye for an eye, and a tooth for a tooth.'"

"I like the way that sounds better," she said. "But more important still, *I hear the words you're not saying.*"

He just looked at her, and she looked at him. They were like two fencers, warily circling around each other to find an opening. She got up, moved over to the window, stared grimly out toward the traffic intersection at the corner ahead. "Green light," she reported. Then she turned toward him with a bitter, puckered smile. "Green light. That means go ahead—doesn't it?"

"Green light," he murmured. "That means go ahead—if you care to. The man that throws the switch in the deathhouse at Sing Sing, what makes him a legal executioner and not a murderer? The modern statutes. The Mosaic Code can have its legal executioners, too, who are also not murderers."

She had come over close to him.

"But never," he went on, looking straight up at her, "exceed or distort its short, simple teachings. Never repay the gun with the knife, or the knife with the club. Then that's murder, no longer the Mosaic Code. In the same way, if the State executioner shot the condemned man on his way to the chair, or poisoned him in his cell, then he wouldn't be a legal executioner any more, he'd be a murderer himself." And he repeated it again for her slowly. "'An eye for an eye, a tooth for a tooth.' Annie Willis met her death by having something withheld from her that her safety depended on. No weapon was used on Annie Willis, remember."

"Yes," she said, "and I know where there's a trunk that belongs to me, down in a basement storage room, seldom entered, seldom used. One of these big theatrical trunks, roomy enough to carry around the props for a whole act. I left it behind when I moved out. I was going to send for it but—" She paused. "And if I came to you, for instance, and said: 'What's been bothering you and me has been taken care of,' how would you receive me—as a criminal under the modern law or a legal executioner under the old one?"

He looked straight up at her with piercing directness. "The modern law failed you and me, didn't it? Then how could I judge you by it?"

She murmured half audibly, as if testing him: "Then why not you? Why me?"

"The injury was done to you, not me. A friend is a personal belonging, a professional disappointment isn't. Nothing was done to me personally. Under the Mosaic Law, a frustrated job can only be repaid by another frustrated job, by making the person who injured you suffer a like disappointment in *his* work."

She laughed dangerously. "I can do better than that," she said softly.

She kept shaking her head, looking at him from time to time as if she still found the situation almost past belief. "The strangest things never get down on the record books! They wouldn't be believed if they did! Here you are, sitting in my room, a man drawing pay from the police department—" She didn't finish it.

"We haven't been talking," he said, getting up.

She held the door open for him. "No," she smiled, "we haven't been talking. You weren't here tonight, and nothing was said."

The door closed and Detective Benson went down the stairs with an impassive face.

What followed was even more incredible. Or, at least, the surroundings it occurred in were. A cop came in to him, at the precinct house three nights later, and said, "There's a lady out there asking for you, Benson. Won't state her business."

Benson said, "I think I know who you mean. Look, Corrigan, you know that little end room on the left, at the back of the hall? Is there anyone in there right now?"

The cop said, "Naw, there's never anyone in there."

"Take her back there, will you?"

He got there ahead of her. She stood outlined in the open doorway first, watching the cop return along the hall, before she'd come in.

He didn't pretend to be going over papers or anything like that. It was one of those blind spots that even the most bustling, overcrowded buildings occasionally have, unused, avoided the greater part of the time by the personnel. He acted slightly frightened. He kept pacing nervously back and forth, waiting for her to enter the room.

When she finally came in and closed the door after her, he said, "Couldn't you have waited until I dropped over to see you?"

"How did I know when you'd be around again? I felt like I couldn't wait another half hour to get it off my chest." There was something almost gloating in the way she looked at him. "Is it safe to talk here?"

He went over to the door, opened it, looked along the passageway outside, closed it again. "It's all right."

She said, half-mockingly, with that intimacy of one conspirator for another: "No dictaphones around?"

He was too on edge to share her bantering mood. "Don't be

stupid," he snapped. "This is the last place I ever expected you to—"

She lit a cigarette, preened herself. "You think you're looking at a cheap ballad singer on a burlesque circuit, don't you?"

"What am I looking at?"

"You're looking at a legal executioner, under the Mosaic Code. I have a case of Biblical justice to report. I had a friend I valued very highly, and she was caused to die by having the skin of her body deprived of air. Now the man who did that to her is going to die sometime during the night, if he hasn't already, by having the skin of *his* body—and his lungs and his heart—deprived of air in the same way."

He lit a cigarette to match hers. His hands were so steady—too steady, rigid almost—that you could tell they weren't really. He was forcing them to be that way. His color was paler than it had been when he first came in.

"What have you got to say to that?" She clasped her own sides in a parody of macabre delight.

"I'll tell you in a minute." He went over to the door, opened it, and looked out again, as if to make sure there was no one out there to overhear. He'd dropped his cigarette on the way over to it.

She misunderstood. "Don't be so jittery—" she began scornfully.

He'd raised his voice suddenly, before she knew what to expect. It went booming down the desolate hallway. "Corrigan! C'mere a minute!" A blue-suited figure had joined him before she knew what was happening. He pointed in toward her.

"Arrest this woman for murder! Hold her here in this room until I get back! I'm making you personally responsible for her!"

A bleat of smothered fury ripped from her. "Why, you dirty, double-crossing—The guy ain't even dead yet—"

"I'm not arresting you for the murder of Frank Willis. I'm arresting you for the murder of his wife, Annie Willis, over a month and a half ago at the New Rotterdam Theater!"

The greater part of it came winging back from the far end of the hallway, along which he was moving fast on his way to try to save a man's life.

They came trooping down single file, fast, into the gloom. White poker chips of light glanced off the damp brick walls from their torches. The janitor was in the lead. He poked at a switch by his sense of memory alone, and a feeble parody of electricity illuminated part of the ceiling and the floor immediately under it, nothing else.

"I ain't seen him since yesterday noon," he told them in a frightened voice. "I seen him going out then. That was the last I seen of him. Here it is over here, gents. This door."

They fanned out around it in a half circle. All the separate poker chips of torchlight came to a head in one big wagon wheel. The door was fireproof; nail-studded iron, rusty but stout. But it was fastened simply by a padlock clasping two thick staples.

"I remember now, my wife said something about his asking her for the key to here, earlier in the evening while I was out," the janitor said. "So he was still all right then."

"Yes, he was still all right *then,"* Benson agreed shortly. "Get that thing off. Hurry up!" A crowbar was inserted behind the padlock; two of the men started to pry. Something snapped. The unopened lock bounced up, and they swung the storage-space door out with a grating sound.

The torchbeams converged inside and lit it up. It was small and cramped, the air musty and unfit to breathe. All the discarded paraphernalia of forgotten tenants over the years choked it. Cartons, empty packing cases, a dismantled iron bed frame, even a kid's sled with one runner missing. But there was a clear space between the entrance and the one large trunk that loomed up, like a towering headstone on a tomb.

It stood there silent, inscrutable. On the floor before it lay, in eloquent meaning, a single large lump of coal brought from the outside part of the basement and discarded after it had served its purpose.

"A blow on the head with that would daze anyone long enough

192

to—" Benson scuffed it out of the way. "Hurry up, fellows. She'd only just left here when she looked me up. It's not a full hour yet. The seams may be warped with age, there's still a slim chance—"

They pushed the scared, white-lipped janitor out of their way. Axe blades began to slash around the rusted snaplock. "Not too deep," Benson warned. "Give it flat strokes from the side, or you're liable to cut in and—Got that pulmotor ready?"

The axes held off at his signal and he pulled the dangling lock off the splintered seams with his bare hands. They all jumped in, began pulling in opposite directions. The trunk split open vertically. A face stared sightlessly into the focused torchbeams, a contorted mask of strangulation and unconsciousness that had been pressed despairingly up against the seam as close as it could get, to drink in the last precious molecule of air.

Willis's body, looking shrunken, tumbled out into their arms. They carried him out into the more open part of the basement, one hand with mangled nails trailing inertly after him. An oxygen tank was hooked up, and a silent, grim struggle for life began in the eerie light of the shadowy basement.

Twice they wanted to quit, and Benson wouldn't let them. "If he goes, that makes a murderer out of me! And I won't be made a murderer out of! We're going to bring him back, if we stay here until tomorrow night!"

And then, in the middle of the interminable silence, a simple, quiet announcement from the man in charge of the squad: "He's back, Benson. He's going again!"

Somebody let out a long, whistling breath of relief. It was a detective who had just escaped being made into a murderer.

The lieutenant came in, holding the confession in his hands. Benson followed.

"She put away?"

"Yes, sir."

The lieutenant went ahead, reading the confession. Benson waited in silence until he'd finished. The lieutenant looked up finally. "This'll do. You got results, but I don't get it. What was this business of her coming here and confiding in you that she'd made an attempt on Willis's life tonight, and how does that tie in with the murder of Annie Willis? You hit the nail on the head, but I miss the connecting links."

Benson said, "Here was the original equation. A wife in the middle, a man and a woman on the ends. She was in the way, but of which one of them? Vilma Lyons claimed it was Willis who had a pash on her. Willis didn't claim anything; the man as a rule won't.

"I watched them to see which would approach the other. Neither one did.

"I still couldn't tell which was which—although my money was still on Willis, up to the very end.

"Here was the technique. When I saw neither of them was going to tip a hand, I tipped it, instead. There's nothing like a shot of good, scalding jealousy in the arm for tipping the hand. I went to *both* of them alike, gave them the same build-up treatment. I was bitter and sore, because I'd muffed the job. It was a mark against me on my record, and so on. In Willis's case, because we'd already held him for it once, I had to vary it a little, make him think I'd changed my mind, now thought it was Vilma, but couldn't get her for it.

"In other words, I gave them both the same unofficial all-clear to go ahead and exact retribution personally. And I lit the same spark to both their fuses. I told Willis that Vilma had taken up with some other guy; I told her he had taken up with some other girl.

"One fuse fizzled out. The other flared and exploded. One of them didn't give a damn, because he never had. The other, having already committed murder to gain the object of her affections, saw red, would have rather seen him dead than have somebody else get him.

"You see, Lieutenant, murder always comes easier the second time than the first. Given equal provocation, whichever one of those two had committed the murder the first time wouldn't hesitate to commit it a second time. Willis had loved his wife. He smoldered with hate when I told him we had evidence Vilma had killed her, but he didn't act on the hints I gave him. It never occurred to him to.

"Only one took advantage of the leeway I seemed to be giving them, and went ahead. That one was the real murderer.

"It's true," he conceded, "that's not evidence that would have done us much good in trying to prove the other case. But what it did manage to do was make a dent in the murderer's armor. All we had to do was keep hacking away and she finally crumbled. Being caught in the act the second time weakened her self-confidence, gave us a psychological upper-hand over her. She finally came through." He indicated the confession the lieutenant held.

"Well," pondered the lieutenant, stroking his chin, "it's not a technique that I'd care to have you men make a habit of using very frequently. In fact, it's a damn dangerous one to monkey around with, but it got results this time, and that's the proof of any pudding."

RED LIBERTY

Red Liberty was originally published in *Dime Detective* in July of 1935 and is a classic whodunit with first-person narration by a working-stiff plainclothesman. This was to be one of many short stories included in a "Landmark Series" collection about New York that never came to fruition. It was included later in the short story collection *Violence*, Part IV "Violence with a Wink", and was retitled *The Corpse in the Statue of Liberty*. This newer version contained the same plot, but with added action at the climax and for the simple sake of staying relevant, Woolrich updated the "slanderous" dialogue so that it matched that of the current era in the fifties.

KATIE MUST HAVE been out of humor to say a thing like that, but it sure rankled. "And that's why you're no further than you are," she went on. "Ten years from now you'll still be a second-grade detective pinching pickpockets. Movies and beer—that's all you ever think of whenever you have any time to yourself. Why don't you improve your mind? Why don't you read a book? Why don't you go to a museum once in a while and look at the beautiful statues?"

I nearly fell over. "Look at statues!" I gasped. "What for?"

I seemed to have her there for a minute. "Why—why, to see how they're made," she said finally, looking bewildered.

There didn't seem to be much sense to it, but anything to keep peace in the family. I reached for my hat and gave a deep sigh. "You win," I said. "I'll try anything once."

Riding down in the sub I got a bright idea. Instead of wasting a lot of time looking at a flock of little statues I'd look at one big one instead and get the whole thing over with. So I got out at the Battery, forked over thirty-five cents for one round-trip ticket and got on the little ferry that takes you down the bay to the Statue of Liberty. It was the biggest statue around, and if there was any truth to what Katie said, it ought to improve me enough to last for the rest of the year.

There were about ten others making the trip with me, and as soon as everyone was on board, the tub gives a peep with its whistle and starts off, graceful as a hippopotamus. First the statue was about the size of your thumb. It came gliding over the water getting bigger all the time, until it was tall as an office building. It was pea-green, just like on the postcards. Finally the ferry tied up at a long pier built on piles that stuck out from the island, and everybody got off. There was another crowd there waiting to get on and go back. It seems the trip is only made once every hour.

It was certainly an eyeful once you got close up under it. The stone base alone was six stories high, and after that there was nothing but statue the rest of the way. There was just room enough left over on the island for a little green lawn with cannonballs for markers, a couple of cement paths, and some benches. But on the other wide, away from the city, there were a group of two-story brick houses, lived in by the caretakers I suppose.

Anyway, we went in through a thick, brutal-looking metal door painted black, and down a long stone corridor, and after a couple of turns came to an elevator. A spick-and-span one too, that looked as if it had just been installed. This only went up as far as the top of the pedestal, and after that you had to walk the other seventeen stories. The staircase was a spiral one only wide enough to let one person through at a time and it made tough going, but several times a little platform opened out suddenly on the way up, with an ordinary park bench placed there to rest on. There was always the same fat man sitting heaving on it by the time I got to it, with not much room left over for anybody else. When I say fat, I mean anywheres from two hundred fifty pounds up. I'd noticed him on the boat, with his thin pretty little wife. "Brother," I said the second time I squeezed in next to him on the bench, "pardon me for butting in, but why do it? You must be a glutton for punishment."

His wife had gone on the rest of the way up without waiting for him. He just wheezed for a long time, then finally he got around to answering me. "Brother," he said with an unhappy air, "she can think up more things for me to do like this. You know the old saying, nobody loves a—"

I couldn't help liking him right off. "Buck up, Slim," I said, "they're all the same. Mine thinks I'm a lowbrow and sends me out looking at statues so I'll learn something."

"And have you?" he wanted to know.

"Yep, I've learned there's no place like home," I told him. "Well, keep your chins up," I said, and with that I left him and went on up.

At the very top you had to push through a little turnstile, and then you were finally up in the head of the statue. The crown or tiara she wears, with those big spikes sticking out, has windows running from side to side in a half-circle. I picked the nearest one and stuck my head out. You could see for miles. The boats in the harbor were the size of match-boxes. Down below on the lawn the cannonballs looked like raisins in a pudding. Well, I stood there like that until I figured I'd gotten my thirty-five cents' worth. The rest were starting to drift down again, so I turned to go too.

At the window next to me I noticed the fat man's pretty little wife standing there alone. He evidently hadn't been able to make the grade yet and got up there with her. She was amusing herself by scribbling her initials or something on the thick stone facing of the window, which was about a foot deep and wider at the outside than at the inside, the tiara being a semicircle. That was nothing. Most people do that whenever they visit any monument or point of interest. All five of the facings were chock-full of names, initials, dates, addresses, and so on, and as time and the weather slowly effaced the earlier ones there was always room for more. She was using an eyebrow pencil or something for hers though, instead of plain lead, I noticed.

By that time we were alone up there. The others were all clattering down the corrugated-iron staircase again, and the ferry was on its way back from the Battery to pick us up. Much as I would have enjoyed waiting to get an eyeful of the shape her stout spouse was going to be in when he got up there, I figured I'd had enough. I started down and left her there behind me, chin propped in her hands and staring dreamily out into space, like Juliet waiting at her balcony for a high-sign from Romeo.

You went down by a different staircase than you came up, I mean it was the same spiral but the outside track this time, and there was no partition between, just a handrail. There were lights strung all along the stairs at regular intervals, of course; otherwise the place would have been pitch-dark. Some were just house bulbs; others were small searchlights turned outward against the lining of the statue, which was painted silver. In other words, anyone that was going up while you were coming down had to pass you in full view, almost rub elbows with you. No one did. The whole boatload that had come out with me was down below by now.

When I got down even with the first resting-platform, with only a rail separating me from it, something caught the corner of my eye just as my head was due to go below the platform level. I climbed back up a step or two, dipped under the railing, and looked under the bench, where it lay. Then I saw what it was and reached in and pulled it out. It was just somebody's brown felt hat, which had rolled under the bench.

I turned it upside down and looked in it. Knox—and P.G. were the initials. But more important, it hadn't been left there yesterday or last week, but just now. The sweat on the headband hadn't dried yet, and there was plenty of it—the leather strip was glistening with it. That was enough to tell me whose it was, the fat guy's. He'd been sitting on this bench when I left him— dripping with exertion—and I remembered seeing this very lid in his hand, or one the same color and shape. He'd taken it off and sat holding it in his hand while he mopped his melting brow.

He hadn't gone on up to where I'd left his wife, for he'd neither arrived while I was still up there nor had I passed him on the way down. It was a cinch he'd given it up as a bad job and gone on down from here, without tackling the last of the seventeen "stories" or twists. Still I couldn't figure how he could come to forget his hat, leave it behind like this, fagged out or not. Then I thought, "Maybe the poor gink had a heart attack, dizzy spell or something and had to be carried down, that's how it came to be overlooked." So I took it with me and went on down to try and locate him and hand it back to him.

I rang when I got to where the elevators started from, and

when the car had come up for me I asked the operator: "What happened to that fat guy, know the one I mean? Anything go wrong with him? I picked up his hat just now."

"He hasn't come down yet," he told me. "I'd know him in a minute. He must be still up there."

"He isn't up above, I just came from there myself. And he's the last guy in the world who'd walk down the six stories from here when there's a car to take him. How do you figure it?"

"Tell you where he might be," said the attendant. "Outside there on the parapet. They all go out there for a last look through the telescope before they get in the car."

"Well, wait up here for a minute until I find out. If he shows up tell him I've got his hat."

I went out and made a complete circuit of the place, then doubled back and did it in reverse. Not a soul on it. It was a sort of terrace that ran around the top of the base, protected by a waist-high stone ledge on all four sides. It was lower down than the head of Miss Liberty of course, but still plenty high.

I went back to the elevator operator. "Nothing doing. You sure you didn't take him down in your car without noticing?"

"Listen," he said. "When he got on the first time he almost flattened me against the door getting in. I woulda known it the second time. I ain't seen him since."

"Are there any lavatories or restrooms on the way up?"

"Naw," he said, "nothing like that."

"Then he musta walked down the rest of the way without waiting for you. Take me down to the bottom—"

"If he did, he's the first one ever did that yet. That's what the elevators are here for." He threw the switch. "Say," he said, and I saw his face light up as if he was almost hoping something would happen to break the monotony of his job, "maybe he—you don't suppose he—"

I knew what he was driving at. "You're trying to tell me he took a jump for himself, aren't you? G'wan, he couldn't have even raised himself up over that stone ledge out there to do it!

And if he had, there'd a been a crowd around him below. Everyone on the island woulda seen him land. I looked down just now. They're all strolling around down there, addressing postcards, taking it easy waiting for the boat."

His face dropped again. "They none of 'em try that from here, they always pick bridges instead. Nothing ever happens here."

"Cheer up, Suicide Johnny," I told him, "your cage will probably fall down the shaft some day and kill everyone in it."

When he let me out I made straight for the concession pavilion down near the pier, where most of the ten who had come out with me were hanging around buying postcards and ice-cream cones, waiting for the ferry to pull in. It wasn't more than fifty yards away by this time, coasting in a big half-circle from the right to get into position, with its engine already cut off.

The fat man wasn't in the refreshment house—one look inside from the doorway told me that. I asked one or two of the others if they'd seen him since they'd come out of the statue. Nobody had, although plenty had noticed him going in—especially on the way up—just as I had.

"He must be around some place," one of them suggested indifferently. "Couldn't very well get off the island until the ferry came back for him."

"No kidding?" I remarked brittlely. "And here I am thinking he went up in a puff of smoke!"

I went around to the other side of the base, following a series of cement walks bordered with ornamental cannonballs. No rotund gentleman in sight. I inquired at the dispensary at the back of the island, and even at one or two of the brick cottages the caretakers lived in, thinking he might have stopped in there because of illness or out of curiosity. Nothing doing.

I completed my circuit of the terraced lawn that surrounds the statue and returned to the front of it again. It had dawned on me by now that I was going to a hell of a whole lot of trouble just to return a man's hat to him, but his complete disappearance was an irritant that had me going in spite of myself. It was the size of the man that burned me more than anything. I wouldn't have minded if it had been somebody less conspicuous, probably wouldn't have noticed him in the first place, but to be as big as all that and then to evaporate completely—

The ferry was in when I got back and the passengers were straggling up the long, almost horizontal gangplank. It hadn't brought anybody out with it this trip, as the statue was closed to visitors after 4:30 each day and this was its last round trip. "Turn this in at the lost-and-found for me, will you?" I said, shoving the hat at one of the soldiers on pier-duty as I went by. "I just found it up there."

"Hand it in at the other end, at the Battery," he said. "That's where they come and claim things."

I was so dead-sure of lamping the lid's owner on the ferry, this being its last trip back, that I hung onto it without arguing and went looking for him in the saloon, or whatever they call the between-decks part of a ferry. Meanwhile the landing platform had been rolled back and we'd started to nose up the bay.

"He's got to be on here," I said to myself. "He's not spending the night back there on the island. And nothing that floats came to take him off between the time we all got off the first time and just now when this thing called back for us." I knew that for a fact, because the ferry only made the run once every hour, on the half-hour, and it was the only one in service. So I went all over the schooner from bow to stern, upstairs, downstairs, inside and out. In the saloon a couple of kids were sitting one on each side of their father, swinging their legs over the edge of the long bench that ran all around it. And a guy who didn't give a hoot about the skyline outside was reading Hellinger in the *Mirror*. Nobody else.

On the port deck the other half-dozen were sitting in chairs, just like they would on a transatlantic greyhound only without rugs, and one or two were leaning over the rail trying to kid themselves they were on an ocean trip. He wasn't there either. Then when I went around to the starboard deck (only maybe it was the port and the other was starboard, don't expect too much from a guy that was never further away than Coney Island), there was his wife sitting there as big as life, all by herself and the only person on that side of the scow which faced good old Joisey. I walked by her once and took a squint at her without stopping. She never even saw me. She was staring peacefully, even dreamily, out at the bay.

Now, I had no absolute proof that she was his wife, or had made the excursion with him at all. He had mentioned his wife to me, so his wife was along with him, no doubt about that. But each time I had overtaken him on one of the benches inside the statue she had gone up just ahead of him and I had missed seeing her. Then when I got up to the top this particular woman had been up there ahead of me scrawling her initials. That much I was sure of. She had been at the next observation window to me with that same "come-and-take-me" far-away look that she had now. But it was only by putting two and two together that I had her labeled as his wife; I had no definite evidence of it. So I stopped up at the other end of the narrow little deck and turned and started back toward her.

I don't care who a guy is or what his job is, it isn't easy for him to accost a woman sitting minding her own business like that, unless he's the masher type—which I'm not. "If she gives me a smack in the puss," I said to myself, "I'm gonna throw this son-of-a—hat in the water and make up my mind I never saw any fat guy; it was just a trick of the lighting effects in the statue!"

I stopped dead in my tracks in front of her and tipped my hat and said: "Pardon me, but I've got y'husband's hat here." I held it out.

She looked me up and down and a lot of little icicles went tinkling along the deck. "I don't know what you're talking about," she said. "I haven't any husband—and I'm not interested in picking one up on a ferryboat in the bay!"

This was enough to sour a saint; it was rubbing it in a little too much. First there's a fat man and his wife. Then there's no fat man. And now it seems there's no wife either. Only a hat.

"I'm no picker-upper," I growled. "Just let's get this straight though. On the way over I distinctly noticed you with a very hefty gentleman. You were talking to each other. You were sitting side by side out on this deck-bench. And you both stood up together when it was time to get off. I remember that distinctly, on account of your shapes reminded me of the number 10. Then later I saw the guy by himself in there. And that's the last; he does a fade-out. Now all I'm trying to do is get this blasted kelly back to—"

The temperature didn't go up any. "Well, why pick on me?" she said. "Why marry me off to him, and turn me into his hatcheck girl in the bargain? Who are you, anyway, the census-taker? All right, a fat clown did sit down next to me on the way out and try to take a shine to me. So what? I never saw him before in my life, don't know his name from Adam. You saw me talking to him all right—I told him a thing or two, only I'm not the kind screams for help and makes a scene. And if he stood up at the same time I did and tried to stick close to me, I outdistanced him once we hit those stairs, don't you worry. And if you think you rate any higher than he did just 'cause your stomach goes in instead of out, think again! Next time I go on an excursion I'm bringing a bulldog along—"

"Oh, just one of these strong, silent women! Not a word to say, eh?" I told her. "Well, suppose you give me your name and address just for fun."

She hoisted herself up and took a quick step away. "I'm going to get a cop!" she burst out.

I side-stepped around and got in front of her. "You've got one," I said, and let the badge slide back into my vest pocket again. "Now are you going to tell me what I asked you?"

"You can't compel me to give you my name if I don't want to!" she said hotly. "Who do you think you're dealing with, some fly-by-night chippy? I don't care whether you're a detec—"

Which was true enough, as far as that goes. But she had me steamed up by now. "Either you identify yourself, or you can consider yourself under arrest!" I didn't have a thing on her, and I knew it. I had no way of proving that what she had told me about the fat man wasn't so. True, he had mentioned his wife to me sitting on the bench in the statue, but he hadn't tagged this particular woman or anyone else in the group as being "it." He hadn't even made it clear whether his wife had accompanied him on the excursion. For all I knew she might be sitting at home at this very moment, just as my own was.

Meanwhile, "— never so insulted in my life!" she was boiling, but she was going through the motions of coming across, with angrily shaking hands. She threw back the lid of her pocketbook and fished around inside it. "I didn't expect a third degree like this," she snapped, "so I didn't bring my pedigree with me! However, I'm Alice Colman, Van Raalte Apartments, Tarrytown. Take it or leave it!"

I felt like two cents by now, especially as I noticed her eyes growing shiny with tears. Even if the fat man had met with foul play, which there was no proof of so far, she hadn't been anywhere near him at the time it happened. She had been away up at the top looking dreamy. I was only doing this because I'd seen them together on the trip out, and she needn't have made me feel like such a lug. I covered it up by going through with what I was doing, taking out my notebook and jotting down the info. "Miss Alice Colman," I said out loud, squinting down my pencil.

"I didn't say that!" she flared. "Oh, let me alone, you dog!" And she whisked herself off down the deck as if she couldn't stand any more. I could see her shoulders shaking as she went. I let her alone after that, didn't try to follow her up.

"Well, well, well," I sighed, "I certainly have the light touch with dolls!" Her last crack, I took it, meant that she was a Mrs. and not a Miss.

If I had any doubts that the fat guy might have turned out to be on the ferry after all, hiding behind a cuspidor or something, and that I had simply missed seeing him until now, they were very soon settled once the tub had tied up at the South Ferry landing. I stationed myself on the lower end of the plank ahead of everyone, and stopped them one by one as they tried to go past. "Police headquarters .... Name, please .... Address. Got anything to back it up?" And I killed the inevitable "What's this for?" each time it came with a terse "None of your business!"

When I was through I had a line on every one who had made the outing with me—at least if anything turned up now I was no longer in the dark. All but the very guy who was missing. And he was still missing. He had definitely not made the trip back on the boat. The Colman person was the last one off, and came sailing by me head in air with the cold remark: "Be sure you follow me— low-down common bully!" I just stood there and looked after her, scratching my head. It was only after she'd gone that I realized she was the only one of the lot who hadn't backed up her name and address with documentary proof.

But meanwhile there was something else I wanted to see about.

I went around to the ticket office in the ferry building; it was closed, of course. Ours had been the last trip of the day. I hammered on the wicket, and then I went around and pounded on the door. Luckily they were still in there, counting the day's receipts or something. I recognized the guy that had sold me my own ticket. "Headquarters, it's all right, lemme in a minute." And when he had, "Now look. Do you remember selling a ticket down the bay to a fat guy, puffy cheeks like this, blue suit, brown hat, when the last boatful went out?"

"Yeah," he said, "yeah, I do."

"How many did he buy? One or two?"

"Two," he said decidedly. "I been selling 'em all day long, but I can remember that all right because he was lamebrained, couldn't count straight. He wanted to tell me four-forty change was coming to him out of a firm. I says, 'Buddy,' I says, 'in my country two times thirty-five adds up to—' "

"Never mind the trailer," I squelched. "Did she—did anyone come up to the window with him when he bought them?"

"Naw, he come up to the window alone and bought two tickets. I didn't see who was with him."

"Being sore at him, you didn't take a gander out the window after him after he moved on? Most ticket-sellers would."

"They were all on line," he explained. "I didn't have time, had to wait on the next rubberneck."

Well, if he'd bought two tickets his wife was with him—he hadn't bought them just because he was overweight himself, that was a cinch. As for his wife, runner-up to himself when it came to staying out of sight, little Alice Colman was elected for the time being. Which added up to this—I was going back to that island. She could hold for awhile. If nothing had happened to him, then it was none of my business whether she was wife, girl-friend, or total stranger to him. But if something had—I wasn't forgetting that she was the only person outside myself I'd seen him talking to.

I beat it outside to the ferry again. It was still there, but fixing to go wherever it is they go for the night when they're not in service. Or maybe it was just going to stay put. But not while I knew it.

A couple of tattooed arms tried to bar my way up the gangplank. "One side," I said, and the badge was getting a high polish just from rubbing against the serge so much, "I gotta see the captain before he slips off his suspenders!"

"He uses safety-pins," he corrected me dryly, "but go ahead—"

He came out of the saloon just then struggling into a lumber-jacket, evidently going ashore to catch up on his suds.

"Say, y'gotta take me back there," I burst out. "Here's what—" And I explained all about the hefty passenger that had gone out and hadn't come back.

He was one person the badge didn't mean a thing to; he was used to being boss of the roost. "Go 'way, man, you're out of your head!" he boomed. "This boat's asleep for tonight, I wouldn't make another run there for St. Peter himself. If he missed it and got left behind, that's his tough luck. He'll just have to wait over until nine in the morning, there are plenty of benches on the island, just like Central P—" and he took the most graceful spiral spit over the rail I had ever seen—and made it.

"But y' don't get what I mean!" I howled, shoving the brown

felt in his face. "He didn't just miss it—something's happened to him. Now give your orders. You know what this means, don't you? You're obstructing—"

"I take my orders from the company," he said surlily, looking longingly in the direction of the dives along South Street. "If that piece of tin means anything why don't it get you a police launch?"

But I wasn't going to be a back-room laughing-stock for the rest of the year in case I did get there with a launch and find the fat guy had stayed behind to pick dandelions or something. I went ashore again and had it out with one of the agents in the ferry house, and he in turn had to telephone one of the higher muck-a-mucks and put it up to him, and then sign an order for me to show the captain.

Some reporters had gotten wind that something was up, in the mysterious way that only reporters can, and a couple of them were already hanging around outside when I came out. "What's the excitement?" they wanted to know, licking their chops. "What's it all about?" "Wotcha doing with two hats?" one of them cracked suspiciously.

"I always carry a spare," I said, "in case the wind blows the first one off."

They looked sort of doubtful, but before they could do anything about it I was back on the ferry and gave orders to keep them off. "Here's your instructions, admiral," I told the captain, who was drooling by this time and biting his nails at the thought of being kept overtime. "I'll buy the first ten rounds," I assured him, "if this turns out to be a wild-goose chase."

"*Hrrmph!*" he growled, and turned around and hollered an order.

Back we plugged.

"How long you gonna be?" he wanted to know as I loped off at the island.

"When I show up again," I promised, "I'll be back." That old fellow could swear.

The thick, chilly-looking, black metal doors that led into the base were shut by this time. I had to get another permit from an officer on the island, and two soldiers were detailed to come with me. The only one who seemed to get any kick out of the proceedings was Suicide Johnny, who was routed out to run us up in the elevator. He was all grins. At last something was happening to break his monotony. "Gee," he said, throwing the switch in the car, "maybe he committed sewercide by hanging himself up there some place!"

"Nuts," I growled, "he couldn't have hoisted himself an inch—not without a derrick. We'll go up to the top," I told my two escorts when we got out of the car. "Start in from there and work our way down." They didn't say anything, but I could read their minds: "This guy was dropped on his head when he was a kid."

We climbed all that weary way back again and finally stood there panting. "He never got up this far," I said when I had my wind back, "because I was up here ahead of him. But I want to take a gander at some of these initials and names scrawled here on the stonework of the windows."

"Aw, them!" said one of the soldiers contemptuously. "Every chump that ever comes up here since the place was built has a crack at that."

"That's just the point," I said. I had a close look, first of all, at what my chief rooter and admirer Alice Colman had written, at the window next to the one I'd been standing at originally. It didn't say Alice Colman, it didn't say any name, but I knew her work. She'd used an eyebrow pencil and the mark it left was dark and greasy, different from the thin, faint pencil marks of the rest of them. It stood out like a headline on a newspaper.

I turned to one of the bored soldiers. "What's today's date?"

"The twenty-third," he said.

That's what I'd thought it was too. But Alice Colman seemed to have gotten her dates mixed. She had it down as the twenty-fourth. Well, that could happen to anyone. But she had the hour right, at least. She'd even put that down—4 o'clock. Some people are like that, though. She'd visited this place at four o'clock and she wanted the world to know.

On top of that, though, came a hitch. She had an address down, and it wasn't her own. It was just five numbers and a letter, all run together. *254W51.* But that wasn't her own address. She'd given me that on the ferry, and I'd checked on it while I was hanging around in the ferry house waiting for the permit to come back here. Yes, the management of the Van Raalte Apartments had told me long-distance over the phone from Tarrytown, that Mrs. Alice Colman was a tenant of theirs. So she hadn't lied to me, yet she'd lied to the world at large when she was making her mark on Lady Liberty. There was something that I didn't get about it.

"Let's go down," I told the soldiers, "I want to look at that bench he was sitting on." By this time they both hated me heartily from the guts outward, I could see, but they turned and led the way.

We never got there, though. About midway between the head and where the bench was—in other words at about where the statue's shoulder came—there was a gap with a chain across it bearing the placard *Public Not Admitted.* I had noticed this twice before, the first time I came up and then later when I had gone down to look for him. Maybe the chain had thrown me off, the undisturbed chain stretched across it. And then, too, until you stood directly before it, it looked far smaller and more inaccessible than it actually was, the way the lights slurred past it and made it seem no more than a fold on the inside of the lady's gigantic metal draperies. This time, though, I stopped and asked them what it was.

"Oh, he ain't up in there!" they assured me instantly. "Nobody's allowed in there. Can't you read what that says? That used to lead up into the arm and torch in the old days. The arm started weakening little by little, so they shut the whole thing off a long time ago. It's boarded up just a little ways past the ch— Hey!" he broke off. "Where you going? You can't do that!"

"I'm going just that little ways between the chain and where the boarding is," I told him, spanning the cable with one leg. "If the arm lasted this long, one more guy ain't going to hurt it, I don't weigh enough. Throw your lights up after me. And don't tell me what I can't do when you see me already at it!"

The thing was a spiral, just like the other staircase that led to the head. Or rather, it started out to be, but at the very first half-turnaround it took, the boarding had already showed up, sealing it from top to bottom. That half-turn, however, cut off their lights, which shone in a straight line like any lights would. A triangle of blackness was left in one corner which they couldn't eliminate, no matter how they maneuvered the torches.

"Come on a little nearer with those things!" I called impatiently. "Come past the chain!"

They wouldn't budge. "Against orders," they called back.

I came down a few steps and reached for a torch myself. "Let me have one of those things. What d'ya think I'm doing, playing hide and seek with you? How we won the last war beats me!" I jumped up again and washed out the stubborn wedge of blackness with the thin beam in my hand.

Sure he was there. And fitted in just as neatly as though the space had been measured off for him ahead of time. In a sitting position on the turn of the steps, back propped against the boarding, legs drawn up under him to help keep him propped. I touched the side of his neck. He was as cold already as the metal statue that made a tomb for him.

"Got him," I shouted laconically. "Come on up and gimme a hand, you two."

"What's he doing up there?" one of those two clucks wanted to know.

"Waiting for judgment day."

They gasped and came on up, orders or no orders.

I bent down and looked at the backs of his shoes. The leather of both heels was scraped and scarred into a fuzz from lift to ankle. The backs of his trousers were dusty all the way to the knees. "Dragged up by the shoulders," I said, "by just one guy. If there'd been two, one of them would have taken him by the feet, like you're going to do getting him down out of here."

"How could one guy, any guy, haul that baby elephant all the way up there?" one of them wanted to know.

"You'd be surprised what one guy can manage to do if he's scared enough and has to work in a hurry," I assured him. "All right, get started. I'll handle your lights. It wasn't done up here anyway, so let's get down before we all take a header into the ocean, arm and all."

It wasn't easy, even for the two of them, to get down with him. Automatically, I figured that eliminated Alice Colman or any other woman as having had any part in it—except as an accessory.

The thing that had done it was lying under him when they got him up off the ground between them—a wicked-looking iron bar wrapped in a stiffened, blood-brown piece of rag. The wound—it was a deadly fracture—was on the side of the head just over the ear. He hadn't bled much, outside of the first splash on the padded weapon itself. The little there was after that had clung to the skin, running down behind the jawbone and into the collar of his shirt, hence nothing on the ground around the bench where the attack had occurred.

I examined the ground around the latter place. The two little tracks his heels had made as he was dragged backwards toward the hiding-place were there plain as day under my flashlight's beam, without the need of any powder or hocus-pocus of any kind. My only wonder was how I'd muffed seeing them when I stooped down to pick up his hat. But of course I hadn't used my torch then.

"Take him on down the rest of the way," I said. "No use parking with him here—it's gotta be done sooner or later anyway."

They loved the job—yeah they did! They must have lost ten pounds apiece in sweat, getting him down those seventeen stories of narrow, spiral staircase. When they were down at the elevator you could hear their heaving all the way up where I was. When I got down myself—I'd waited on the murder bench until the way was clear, no use dogging their footsteps an inch at a time— Suicide Johnny, with the body tucked into his car and the two guards in a state of collapse alongside of it, was wreathed in smiles. His fondest dream had come true. Something had at last happened. "Gee!" he kept murmuring. "Gee! A moider!"

I had Fatty carried over to the barracks, and an apoplectic-looking guy of Spanish War vintage whose collar was too tight for him came out to see what it was all about.

"Sorry to bother you," I said, "but there's just been a crime committed on your jurisdiction—man murdered up in the statue."

"Who are you, sirrr?" he boomed like a twenty-one gun salute. I felt like I was going to be shot at sunrise for daring to find anything the matter around his diggings.

"Denton, New York Homicide," I told him.

"Are you sure, sirrrr?" the old rooster crowed. He meant about the murder, not who I was. He wasn't going to believe me until he saw it with his own eyes, so I took him over and showed it to him.

"Now, just where do I stand?" I said, resting my hand on the stiff's knee.

"This, sirr," he orated, "is United States Government property. This is a matter for the Federal inves—"

I'd expected that. "Oh, so I get the air!" I interrupted heatedly. "After I been up and down that blank statue eighty-six times today. O.K., you put who you want on it. I'm going right ahead with it on my own. And we'll see who comes out ahead!" I got as far as the door, then I turned around and fired at him: "I'll even give your guy a head-start, just so you can't accuse me of withholding information. This guy is tagged Colman. He lived until today at the Van Raalte Apartments, Tarrytown, with his wife, who is thin, blond, pretty, blue eyes, about twenty-eight, and very ritzy front. But you won't find her there any more, so you can tell your guy to save his carfare. She didn't do it anyway. But if you want to get hold of her, and the guy that actually did it, I'll tell you where to look for them—"

"Where, sirrr?" he boomed like a great big firecracker.

"Today is Wednesday, isn't it?" I answered detachedly. "Well, send your guy around to Centre Street, say day after tomorrow, that would be Friday. We'll be holding 'em both for you down there by that time. No trouble at all, Field Marshal." He sort of blew up internally, so I got out before he did anything about calling a firing squad.

I ducked into the statue again, for what I hoped was the last time, and decided to make Suicide Johnny useful, since he seemed to be enjoying himself so. "How would you like to help?" I said. "Come on up with me."

When we got all the way up to the head, I took out my pocket notebook and opened it at the page where all the names were, the names I'd collected from the ten (eight really, excluding the two kids with their father) who had made the trip here and back on the ferry. Excluding Colman himself and his wife (who couldn't have been an actual participant for reasons I've already given) that left six. Excluding two other women who'd been in the group, that boiled it down to four. Now the name, of course, was going to be phony—I mean the name the actual murderer had handed me—that was a pushover. But that didn't matter. All I wanted was to connect the right guy with any name, phony or otherwise, just so I could remember something about what he'd looked like. Any little thing at all.

"You take a pencil," I told Suicide, "and each time I call out a name, you cross off the corresponding one written down there in that book. That's all."

"Gee!" he said. "I'm helping a real detective!"

"My chief," I answered drily, "sometimes has grave doubts about that. Ready? Let's go." I started going over the window-ledges inch by inch. They were crawling with names and initials, but I finally located one that matched one in the notebook. Johnny promptly crossed it out. Then another. Then a triple initial that matched. "Don't cross yet," I warned him, "just put a check next to that."

Well, when we got through, we had nine of the ten names, women, kids and all. Each and every one of them had scribbled their names as mementoes on the stone work. "Now, which one's left over?" I asked Suicide.

He screwed up his face and read off: "Vincent Scanlon, 55 Amboy Street, Brooklyn, real estate."

"On circumstantial alone, that's my guy."

"Hully mackerel!" said the enraptured Johnny. "Can y'tell just by hearing his name like that?"

"His name ain't Scanlon, he don't live on Amboy Street, and he's not in real estate," I tried to explain. "But he's the only one of the bunch that didn't come up here and scrawl his John Hancock. Me and the fat guy were the last ones coming up the stairs. When I left him on the bench he was still alive. When I got up here myself even his wife was up here ahead of me, and all the others had finished their signatures and were on their way down again. Therefore, this guy who tags himself Scanlon was the murderer. Don't you understand, he never went all the way to the top. He either came up the stairs behind me and the fat guy, or else if he was ahead of us switched into the opening that leads up into the arm, let everyone else go by, and then crept down again to where the bench was—and did his dirty work the minute the coast was clear."

I took a notebook from him, hold it open before me, and did my damndest to try and separate the party that had given me that name from the other ten. I tried to remember some feature about him, some detail, anything at all, and couldn't, no matter how I racked my brains. There had been too many of them at one time, all getting off the ferry at once, all stopping in front of me just for a half-minute or so. He should have been nervous, just coming away from doing a thing like that, should have been pale, tense, jumpy, anything you want to call it—should have given himself away in some way, if not right then, then now that I was thinking back over it. But he either hadn't, or—what was more likely—I was pretty much of a wash-out at my own business. I couldn't even get him by elimination, the way I had gotten his phony name. One or two of the others started to come clear—the father of the two kids, the two other women besides Alice Colman—but not him. I might just as well have written down that name out of my own head for all I could remember of the man who had given it to me.

I took another look at Alice Colman's regards to the statue and wondered why she hadn't put her name down with it, and how she had come to be mixed up on her dates the way she had. And why a different address from her own. Of course the obvious answer was that she knew g.d. well what was taking place on that stairway below at the time, and was too nervous to know what she was doing. But she hadn't acted nervous at all, she had just acted dreamy. So that probably wasn't the answer at all. And just for luck I transcribed the thing into my notebook exactly as it stood in eyebrow pencil. 4/24/35/4 and then, 254W51. Wrong date, right hour, wrong address, no name.

"I take it all back, Johnny," I said wearily. "Kick me here— and here. The guy did come up here after all—and right on top of what he did too."

"But he didn't write nothing—you looked all over them wind—"

"He didn't come up here to write, he came to read." I pointed at it. "He came to read that. Let's go down. I guess I can keep my promise to General Lafayette down there after all."

When I got ashore I halfheartedly checked Colman at the Tarrytown Apartments once more. No, neither Mr. nor Mrs. had come back yet, they told me after paging them on the house phone. I didn't tell them so, but they might just as well have hung out a to-let sign and gotten ready to rent that apartment all over again. He wasn't coming back any more because he was spending the night at the morgue. And she wasn't coming back any more either—because she had a heavy date at 4. As for Scanlon's Amboy Street address, I didn't even bother with it. Have to use your common sense once in awhile. Instead I asked Information to give me 254 West 51st Street, which was the best I could make out of the tag end of her billet-doux.

"Capital Bus Terminal," a voice answered at the other end.

So that's where they were going to meet, was it? They'd stayed very carefully away from each other on the ferry going back, and ditto once they were ashore in New York. But they were going to blow town together. So it looked like she hadn't had her days mixed after all, she'd known what she was doing when she put tomorrow's date down. "What've you got going out at four?" I said.

"A.M. or P.M.?" said the voice. But that was just the trouble, I didn't know myself. Yet if I didn't know, how was he going to know either? I mean Scanlon. The only thing to do was tackle both meridians, one at a time. A.M. came first, so I took that. He spieled off a list a foot long but the only big-time places among them were Boston and Philly. "Make me a reservation on each," I snapped.

"Mister," the voice came back patiently, "how can you go two places at once?"

"I'm twins," I squelched and hung up. Only one more phone call, this time to where I was supposed to live but so seldom did. "I may see you tomorrow. If I came home now I'd only have to set the alarm for three o'clock."

"I thought it was your day off."

"I've got statues on the brain."

"You mean you would have if you had a—" she started to say, but I ended that.

I staggered into the bus waiting room at half past three, apparently stewed to the gills, with my hat brim turned down to meet my upturned coat collar. They just missed ouch other enough to let my nose through, the rest was shadow. I wasn't one of those drunks that make a show of themselves and attract a lot of attention, I just slumped onto a bench and quietly went to sleep. Nobody gave me a first look, let alone a second one.

I was on the row of benches against the wall, not out in the middle where people could sit behind me. At twenty to four by the clock I suddenly remembered exactly what this guy Scanlon had looked like on the ferry that afternoon. Red hair, little pig-eyes set close together—what difference did it make now, there he was, valise between his legs. He had a newspaper up over his face in a split second, but a split second is plenty long enough to remember a face in.

But I didn't want him alone, didn't dare touch him alone until she got there, and where the hell was she? Quarter to, the clock said—ten to—five. Or were they going to keep up the bluff and leave separately, each at a different time, and only get together at the other end? Maybe that message on the statue hadn't been a date at all, only his instructions. I saw myself in for a trip to Philly, Boston, what-have-you, and without a razor, or an assignment from the chief.

The handful of late-night travelers stirred, got up, moved outside to the bus, got in, with him very much in the middle of them. No sign of her. It was the Boston one. I strolled back and got me a ticket, round-trip. Now all that should happen would be that she should breeze up and take the Philly one—and me without anyone with me to split the assignment!

"Better hurry, stew," said the ticket seller handing me my change, "you're going to miss that bus."

"Mr. Stew to you," I said mechanically, with a desperate look all around the empty waiting room. Suddenly the door of the ladies' restroom flashed open and a slim, sprightly figure dashed by, lightweight valise in hand. She must have been hiding in there for hours, long before he got here.

"Wait a minute!" she started to screech to the driver the minute she hit the open. "Wait a minute! Let me get on!" She just made it, the door banged, and the thing started.

There was only one thing for me to do. I cut diagonally across the lot, and when the driver tried to make the turn that would take him up Fifty-first Street I was wavering in front of his headlights. Wavering but not budging. "Wash'ya hurry?" I protested. His horn racketed, then he jammed on his brakes, stuck his head out the side, and showed just how many words he knew that he hadn't learned in Sunday School.

"Open up," I said, dropping the drunk act and flashing my badge. "You don't come from such nice people. And just like that"—I climbed aboard—"you're short three passengers. Me—and this gentleman here—and, let's see, oh yeah, this little lady trying so hard to duck down behind the seat. Stand up, sister, and get a new kind of bracelet on your lily-white wrist."

Somebody or other screamed and went into a faint at the sight of the gun, but I got them both safely off and waved the awe-stricken driver on his way.

"And now," I said as the red tail lights burned down Eighth Avenue and disappeared, "are you two going to come quietly or do I have to try out a recipe for making goulash on you?"

"What was in it for you?" I asked her at Headquarters. "This Romeo of yours is no Gable for looks."

"Say lissen," she said scornfully, accepting a cigarette, "if you were hog-tied to something that weighed two hundred ninety pounds and couldn't even take off his own shoes, but made three grand a month, and banked it in your name, and someone came along that knew how to make a lady's heart go pit-a-pat, you'd a done the same thing too!"

I went home and said: "Well, I've gotta hand it to you. I looked at a statue like you told me to, and it sure didn't hurt my record any." But I didn't tell which statue or why. "What's more," I said, "we're going down to Washington and back over the week-end."

"Why Washington?" my wife wanted to know.

"Cause they've got the biggest of the lot down there, called the Washington Monument. And a lotta guys that think they're good, called Federal dicks, hang out there and need help."

PREVIEW OF DEATH

Preview of Death was originally published in *Dime Detective* in November of 1934. This story was inspired by Woolrich's less successful screenwriting career, and the fascination gained from the death of actress Martha Mansfield on the set of *The Warrens of Virginia* in 1923. The popularity of this story comes from the combination of pulp and noir elements, coupled with a bizarre death. Woolrich also used this literary device in *Times Square* for the character of the lead actress. In the late 50's, this story was updated and heavily rewritten as *Screen-Test* to be included in Dodd Mead's 1956 collection entitled *Nightmare*.

IT WAS WHAT somebody or other has called life's darkest moment. My forehead was dripping perspiration and I stared miserably down at the floor. "But, Chief," I said when he got all through thundering at me, "all I had was a couple of beers and besides I wasn't on duty at the time. And how was I to know that that wasn't the right way out of the place? I only found out it was a plate-glass window when I came through on the other side of it. And my gun didn't go off, you can look for yourself. It was some car out in the street that back-fired just then and made everybody clear out in such a hurry. You're not going to break me for that, are you?"

"No," he said, "but I'm going to give you a nice quiet assignment that'll keep you out of trouble for awhile. You're going to look after Martha Meadows from now on, she's been getting threatening letters and her studio just called and asked us to furnish her with protection. That's you until further orders."

"I resign," I said when I heard that.

He switched his cigar from the left-hand corner to the right-hand corner without putting a finger to it, leaned half-way across his desk at me, and went into another electrical storm. A lot of fist-pounding on the mahogany went with it. You couldn't hear yourself think, he was making that much noise. "Resign? You can't resign! Over my dead body you'll resign! What d'ya think this squad is, a game of in-again out-again Finnigan?"

"But-but Chief," I pleaded, "bodyguard to a-a movie actress! All the rest of the boys will laugh at me, I'll never be able to live it down! And what'll the wife say? Dock me, break me-anything but that!"

He rattled some papers around and held them up in front of his face. Maybe to keep from weakening, I don't know. *"Ahem-*

now not another word out of you, Galbraith. Off you go. Get right out there and don't let her out of your sight until further notice. Remember, your job isn't to trace these threats or track down whoever sent 'em, it's just to keep your eye on Martha Meadows and see that nothing happens to her. You're responsible for her safety."

"O.K., Chief," I sighed, "but I really should be wearing a dog collar."

No doubt about it, I was the unhappiest, most miserable detective that ever started out on an assignment as I walked out of headquarters that day and got in a taxi. The sooner I got busy on the job, I figured, the sooner the chief might relent and take me off it. The taxi, and everything else from now on, was at Miss Meadows' own personal expense, but that didn't make me like her any the better. Without actually wishing her any harm, I was far from being a fan of hers at the moment.

The studio, on Marathon Street, looked more like a library than anything else from the outside. The gateman picked up a phone, said: "From headquarters, to see Miss Meadows," and everything opened up high, wide and handsome. I passed from hand to hand like a volley-ball getting to her; and all of them, from the gateman right on up, seemed glad that I had been sent over to look after her. You could tell she was well liked.

She was in her bungalow dressing-room resting between scenes and having her lunch when they brought me in. Her lunch was a malted milk and a slice of sponge cake – not enough to keep a canary alive. She had a thick make-up on, but even at that she still looked like somebody's twelve-year-old sister. You sort of wanted to protect her and be her big brother the minute you set eyes on her, even if you hadn't been sent there for just that purpose – the way I had. I'm Jimmy Galbraith from headquarters, Miss Meadows," I said.

She gave me a friendly smile. "You don't look a bit like a detective," she answered, "you look like a college boy."

Just to put her in her place I said: "And you don't look a bit like a screen star, you look like a little girl in grade school, rigged up for the school play."

Just then a colored woman, her maid I guess, looked in and started to say, "Honey lamb, is you nearly-" Then when she saw me she changed to: "Look here, man, don't you bring that cigarette in here, you want to burn that child up?" I didn't know what she meant for a minute, I wasn't anywhere near Meadows.

"Hush up, Nellie," Martha Meadows ordered with a smile. "She means this," Meadows explained, and pointed to her dress: "It has celluloid underneath, to stiffen it. If a spark gets on it—" She was dressed as a Civil War belle, with a wide hoopskirt the size of a balloon. I pinched the cigarette out between my fingers in a hurry.

"Just cause it ain't happen', don't mean it can't happen," snapped the ferocious Nellie, and went about her business muttering darkly to herself. The dressing-room telephone rang and Meadows said: "Alright, I'm ready whenever you are." She turned to me. "I have to go back on the set now. We're shooting the big scene this afternoon."

"Sorry," I said, "but I'll have to go with you, those are my orders."

"It's agreeable to me," she said, "but the director mayn't like outsiders watching him. He's very temperamental, you know."

I wasn't even sure what the word meant, so I looked wise and said: "He'll get over it."

She started up and the three of us left the bungalow. I let the maid and her go in front and followed close behind them. They walked along a number of lanes between low one-story studio buildings and finally came to a big barn of a place that had sliding doors like a garage and a neat little sign up: *Set VIII, Meadows, Civil War Picture.* People were hanging around outside, some in costume and some not. They made way for her respectfully and she passed through them and went in. She bowed slightly to one or two and they nearly fell over themselves bowing back.

Inside, the place had a cement floor criss-crossed over with a lot of little steel rails like baby train tracks. They were for moving heavy camera trucks back and forth, and cables and ropes and wires and pulleys galore were dangling from the rafters. Canvas back-drops were stacked, like cards, up against the walls. But it wasn't out here they were going to shoot the scene at all. There was a sound-proof door with a red light over it leading in to the "stage" itself, where the action was to take place.

Before we got to it, though, a bald-headed man in a pullover sweater came up to Meadows. He was about five feet tall and with a beak like an eagle's. A girl carrying a thick notebook, like a stenographer's dictation pad, was following him around wherever he went. I had him spotted for the director as soon as I looked at him.

"Who is this man?" he asked – meaning me. Then, when she told him, he raised both hands to his head and would have torn out some hair, only, as I said before, he was bald. "No," he said, "I cannot work! There are too many people hanging around the stage already! First it was your colored maid. Now a detective! Who will it be next?"

A big argument started in then and there about whether I was to go in or stay out, with Meadows taking my part and the script-girl trying to calm the director down. "Now, Stormy," she kept saying, "please don't excite yourself, this isn't good for you, remember how sensitive you are!" Finally I cut the whole thing short by saying I'd phone the chief and leave it up to him, as he was the one who had given me the assignment. But there was no telephone in the place and I had to go outside and call up headquarters from the studio cafeteria next door.

The chief went off like a firecracker. "What's the matter with them anyway? First they ask me for a bodyguard for her, then they start shooing him away. You go in there, Gal, and if they try to keep you out, quit the case cold and report back here to me. I'll wash my hands of all responsibility for her safety!" Which was music to my ears, as I hadn't liked the job from the start.

Sure enough, when I got back, the sound-proof door was already closed, the red light was on above it to warn that "shooting" was going on, and they had all gone in without waiting. There was a guard stationed outside the door to keep people from opening it by accident.

"She left word for you to wait out here," he told me. "Stormann bullied her into going in without you."

"Oh, he did, did he?" I burned. "The little shrimp! Who does he think he is? He may be the whole limburger around here but he isn't even a bad smell to us down at headquarters!" The chief had told me what to do, but Stormann's opposition somehow got my goat so beautifully that instead of quitting I hung around, just for the pleasure of telling him a thing or two when he came out. To crash in now would have ruined the scene, cost the company thousands of dollars, and maybe gotten Meadows in bad with her bosses; so I didn't have the heart to do it.

"They'll be through about four," the guard told me. It was now a little before two.

Whether I would have stuck it out for two whole hours, outside that door, just to bawl Stormann out – I don't know. I never will know. At 2:10 or thereabouts the door suddenly opened from the inside without any warning and through it came the horrible unearthly screams of the dying. Nothing could scream like that and live very long.

"Something's happened!" he blurted. "That's not in the scene! I know,

It was Meadows' maid. Only she was almost white now. Her voice was gone from fright. "Oh, somebody – quick, somebody!" she panted. "I've been hammering on this door-" But she wasn't the victim. The screaming went right on behind her.

I rushed in, the guard with me. The sight that met us was ghastly. Martha Meadows, with the cameras still playing on her, was burning to death there before everyone's eyes. She was a living torch, a funnel of fire from head to foot, and screaming her life away. She was running blindly here and there, like some kind of a horrible human pin wheel, and they were all trying to overtake her and catch her to throw something over her and put the flames out. But she was already out of her head, mad with agony, and kept eluding them, ducking and doubling back and forth with hellish agility. What kept her going like that, with her life going up in blazing yellow-white gushes, I don't understand. I'll see that scene for years to come.

But I didn't stand there watching. I flung myself at her bodily, head first right into the flames in a football tackle. With stinging hands I grasped something soft and quivering behind that glow that had once been cool, human flesh. The pillar of fire toppled over and lay horizontal along the ground, with the flames foreshortened now and just licking upward all around it like bright scallops. With that, a blanket or something was thrown over her, and partly over me, too. As it fell with a puff of horrid black smoke spurting out all around the edges, the last scream stopped and she was still.

I held my breath, so as not to inhale any of the damned stuff. I could feel rescuing hands beating all around the two of us through the blanket. After a minute I picked myself up. My hands were smarting, my shirt cuffs were scorched brown in places and peeling back, and sparks had eaten into the front of my suit. Otherwise I was alright. But what lay under the blanket didn't move. Five minutes ago one of the most beautiful girls in America, and now something it was better not to look at if you had a weak stomach.

As if in gruesome jest, the winking eyes of the cameras were still turned upon her and, in the deathly silence that had now fallen, you could hear the whirring noise that meant they were still grinding away. No one had thought of signaling them to stop.

The guard who had been outside the door, though, had had the presence of mind to send in a call for help even before the flames had been beaten out. The studio had a first-aid station of its own a door or two away, and two men arrived with a stretcher and carried her out with them, still under the blanket. Nellie went with them, bellowing like a wounded steer and calling: "Oh, Lawd, oh Lawd, don't do this to my lamb! Change yo' mind, change yo' mind!"

Stormann was shaking like a leaf and incoherent with shock, and had to be fed whiskey by one of the electricians. The girl with the notebook, the script-girl, was the only one there who seemed to have kept her head about her. I went up to her, dabbing some oil they'd given me onto the red patches on the back of my hands and wrists, and asked: "How'd it happen?"

It turned out she wasn't as bright as I thought she'd be. "It happened right here," she said. "I was following very closely, the way I'm supposed to—that's my job." I looked to find out where "here" was, but instead of pointing any place on the set, she was pointing at her book.

"See – where it says 'Oh won't he ever come?' That's her line. She's supposed to be waiting by the window for her lover. Well, she spoke it alright, and then the next thing I knew, there was a funny flickering light on the pages of my book. When I looked up, I saw that it was coming from her. She had flames all over her. Well, just from force of habit, I quickly looked back at the book to find out whether or not this was part—"

I gave her up as a complete nut. Or at least a very efficient script-girl but a washout otherwise. I tackled Stormann next. He was on his third or fourth bracer by now and wringing his hands and moaning something about: "My picture, my beautiful picture"

"Pull yourself together," I snapped. "Isn't there anyone around here who has a heart? She's thinking about her book, you're thinking about your picture. Well, I'm thinking about that poor miserable girl. Maybe you can tell me how it happened. You're the director and you're supposed to have been watching what went on!"

Probably no one had ever spoken to him that way in years. His mouth dropped open. I grabbed him by the shoulder, took his snifter away from him, and gave him a shake. "Let me have it, brother, before I go sour on you. I'm asking you for your testimony – as a witness. You can consider this a preliminary inquest."

I hadn't forgotten that it was his doing I'd been kept out of here earlier, either. Seeing that he wasn't up against one of his usual yes-men, he changed his mind and gave until it hurt. "No one was near her at the time, I can't understand what could have caused it. I was right here on the side-lines where I always sit, she was over there by that win-"

"Yeah, I know all that. Here's what I'm asking you. Did you or did you not see what did it?" Not liking him, I got nasty with him and tapped him ten times on the chest with the point of my finger, once for each word, so it would sink in. The idea of anyone doing that to him was so new to him he didn't dare let out a peep. "No," he said, like a little kid in school.

"You didn't. Well, was anyone smoking a cigarette in here?"

"Absolutely not!" he said. "No director allows it, except when the scene calls for it. The lenses would pick up the haze-"

"Did she touch any wires, maybe?"

"There aren't any around, you can see for yourself. This whole thing's supposed to be the inside of an old mansion."

"What about this thing?" I picked up a lighted oil lamp that was standing on the fake window sill, but when I looked, I saw that it had an electric pocket-torch hidden in it. I put it down again. "Who was playing the scene with her? She wasn't alone in it, was she?"

"Ruth Tobias. That girl crying over there." I let him go back to his pain-killer and went over to tackle her. She was having grade-A mysteries across the back of a chair, but, as I might have known, on her own account, not poor Meadows'.

"Two whole years-" she gurgled, "two whole years to make a come back. I've waited – and now, look! They won't hire me again. I'm getting older –"

"Alright sis, turn off the faucets," I said. "Uncle wants to ask you something. What happened to her?"

She had on one of the same wide dresses as the kid had, but she was gotten up to look older-black gloves and a lorgnette with her hair in a cranky knot. At that, she wasn't out of her twenties yet, but looked as though she'd been used as a filling-station for a bootlegger while she was out of work the last few years.

"I played her older sister," she sniffled, "although they really had a nerve to cast me in an older part like that. I had to take anything I could get. I was in that rocker there on the set, facing her way. I'm supposed not to approve of the fellow she's intending to run off with, but all I do to show it is to keep rocking back and forth. She had her back to me, over at the window – I tell you I was looking right at her and all of a sudden, *ffft,* she was on fire from head to foot! As quickly as that, and for no earthly reason that I could make out! All I had time to do was jump back out of the way myself-"

"You would," I thought, but without saying so.

She gave me a sort of a come-on smile and said: "You're not a bad-looking guy at all for a detective."

"That's what my wife and eighteen kids tell me," I squelched her.

"Hmf," she said, and went over to chisel a drink from Stormann.

Just then they sent word in that, impossible as it sounded, Meadows was still breathing. She was going fast, though – just a matter of minutes now. They'd given her morphine to kill the pain.

"Is she conscious or out?" I asked.

"Semi-conscious."

"Quick then, let me have a look at her before she goes!"

It was a slim chance, but maybe she, herself, knew what or who had done it. Maybe she, alone, of all of them, had seen what caused it and hadn't been able to prevent it in time to save herself.

On my way out, I collared the guard, who was back at the door again keeping out the crowd of extras and employees who had heard the news.

"Consider yourself a deputy," I said to him in an undertone. "See that they all stay where they are until I get back. Whatever you do, see that nothing's touched on that set – not even a match stick. Keep everything just the way it is-"

It was a monstrous thing they showed me in that bed, dark as the room was. Without eyes, without ears, without nose, without any human attribute. An oversized pumpkin-head, a Halloween goblin, made of yards and yards of interlaced gauze bandaging. It stood out whitely in the greenish dimness cast by the lowered shades. A crevice between the bandages served as a mouth. Atop the sheets were two bandaged paws. She was conscious, but partly delirious from the heat of the burns and "high" from the morphine that kept her from feeling the pain in her last moments. The faithful Nellie was there beside her, silent now and with her forehead pressed to the wall.

I bent close to the muffled figure, put my face almost up against the shapeless mound that was Martha Meadows, to try to catch the garbled muttering which came through the bandages. I couldn't make it out. "Martha Meadows," I begged, "Martha Meadows, what caused the accident?"

The muttering stopped, broke off short. I couldn't tell whether she'd heard me or not. I repeated the question. Then suddenly I saw her head move slowly from side to side, slowly and slightly. "No – accident," she mumbled. Then she repeated it a second time, but so low I couldn't catch it any more. A minute later her head had lolled loosely over to the side again and stayed that way. She'd gone.

I went outside and stood there, lost in thought. I hadn't found out what I'd come to find out – what did it – but I'd found out something else, much more important. "No – accident" meant it had been done purposely. What else could it mean? Or was I building myself a case out of thin air? Delirium, morphine—and a shaking of the head in her death-throes that I'd mistaken for "no"? I tried to convince myself I was just looking for trouble. But it wouldn't work. I had an answer for every argument. She'd known what I was asking her just now. She hadn't been out of her mind.

Death will strike during unconsciousness or sleep, maybe, but never during delirium. The mind will always clear just before it breaks up, even if only an instant before. And hadn't she gotten threatening letters and asked for protection? Anyway, I told myself, as long as there *was* a doubt in my mind, it was up to me to track it down until there *wasn't* any doubt left-either one way or the other. That was my job. I was going to sift this thing down to the bottom.

Nellie came out. She wasn't bellowing now any more like she had been on the set. "They musta been casting her in heaven today, but they sure picked a mis'able way to notify her," she said with a sort of suppressed savagery. "I'm gonna buy me a bottle a' gin and drink it down straight. If it don't kill me the fust time, I'll keep it up till it do. She'll need a maid on the set up there fust thing and I ain't gonna leave her flat!" She shuffled off, shaking her head.

I was hard-hearted enough to go after her and stop her. "That's all right about heaven, auntie, but you don't happen to know of anyone down below here who had a grudge against her, do you?"

She shook her head some more. "Stop yo' mouth. She was everybody's honey. Didn't she even go to the trouble of axing 'em and coazing 'em to give that Miss Tobias a job in her picher on account of she felt sorry for her cause she was a back-number and nobody wanted her no-how?"

"What about those threats she got, where are they?"

"She turned 'em over to her supe'visor. They weren't nothing,

"You were there when it happened. What'd *you* see?"

"Weren't nothing to see. 'Pears like it musta been some of this here sponchaneous combusting."

That gave me an idea, but I hung it up to dry for a while. I rang headquarters and spilled what had happened to the chief. "Something new—an invisible accident. Right under everybody's nose and yet nobody saw it. Guess I better stay on it for a while, don't you?"

"You park your can on it till it breaks. I'll let the studio hot-shots know."

When I got back to the set they were all there yet – all but 'Stormann and Tobias! "I thought I told you-" I snarled in the guard's ear.

"They'll be right back," he whined, "they told me so. Stormy only stepped next door to get some more liquor. The electrician that was supplying him ran out of it. And she went to take off her costume. She got jittery because Stormy was nervous and started smoking around her. After what happened to- Besides, they weren't under arrest. Nobody here is, and you don't know Stormy. If I'd a' tried to stop him, it woulda been good-bye to my job—"

They were back in no time at all. Tobias was back first and I made a mental note of that. Since when does it take a man longer to dig up some liquor than it does a woman to change clothes from head to foot – besides, scraping off a stage make-up in the bargain? That was another little chip stacked against Stormann. I had three of them so far. He hadn't wanted Meadows to bring me on the set with her. He bullied her into going in alone while my back was turned. And lastly he'd found an excuse for leaving the set, taking him longer to get back than it had a conceited frail, like Tobias, to do herself over from head to toe.

The ace turned up when I checked up on the electrician who'd been supplying him.

"Why, no," he admitted, "I got another bottle left. I told him so, only he got a sudden notion his own was better quality and went out after it."

What a dead give-away that was!

He had the staggers when he showed up, but he had enough decency left to straighten up when he saw me and breathe: "How is she?"

I made the announcement I'd been saving until he got there—to see how he'd take it.

"I'm sorry to say – she's quit."

I kept my eyes on him. It was hard to tell. Plop! went the bottle he'd brought in with him and he started folding up like a jack knife. They picked him up and carried him out. It might've been the drink – but if he hadn't wanted to be questioned, for instance, it was the swellest out he could've thought up.

Maybe I should and maybe I shouldn't have, but I'm frank to admit I stuck a pin in him before they got him to the door – just to see. He never even twitched.

I turned a chair around backwards, sat down on it, and faced the rest of them. "I'm in charge of this case now," I said, "by order of police headquarters and with the consent of the studio executives. All I'm going to do, right now, is repeat the question I've already asked Mr. Stormann, Miss Tobias, Nellie, and the script-girl. Did any of you see what caused it'?" This meant the electricians, stage-hands, and the two cameramen. They all shook their heads.

I got up and banged the chair down so hard one leg of it busted off. "She wasn't six feet away from some of you!" I bawled them out. "She was in the full glare of the brightest lights ever devised! All eyes were on her watching every move and she was the center of attraction at the time! She burned to death, and yet no one saw how it started! Twenty-five pairs of human eyes and they might as well have all been closed! Well, there's one pair left – and they won't let him down."

I suppose they thought I meant my own. Not by a damn sight. "Now clear out of here, all of you, and don't touch anything as you go!" I pointed to the chief electrician. "You stay and check up on those lights for defects – one of 'em might have got overheated and dropped a spark on her. And don't try to hold out anything to save your own skin. Criminal carelessness is a lot less serious than obstructing an agent of justice!" I passed my handkerchief to the guard. "You comb the floor around where she was standing. Pick up every cigarette butt and every cinder you find!"

The rest of them filed out one by one, giving me names and addresses as they went. I wasn't worried about getting them back again if I wanted them. They all reacted differently. Some were frightened, some just curious, some cracking wise. The script-girl's nose was still buried in her book. She hardly looked up at all. Tobias glided by me with a little extra hip-action and purred over her shoulder: "Lots of luck, Handsome. And if you find out you were mistaken about those eighteen kids of yours, look a lady up sometime."

"Thirtieth of next February," I told her.

The chief cameraman came out of his booth with a round, flat, tin box-packed under his arm.

"Where you going with that?" I asked him.

"Drop it in the ash can on my way out," he said. "It's what we took today, no good now any more."

"Ashcan-hell," I snapped. "Those machines of yours are the other pair of eyes I told you about! How soon can you develop that stuff?"

"Right away," he told me, looking surprised. "But we can't use this roll – it's got her whole death-scene on it and it'll turn your hair white just to look at it."

"You do it yourself," I warned him, "don't call anybody in to help you. And don't touch it, leave it just the way it is. Can I trust you?"

"Meet me in half an hour in projection room A," he said. "She was a swell kid."

The electrician came down from way up high somewhere and reported the lights all jake. No crossed wires, not a screw out of place anywhere.

"You dig up a typewriter and get that all down on paper, sign it, have a notary witness it, and shoot it in to me at headquarters— Galbraith's the name. It better be on the level, the pay-off is withholding information from the authorities." Which didn't mean anything, but it was good enough to throw a scare into him. I never saw anyone take it on the lam so quick in my life.

The guard passed me my handkerchief back with a cigarette butt, a wire frame, and a lot of little pieces of glass in it.

"The butt's Stormann's," he pointed out. "He was smoking it after it was all over. I saw him throw it down and step on it before he went after that liquor. I remember because Tobias yapped 'Don't come near me with that thing! You want it to happen to me, too?"

I wondered if that remark meant anything. Did he *want* it to happen to her, too? Get the point? I knew what the pieces of glass and the frame were right away – a busted lorgnette like I had seen Tobias fiddling with.

"Meadows had it around her neck I guess," he suggested, "and it fell and smashed when she started to run around crazy."

I felt like telling him he didn't know his ears from his elbow, but I kept quiet about it. These pieces of glass were clear, that burning celluloid would have smoked them up plenty if they had been anywhere near Martha Meadows. But there was an easy enough way of settling that.

"Get the wardrobe-woman in here and tell her to bring a complete list of every article she furnished Meadows and Tobias for this picture."

She was a society-looking dame, with white hair, and had had her face lifted. She had typewritten sheets with her.

"Did you supply Meadows with a lorgnette?"

"Why no," she said. "Young girls didn't wear them even in those days."

"But Tobias wore one. Is this it?" I showed her the pieces.

"It must be," she returned. "She turned in her costume a little while ago and explained that she'd broken her lorgnette while that awful thing was happening to poor Martha. You see I have everything else crossed off but that. We usually charge players for anything that isn't returned to us, but in this case of course nothing like that will happen."

That explained something that had bothered me for a minute or two. Because I'd distinctly seen the lorgnette on Tobias *after* the accident, when she was making those first passes at me. She must have broken it later – while I was outside in the infirmary with Meadows. But a chiseler like her who would cadge a drink from Stormann would try to make them believe it had happened during all the excitement – to get out of paying for it.

"You keep those two lists just the way they are now, I may want to see them again." I folded up the handkerchief with the pieces of broken glass and put it away in my pocket.

A kid came in and said: "The rushes are ready for you in

projection room A," and took me over there.

It had rows of seats just like a miniature theatre and a screen on one wall. I closed the door and locked the cameraman and myself in.

"It's ghastly," he said, "better hang on tight."

"Run it through at normal speed first," I said. "I'll see if I can stand it."

I sat down in the front row with the screen almost on top of me. There wasn't much to it at regular speed-about five minutes worth of picture-what they call a "sequence." It was pretty grisly at that. It opened on Tobias sitting there in the rocker, broadside to the camera. Meadows came in almost at once.

"I'm going away with him tonight," she said.

Tobias opened her lorgnette and gave her the once-over through it. Meadows went over to the window, and the camera followed her part of the way. That left Tobias over at the left-hand side of the screen and partly out of the picture, with just one shoulder, arm, and the side of her head showing. She started to rock buck und forth and tap her lorgnette against the back of her hand. I had my eyes glued to Meadows though. She turned around to look at her "sister."

"Oh, won't he ever come?" she said.

Her face sort of tightened up-changed from repose to tenseness. A look of horror started to form on it, but it never got any further. Right then and there the thing happened.

The best way I can describe it is, a sort of bright, luminous flower seemed to open up halfway down her dress, spreading, peeling back. But the petals of it were flame. An instant later it was all over her, and the first screams of a voice that was gone now came smashing out at my eardrums. And in between each one, the hellish sound-track had even picked up and recorded the sizzling that her hair made.

"Cut!"

I turned around and yelled back at him: "For Pete's sake, cut, before I throw up!" and I mopped my drenched forehead. "I did twice–while I was processing it," he confessed, looking out of the booth at me.

It hadn't told me a thing so far, but then I hadn't expected it to – the first throw out of the bag.

"Go back and start it over," I shivered, "but, whatever you do, leave out that finale! Take it up where she turns at the window. Slow motion this time. Can you hold it when I tell you to?"

He adjusted his apparatus. "Say when," he called.

The figures on the screen hardly moved at all this time, eight times slowed down. They drifted lazily – sort of floated. I knew the place. To look for on Meadows' dress now, and I kept my eyes focused on it and let everything else ride. A moment later something had shown up there.

"Hold it!" I yelled, and the scene froze into a "still."

Now it was just a magic-lantern slide, no motion at all. I left my seat and stood close up against the screen, keeping to one side so my own shadow wouldn't blur out that place on her dress. No flame was coming from it yet. It was just a bright, luminous spot, about the size and shape of a dime.

"Back up one!" I instructed. "One" meant a single revolution of the camera. The scene hardly shifted at all, but the pin-point of light was smaller-like a pea now. You couldn't have seen it from the seat I'd been in at first.

Two heads are better than one. I called him out and showed it to him. "What do you make of this? It's not a defect in the film, is it?"

"No, it's a blob of light coming to a head at that place on her dress. Like a highlight, you might say. A gleam." Which is what I'd had it figured for, too.

"Go three forward," I said, "and then hold it."

He came out again to look. It was back to the size of a dime again, and only a turn or two before the flames were due to show up. "There's heat in it!" I said. "See that!" The white spot had developed a dark core, a pin-head of black or brown.

"That's the material of the dress getting ready to burn. See that thread coming out of the dot? Smoke – and all there'll ever be of it, too. Celluloid doesn't give much warning."

So far so good. But what I wanted to know was where that gleam or ray was coming from. I had the effect now, but I wanted the cause. The trouble was you couldn't follow the beam through the air – to gauge its direction. Like any beam of light, it left no trail – only showed up suddenly on her dress. The set-up, so far, seemed to fit Nellie's theory of spontaneous combustion perfectly. Maybe one of the powerful Klieg lights, high overhead and out of the picture, had developed some flaw in its glass shield, warping one of its rays. But the electrician had gone over them afterward and given them all a clean bill of health.

"Start it up again," I said wearily. "Slow motion," and went back and sat down. I was farther away now and had a better perspective of the thing as a whole; maybe that's what did it.

As the scene on the screen thawed and slowly dissolved into fluid motion once more, it gave the impression for a moment of everything on it moving at once. Therefore it was only natural that the one thing that *didn't* move should catch my eye and hold it. Tobias' lorgnette, and the wrist and hand that held it. The three objects stayed rigid, down in the lower left-hand corner of the screen, after everything else was on the go once more. The chair she was in had started to rock slowly buck und forth, and her body with it, but the forearm, wrist, hand and lorgnette stayed poised, motionless. There was something unnatural about it that caught the eye at once. I remembered she had opened the scene by tapping her lorgnette *as well as* rocking.

Now, with the fire due to break out any second, she was only rocking. The lorgnette was stiff as a ramrod in her grasp. Not that she was holding it out at full length before her or anything like that, she was holding it close in, unobtrusively, but straight up and down – a little out to one side of her own body. Maybe the director's orders had been for her to stop fiddling with it at a certain point. Then again maybe not. All I wanted to find out was at what point she had stopped tapping and playing with it. I had been concentrating on Meadows until now and had missed that.

"Whoa, back up!" I called out to him. "All the way back and

then start over – slow."

I let Meadows go this time and kept my eye on Tobias and her lorgnette. The minute I saw it stop – "Hold it!" I yelled and ran over to the screen and examined Meadows' dress. Nothing yet. But in three more revolutions of the camera that deadly white spot had. Already showed up on the celluloid-lined hoopskirt. Effect had followed cause too quickly to be disregarded.

"Lights!" I roared. "I've got it!"

He turned a switch, the room blazed all around me, and I took that handkerchief out of my pocket and examined the pieces of glass it held. Some were thicker than others – the lens had therefore been convex, not flat. I held one up and looked at my cuff through it. The weave stood out. A magnifying glass. I held it about a foot away from the back of my hand, where I'd already been burned once this afternoon, and even with the far weaker lights of the projection-room working through it, in about thirty seconds something bit me and I jumped.

He'd come out and was watching what I was doing. "Pack that film up again in the box the way you had it," I said. "I'll be back for it in a minute. I'm taking it down to headquarters with me!"

"What'd you find out?" he asked.

"Look it up in tomorrow morning's papers!"

I called Tobias' dressing-room. "How's the lay of the land?" I greeted her.

She knew me right away. "I know, it's Handsome."

"I was wrong about those eighteen kids," 1 told her. "I counted 'em over – only nine."

She sure was a hard-boiled customer. "Nine to go," she said cheerfully. "When will I see you?"

"I'll pick you up in about twenty minutes."

"Where we going?" she cooed when she got in the car.

"You'll find out."

Then when we got there, she said: "Why, this looks like police headquarters to me."

"Not only does, but is," I told her. "Won't take a minute, I just want to see a man about a dog."

"Wouldn't you rather have me wait outside for you?"

I chucked her under the chin. "I'm getting so fond of you I want you with me wherever I go. Can't stand being without you even for five minutes."

She closed her eyes and looked pleased and followed me in like a lamb. Then when the bracelets snapped on her wrists she exploded: "Why you dirty doublecrossing—I thought you said you wanted to see a man about a dog."

"I do," I said, "and you're the dog."

"What're the charges?" the chief asked.

"Setting fire to Martha Meadows with a magnifying glass and causing her to burn to death. Here's the glass she used; picked up on the set. Here's the original harmless glass that was in the frame before she knocked it out; picked up in the trashbasket in her dressing room. The film, there in the box, shows her in the act of doing it. She's been eaten away with jealousy ever since she faded out and Meadows stepped into her shoes."

I never knew a woman knew so many bad words as she did; and she used them all. After she'd been booked and the matron was leading her away she called back: "You'll never make this stick. You think you've got me, but you'll find out!"

"She's right, Gal," commented the chief, after she'd gone. "The studio people'll put the crusher on the case before it ever comes up for trial. Not because they approve of what she's done—but on account of the effect it would have on the public."

"She may beat the murder rap," I said, "but she can't get around these." I took a bundle of letters and a square of blotting-paper out of my pocket and passed them to him. "Wrote them in her very dressing room at the studio and then mailed them to Meadows on the outside, even after Meadows had gotten her a job. The blotting-paper tells the story if you hold it up to a mirror. She didn't get rid of it quickly enough."

"Good work, Gal," the chief said: and then, just like him, he takes all the pleasure out of it. "Now that you're in for promotion, suppose you step around to that grill and pay the guy for that plate-glass window you busted."

CORNELL WOOLRICH

George Hopley-Woolrich (4 December 1903 – 25 September 1968) is one of America's best crime and noir writers who sometimes wrote under the pseudonyms William Irish and George Hopley. He's often compared to other celebrated crime writers of his day, Dashiell Hammett, Erle Stanley Gardner and Raymond Chandler.

Born in New York City, his parents separated when he was young and he lived in Mexico for nearly a decade with his father before returning to New York City to live with his mother, Claire Attalie Woolrich.

He attended New York's Columbia University but left school in 1926 without graduating when his first novel, *Cover Charge*, was published. *Cover Charge* was one of six of his novels that he credits as inspired by the work of F. Scott Fitzgerald. Woolrich soon turned to pulp and detective fiction, often published under his pseudonyms. His best known story today is his 1942 *"It Had to be Murder"* for the simple reason that it was adapted into the 1954 Alfred Hitchcock movie *Rear Window* starring James Stewart and Grace Kelly. It was remade as a television film by Christopher Reeve in 1998.

Woolrich was a homosexual but in 1930, while working as a screenwriter in Los Angeles, he married Violet Virginia Blackton (1910-65), daughter of silent film producer J. Stuart Blackton. They separated after three months and the marriage was annulled in 1933.

Woolrich returned to New York where he and his mother moved into the Hotel Marseilles (Broadway and West 102nd Street). He lived there until her death on October 6, 1957, which prompted his move to the Hotel Franconia (20 West 72nd Street). In later years he socialized on occasion in Manhattan but alcoholism and an amputated leg, caused by an infection from wearing a shoe too tight which he left untreated, turned him into a recluse. Thus, he did not attend the New York premiere of Truffaut's film based on his novel *The Bride Wore Black* in 1968 and, shortly thereafter, died weighing only 89 pounds. He is interred in the Ferncliff Cemetery in Hartsdale, New York.

Woolrich bequeathed his estate to Columbia University to endow scholarships in his mother's memory for journalism students.

Publisher's Note

The Author and Renaissance Literary & Talent have attempted to create this book with the highest quality conversion from the original edition. However, should you notice any errors within this text please e-mail corrections@renaissancemgmt.net with the title/author in the subject line and the corrections in the body of the email. Thank you for your help and patronage.

Made in the USA
Las Vegas, NV
03 November 2020